THE
BOY
IS
BACK

BOOKS BY MEG CABOT

The Princess Diaries series

The Mediator series

Heather Wells series

The Boy series

Overbite

Insatiable

Ransom My Heart (with Mia Thermopolis)

Queen of Babble series

She Went All the Way

The 1-800-WHERE-R-YOU series

All-American Girl series

Nicola and the Viscount

Victoria and the Rogue

Jinx

How to Be Popular

Pants on Fire

Avalon High series

The Airhead series

Allie Finkle's Rules for Girls series

From the Notebooks of a Middle School Princess series

THE
BOY
IS
BACK

MEG CABOT

wm

WILLIAM MORROW

An Imprint of HarperCollins Publishers

THE BOY IS BACK. Copyright © 2016 by Meg Cabot, LLC. All rights reserved. Printed in the United States of America. No part of this book may be used or reproduced in any manner whatsoever without written permission except in the case of brief quotations embodied in critical articles and reviews. For information, address HarperCollins Publishers, 195 Broadway, New York, NY 10007.

HarperCollins books may be purchased for educational, business, or sales promotional use. For information, please email the Special Markets Department at Spsales@harpercollins.com.

FIRST EDITION

Designed by Ruth Lee-Mui

Library of Congress Cataloging-in-Publication Data has been applied for.

ISBN 978-0-06-237877-4 (paperback)
ISBN 978-0-06-266120-3 (Schuler signed edition)
ISBN 978-0-06-249077-3 (hardcover library edition)

16 17 18 19 20   DIX/RRD 10 9 8 7 6 5 4 3 2 1

EPIGRAPH

A man does not recover from such devotion of the heart to such
a woman! He ought not; he does not.
 —Jane Austen, *Persuasion*

THE
BOY
IS
BACK

MovingUp!
SENIOR MOVE MANAGEMENT CONSULTANTS, LLC

PRESIDENT AND CEO
BECKY FLOWERS

CFO
NICOLE FLOWERS

OFFICE MANAGER
BEVERLY FLOWERS

STEWART
FAMILY TREE

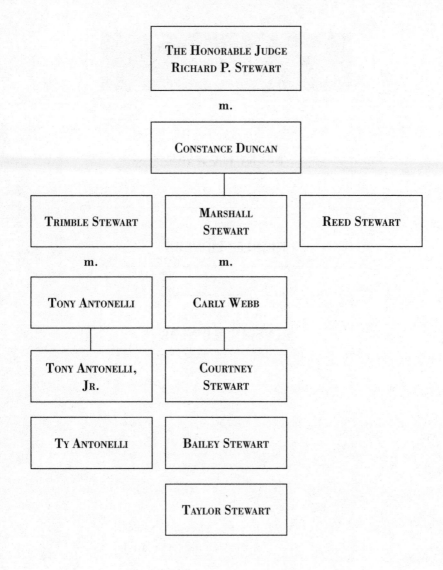

THE HONORABLE JUDGE
RICHARD P. STEWART

m.

CONSTANCE DUNCAN

TRIMBLE STEWART

MARSHALL
STEWART

REED STEWART

m.

m.

TONY ANTONELLI

CARLY WEBB

TONY ANTONELLI,
JR.

COURTNEY
STEWART

TY ANTONELLI

BAILEY STEWART

TAYLOR STEWART

The Bloomville Herald

The Tri-County Area's Only
Daily Newspaper
• Monday, March 13 • Vol. 139 •
Still Only 50 Cents!

CRIME REPORT

Information in the Crime Report is obtained from calls logged by the Bloomville Police Department.

Shelby Park, Bloomville—Resident **Beverly Flowers** reported a man camping illegally who also appeared to be intoxicated. Officer Corrine Jeffries issued a warning and a fine.

11th and Main, Bloomville—Resident **Summer Hayes** reported a barking dog. Officer Henry De Santos dispatched to investigate. A warning was given to the dog's owner.

Old Towne Mall, Bloomville—Server **Tiffany Gosling** reported that **Judge Richard P. Stewart** and his wife, **Mrs. Constance D. Stewart**, of Country Club Road, attempted to pay for a meal at Shenanigans Neighborhood Bar and Grill with a postage stamp. Officer Corrine Jeffries responded. Couple was arrested and taken to Bloomville City Jail for processing.

BECKY FLOWERS	10:45AM	96%
TODAY	ALL	MISSED

From: Nicole@MovingUp.com
Date: March 13 10:24:11 AM EST
To: Becky@MovingUp.com
Subject: Crime Report

Beck. Go to this link.

http://www.bloomvilleherald.com/crimereport

From: Becky@MovingUp.com
Date: March 13 10:26:15 AM EST
To: Nicole@MovingUp.com
Subject: Re: Crime Report

I don't have time right now, Nicole. I'm driving to my 11:00 consultation with Mrs. Blumenthal about her mother, remember?

BECKY FLOWERS, CSMM
Moving Up! Consulting LLC, President

Sent from my handheld device, please excuse typos

Nicole F   10:28 AM
If you were actually driving, you wouldn't be checking your phone. I know you. You never break the law. You clearly took I-65 (even though I warned you not to since it's under construction), and now you're stuck in traffic.

You HAVE to go to that link right now. It's about Reed Stewart. . . .
♨ ♥

Becky F   10:30 AM
Why would I want to read something about a guy I broke up with ten years ago, and haven't thought of since?

Nicole F   10:31 AM

Oh, right. You don't think about Reed Stewart at all.

That's why you still have your prom photo with him on the bulletin board above the treadmill, and every time Reed is in a tournament, you record it.

Becky F   10:32 AM

I happen to be at my ideal weight in that photo and am using it for inspiration.

And I record EVERY golf tournament. Graham asked me to take lessons with him at the public range this summer. We both think it will be a good way to pick up new clients.

Nicole F   10:33 AM

The lumbersexual plays GOLF?

Oh, wait, of course he does. Everyone knows a lumbersexual is just a metrosexual with a neatly trimmed beard. Why wouldn't he enjoy a sport that is a symbol of everything that's wrong about our country, a metaphor for our greed, disregard for the environment, and historic oppression by the patriarchy?

Becky F   10:33 AM

Did you skip breakfast again this morning?

Nicole F   10:33 AM

For your information, I had a cinnabun from the café at Bloomville Books.

Becky F   10:33 AM

Well, you obviously need more protein. I've asked you repeatedly to stop calling Graham a lumbersexual.

Nicole F   10:33 AM

Would you prefer that I call him a cheesemonger?

Becky F 10:34 AM

You know that Graham isn't a cheesemonger. He is the successful owner-operator of the only wine and cheese boutique in a fifty mile radius.

Nicole F 10:34 AM

Seriously? That's what he's calling it? A boutique? He so needs to get over himself. It's a wine bar, Beck. A wine bar that also serves cheese and has a really dumb name.

Becky F 10:34 AM

What's wrong with the name Authentic?

And you seem surprisingly hostile towards the patriarchy for someone who is currently dating a cop.

Nicole F 10:34 AM

What's wrong with the name Authentic? How about everything. It implies that wine and cheese sold elsewhere is inauthentic, which is factually incorrect. The wine and cheese I buy at Kroger is as authentic as the wine and cheese Graham sells at his place.

And if you're talking about Henry, yes, I suppose he is one of the oppressors. But he looks AMAZING in his uniform—and out of it.

Becky F 10:35 AM

Nic, honestly, you have got to eat less sugar in the morning.

And you were right about I-65. I'm stuck in what looks like a war zone between a concrete railing, a backhoe, and a jackhammer that is pounding so loudly I can hardly hear myself think.

Could you please call Mrs. Blumenthal for me and let her know I'm going to be late? I'd do it, but all she'd hear is jackhammering.

Nicole F   10:36 AM

Fine, I'll call Mrs. Blumenthal for you, but only if you click on that link.

Seriously, you HAVE to, Beck. It's not even about Reed. It's about his parents.

And it's all anyone in town is going to be talking about tonight at the tasting at AUTHENTIC.

Becky F   10:36 AM

OK. But please don't use all caps. You're 24 now, not 12.

Nicole F   10:37 AM

Just do it. Click it. Cliiiiiiiiiiiiiiiiiiiiiiiiiiiiiiiick it. 👆

Becky F   10:38 AM

I said I would! ☹

Becky F   10:45 AM

Where are you? There's a break in the jackhammering and I've been trying to reach you. Why aren't you picking up?

Becky F   10:46 AM

Seriously, where are you? I need to talk about this before they—oh, ugh, too late! Either let us move or STOP WITH THE HAMMERING!

Becky F   10:47 AM

Anyway, Nic, this has to be some kind of mistake. Reed's parents would never do something like that.

Could you call Henry and just double check with him that the paper got this story right? He must know someone who was at the station last night when the Stewarts were brought in. Because there is no way this story about them can be true.

Becky F	10:49 AM

Oh, they stopped hammering again! Call me! CALL ME ASAP!

Becky F	10:51 AM

Nicole, it's not that I care or anything, but Judge Stewart married half the people in this town, including Mom and Dad. The courthouse is named after him.

So there is no way a man of his stature is going to try to con Tiffany Gosling of all people out of a restaurant bill. There is just no way.

Where did you go, anyway? You better not have made a run back to Bloomville Books for more cinnabuns. You know we can't leave the phones unstaffed . . . or even worse, let Mom answer them. Remember what happened last time!

Becky F	10:53 AM

And even if it IS true, Judge Stewart couldn't possibly have known the stamp was only worth $4! He would never cheat a waitress, especially Tiffany. If I remember correctly, her mom was the one who had a trailer in that park that was being bought out by those developers, and Judge Stewart ruled that the developers had to pay her the cost of the trailer AND the land it was sitting on if they wanted her to move. So now she's living in a condo in Tucson.

I mean, honestly, why would he go to all the trouble of saving Tiffany's mom just so he could cheat her daughter?

Where are you?????

Nicole F	10:55 AM

Sorry. I'm on the office line with Mrs. Blumenthal. I called her, like I said I would. Boy, is she a talker, or what? I can't remember if we're going to need to order a Dumpster for her mom or what? I know how you love a Dumpster. ☺

Becky F   10:55 AM

No to the Dumpster for Mrs. B. She's the one who hoards Princess Diana memorabilia, remember? She'll be able to take most of it to her new retirement home, and whatever's left her daughter wants us to try to sell online.

But who even cares about that? What about the Stewarts? Have you talked to Henry about them? Are they really under arrest? What's happening???

Nicole F   10:55 AM

Whoa, whoa, whoa. That's a lot of questions for someone who hasn't even thought about Reed Stewart in ten years. ☺

Becky F   10:56 AM

Stop it! I can not care about Reed Stewart and still be concerned about his parents. What did Henry say???

Nicole F   10:57 AM

☺ Henry says a buddy of his was working the night shift when the Stewarts were brought into the station.

He said Judge Stewart seemed to have no idea what was happening. He was smiling and waving to everyone and handed the booking officer their doggie bag from Shenanigans and asked if he could keep it in the staff fridge until he and Mrs. S made bail, because it had mozzarella sticks in it.

He said they were both super cheerful about getting arrested, like it was all a big joke.

Becky F   10:57 AM

Nicole! OMG! That's terrible.

Nicole F   10:58 AM

Yeah, it's definitely not good. Although Henry says it's a pretty popular con these days.

Becky F   11:00 AM

What is? What are you talking about?

Nicole F   11:00 AM

Faking dementia in order to scam restaurants out of free meals.

Henry says that's why Tiffany called the cops in the first place. She didn't want to, but the night manager made her. This is the third time this year something like this has happened at Shenanigans . . . although usually the customers find "worms" in their salad.

Becky F   11:01 AM

What? NO! Nicole, I hope you let Henry know that the Stewarts aren't like that. They're the loveliest, most generous people alive. They would never try to scam a restaurant out of a free meal. Remember when they gave me that gold Gucci watch for my 18th birthday? I'd only been dating Reed for a month at the time, but I think they felt bad for me, because Dad had just gotten diagnosed.

Plus, they live in a mansion! It's listed with the National Register of Historic Places. They belong to the country club.

People like that do not knowingly rip off Shenanigans.

Nicole F   11:02 AM

Uh, no offense, Beck, but rich people—even judges—do commit crimes.

Reed certainly did, as I think you, of all people, would remember.

Becky F   11:02 AM

Not funny.

And I don't see how someone in our line of work—who sees elderly people suffering from dementia every day—can not be aware that this is EXACTLY what this could be.

Nicole F   11:02 AM

And I don't see why someone who claims to be so over her ex—especially an ex who treated you the way Reed did—is so concerned about his parents.

Becky F   11:03 AM

I told you: Because however Reed Stewart might have treated me, his parents were always very kind. They don't deserve to have their reputations ruined over what sounds to me like a little misunderstanding. Or possibly senile dementia.

Nicole F   11:03 AM

Um, it's the Bloomville Herald, Becky. Hardly anyone reads it, let alone gets their reputation ruined over it. I sent you that link because I thought you'd find it funny. I didn't think you'd get so upset about it.

The fact that you ARE so upset makes me worried.

Becky F   11:03 AM

Worried about what?

Nicole F   11:04 AM

Worried about how you're going to react if his parents DO have senile dementia or whatever, and Reed comes back after all these years to deal with them. I'm dating a cop, not a lawyer.

Becky F   11:05 AM

What are you talking about?

Nicole F   11:05 AM

Well, Henry can't get you off for vehicular manslaughter if you decide to finally get revenge on Reed for what he did to you on prom night. ☺

Becky F   11:06 AM

Oh, ha ha. Very funny.

You know, Reed's got two siblings who still live right here in Bloomville. I'm sure they're going to handle it—if there's anything to handle, which I doubt, since, like I said, the whole thing is probably nothing but a silly misunderstanding.

Nicole F   11:07 AM

So what you're saying is that if Reed came back, it would make no difference to you.

Becky F   11:07 AM

Right. I'm in a committed relationship, remember?

Nicole F   11:08 AM

I remember. With the lumbersexual.

Becky F   11:08 AM

Stop calling him that!

And what happened with Reed was ages ago. Would you like to be constantly teased and reminded about the guys YOU dated in high school?

Nicole F   11:08 AM

Ew, no.

Becky F   11:08 AM

I rest my case.

OK, traffic's starting to move. Gotta go. I'll pick up salads for us for lunch on the way home.

Nicole F   11:09 AM

DON'T GET THEM FROM SHENANIGANS!

Becky F   11:09 AM

Don't worry, I won't.

Or will I? ☺

————————————————Today————————————————

Summer Hayes   11:29 AM

Hi, Carly! It's been forever, hasn't it? So, I saw that Bailey still insists on wearing that Chief Massasoit costume everywhere, even though the Thanksgiving play was ages ago. You poor thing ;-)

Slightly off topic, isn't Judge Stewart your father-in-law? I'm so sorry.

☺ Summer ☺
Britney's Super Mom!

From: Carly Stewart@StewartRealty.com
Date: March 13 12:06:26 PM EST
To: Summer Hayes <BestMomEva89@yogamommy.com>
Subject: Judge Stewart

Hi, Summer. Yes, Bailey is very fond of her Chief Massasoit costume. I don't see what's wrong with that. If it weren't for Chief Massasoit bringing the Pilgrims all that venison on Thanksgiving, our country probably wouldn't exist, because our forefathers would have starved to death.

Anyway, yes, Judge Stewart is my father-in-law. Why are you sorry about that?

Carly R. Stewart | Accountant | Stewart Realty | 801 South Moore Pike, Bloomville, IN 47401 | phone (812) 555-8722 | Please visit StewartRealty.com for all your realty needs

---

From: Summer Hayes <BestMomEva89@yogamommy.com>
Date: March 13 12:15:03 PM EST
To: Carly Stewart@StewartRealty.com
Subject: Re: Judge Stewart

Just so you know, Carly, one of the parents complained at the last soccer game that she found it culturally insensitive of Bailey to be wearing that costume, especially considering the fact that your family, as far as any of us know, isn't Native American.

And then when Bailey took it upon herself to perform that war dance— or whatever it was—at halftime, numerous parents from the opposing team expressed concern. The Bloomville Girls Soccer League's mascot is a chipmunk, not a Wampanoag Indian chief who never even lived in Southern Indiana.

I know how busy you must be as a working mom, and probably simply haven't realized any of this—just like you haven't realized that today's Crime Report in the *Bloomville Herald* features a story about your in-laws having been arrested last night at Shenanigans at the Bloomville Mall—but it would really help if you'd have a discussion with your daughter about cultural insensitivity to indigenous peoples.

Thanks!

☺ Summer ☺
Britney's Mommy

CARLY STEWART	12:45PM	92%
TODAY	ALL	MISSED

Carly Stewart — 12:22 PM
GET IN HERE NOW.

Marshall Stewart — 12:25 PM
Can't. I'm in that meeting with the Patels.

I think they're going to bite on the Thomas property! They haven't even asked about the water damage!

Carly Stewart — 12:27 PM
YOUR PARENTS GOT ARRESTED AT SHENANIGANS LAST NIGHT.

Marshall Stewart — 12:30 PM
FUUUUUUUUUUUUUUUDDDDDGGGGGGEE

Marshall Stewart — 12:30 PM
Fudge. I mean fudge. Stupid autocorrect!

How could this have happened?

Carly Stewart — 12:30 PM
What do you mean how could this have happened? I've been warning you since Christmas that something like this was going to happen. But do you ever listen to me? No.

Marshall Stewart — 12:30 PM
What are you talking about?

Carly Stewart — 12:30 PM
What part can't you figure out? The part where my high school nemesis just informed me that my in-laws were arrested last night, or the part where you refuse to admit your parents need professional help?

Marshall Stewart   12:31 PM
My father is a very intelligent man. He's just eccentric.

Carly Stewart   12:31 PM
Marshall, your father took a left turn past eccentric and pulled into Crazy Town six months ago. And now everyone in Bloomville knows it but you.

Marshall Stewart   12:32 PM
You're enjoying this, aren't you?

Carly Stewart   12:32 PM
Enjoying that my mother-in-law, who gave me knives for my last birthday, is in jail? How could you imagine such a thing?

Marshall Stewart   12:33 PM
Those were really expensive knives. They cost like $80.

Carly Stewart   12:33 PM
Don't you have slightly more important things to worry about right now than how much your mother spent on her last birthday gift to me? Like where your parents are, and what the Patels think you're doing while you're texting me?

Marshall Stewart   12:33 PM
The Patels think I'm looking up zoning restrictions. They want to put in a pool.

But I guess that's a good question. Where are my parents now?

Carly Stewart   12:34 PM
The Patels can't put in a pool unless they build a ten-foot retaining wall. That house is in a historic floodplain. Remember, we had this exact same problem when the Greenwalds wanted to make an offer last year?

Marshall Stewart   12:34 PM

I AM AWARE OF THAT, CARLY. WHERE ARE MY PARENTS???

Carly Stewart   12:34 PM

Oh, NOW you're concerned. I have been telling you since Christmas that there is something wrong with your parents, but you wouldn't listen.

"They're just eccentric." "They like collecting." "It's totally normal to own that many ceramic cat figurines."

Why do I have to do everything in this relationship? WHY? You DO have other family members, including a sister who is co-counsel at your father's private law office.

Not that she would deign to answer the phone when I called to ask the exact question you just did—where are your parents.

Marshall Stewart   12:35 PM

Don't bring my sister into this. And what did you mean you warned me about this at Christmas? What happened at Christmas?

Carly Stewart   12:35 PM

You mean when your parents invited us over for dinner and we saw all those turkey carcasses sitting out on the front lawn leftover from when they had us for Thanksgiving?

You didn't find that odd?

Marshall Stewart   12:36 PM

Mom said she left them out there for the cats.

Carly Stewart   12:37 PM

Marshall. Your parents don't own any cats.

Marshall Stewart   12:37 PM

Oh.

Well, I guess they do now.

Carly Stewart   12:38 PM

Yes. Every cat in the neighborhood.

Now can we please admit that your parents have a problem and DO something about it? Because I personally can't stand the idea of Summer Hayes dishing about my in-laws on Facebook. Which, FYI, she's been doing, in between complaining about Bailey and her Chief Massasoit costume.

Marshall Stewart   12:38 PM

What's wrong with Bailey's Chief Massasoit costume? Besides the fact that it's filthy because she refuses to take it off?

Carly Stewart   12:38 PM

Summer Hayes says other parents have been complaining that it's culturally insensitive.

Marshall Stewart   12:38 PM

Great. I'm going to kill myself.

Right after I kill those other parents. And then my own parents.

Do you realize the Patels may be the last clients we ever have? Every single other person in this town knows that the Honorable Judge Richard P. Stewart is my father.

Which means that every single person in this town with a Stewart Realty sign on their front lawn will probably be stuffing it into their recycling bin tonight, since they aren't going to want to associate with the son of a known felon.

Carly Stewart   12:38 PM

Now you're overreacting. We don't even have the whole story yet. Your parents are innocent until proven guilty, right? That's what your dad always said about the people he saw in court every day, anyway.

Marshall Stewart   12:39 PM
Yeah, and look what happened to most of them.

GUILTY.

Carly Stewart   12:39 PM
Stop it. This town, like your dad, has always been pretty forgiving. They forgave your brother Reed, didn't they? He used to be the most hated boy in Bloomville.

Now he's their golden child. They have the shoes he wore in the US Open hanging on the wall at Antonelli's Pizza!

Marshall Stewart   12:40 PM
Carly, my sister is married to the owner of Antonelli's.

Remember what the therapist said? There's a difference between being supportive and being condescending.

Have you been able to reach Trimble? Reed? Anyone?

Carly Stewart   12:40 PM
The receptionist says your sister got called to a meeting at her kids' school and can't be disturbed—something going on with Ty.

And your brother's phone goes instantly to voice mail. I suppose, since he's on California time, he isn't up yet.

P.S. The therapist ALSO said you have anger issues and need a hobby.

Marshall Stewart   12:41 PM
Reed is up. He's probably already out on the links, hitting balls. That bastard.

And if Ty is anything like her mother was when SHE was 14, I BET she got called to a meeting at her school.

Look, how many subscribers to the Bloomville Herald can there even be? 5,000? 2,000?

Carly Stewart   12:42 PM

I don't know. Not that many. Aren't they always complaining about how nobody reads newspapers anymore? Journalists are getting laid off right and left, I heard.

Marshall Stewart   12:42 PM

Right! So long as no one on social media picks up on the story, we'll be fine. This whole thing is probably nothing. A mountain out of a molehill.

Carly Stewart   12:42 PM

Marshall, that's what you've been saying about your parents for months now, and look what's happened. I think you're in denial. They need help. Serious help.

Marshall Stewart   12:42 PM

Come on. They're fine. Dad's the smartest guy who ever lived in this town. And Mom's great! I bet this whole thing was a misunderstanding, and by dinnertime, it will all have blown over, and we'll be having a good laugh over it with Mom and Dad. Wait and see. ☺

NEWYORKJOURNAL.COM

Where the World Goes For Its News, Celebrity Buzz, LOLs, and More

DUMBASS OF THE WEEK

Be glad the only embarrassing thing *your* parents ever do is post your old baby photos on Facebook!

The Honorable Judge Richard P. Stewart and his wife, both 75 and natives of Bloomville, Indiana, enjoyed their romantic dinner at their local Shenanigans Neighborhood Bar and Grill last night so much, they decided to pay for it in a very special way.

When waitress Tiffany Gosling (also of the delightfully named Bloomville) went to their table after the couple had left, she found a postage stamp attached to the bill (in lieu of the more customary form of payment, money). Along with the stamp was a note that said:

> Thank you for the lovely meal. Please accept this rare two cent commemorative postal stamp of our nation's first president, George Washington, as payment for the meal. It is worth over $400.

At first Tiffany was thrilled . . . until she looked up the true value of the stamp.

Turns out two-cent George Washington stamps, issued between 1922 and 1938, are not rare at all. The couple had left a stamp worth $4 for a $59 meal, not even enough to cover Tiffany's tip.

The manager called the police, who arrived and were taking a report when the Stewarts returned: the good judge had forgotten his doggie bag.

The couple was charged with collusion, fraud, unauthorized assumption of ownership of personal property of others, and of being . . .

NY JOURNAL'S DUMBASS OF THE WEEK

Your reaction?

LOL	Fail	WTF
128,357	712	12,455

REED STEWART	6:45PM	2%
TODAY	ALL	MISSED

Carly 9:22 AM
Missed Call

Carly 9:45 AM
Missed Call

Marshall 10:05 AM
Missed Call

From: Dolly Vargas <D.Vargas@VTM.com>
Date: March 13 10:22:10 AM PST
To: Reed Stewart@reedstewart.com
Subject: Lyrexica Offer

Darling, where are you? Why aren't you picking up? Did you get my voicemails? I've left four of them. I've got some exciting news: you've got another endorsement offer. This one is for a product called Lyrexica. It's for male pattern baldness.

And before you start, yes, I know. I *know* you don't have male pattern baldness.

But no one actually *uses* the products they endorse. That's why they want you: There aren't that many athletes with hair as thick and lustrous as yours.

Well, except for that idiotic Cobb Cutler, but as we both know, Cutler would hardly make a good spokesperson for anything. Did you see that statement he released earlier about that Russian model bride of his? I don't know why his people let him write his own social media posts (although I must admit I'm glad they do, as they provide me with no end of entertainment).

In any case, I believe you owe me $5. I told you that marriage wouldn't last.

Anyway, I know how you feel about pharmaceutical products, but they're offering *six figures*, darling.

And I don't think you can afford to be choosy after what happened last year at Augusta.

Call me soon! I can't wait to get back to those suits with a counter offer.

XOXOX

Dolly
Dolly Vargas
Vargas Talent Management
Los Angeles, CA

> **Marshall 11:17 AM**
> Missed Call

> **Marshall**   11:52 AM
> Dude where are you? Pick up.

> **Marshall**   12:39 PM
> Srsly dude, this is not cool. Call me.

> **Marshall**   1:27 PM
> Dude where are you? Mom and Dad got arrested. MOM AND DAD ARE IN JAIL. Pick the fudge up. I mean fudge. I mean fudge. I HATE THIS PHONE.

> **Marshall**   2:14 PM
> Oh great now. It's on the Internet. MOM AND DAD HAVE BEEN NAMED DUMBASS OF THE WEEK. Our parents are dumbasses.
>
> Not that we didn't know this already (remember all the times they forgot to pay the electric bill and we had to have Christmas in the dark?), but it's a little disturbing to have it announced to the ENTIRE INTERNET. WHERE ARE YOU?

Enrique Alvarez   2:37 PM

Boudro. Did you want chili on that? If you don't text back in one minute, you're getting chili on your dog. That is what happens when you send your caddy for your lunch and you also forget to give him money. AGAIN.

Marshall   3:05 PM

Oh great. Now it's the lead story on the evening news. Jackie Monroe of Channel 4 WISH-TV is talking about our parents. OUR PARENTS!!!!

Now even people who don't have the Internet are going to know. If there is anyone who doesn't have the Internet, which I guess is only you because YOU NEVER CHARGE YOUR PHONE.

From: Dolly Vargas <D.Vargas@VTM.com>
Date: March 13 4:10:10 PM PST
To: Reed Stewart@reedstewart.com
Subject: Lyrexica Offer

Why haven't you replied about the Lyrexica offer? Is it because you're worried about it ending up in a class action lawsuit like Paryxica? Don't. This stuff has actually been tested on humans, apparently, with no ill effects.

Well, so far.

And what are these rumors I'm hearing about *your parents* being those people in that hick little town who tried to scam that restaurant? They aren't true, are they?

Because you know if they are, it would be *brilliant.* I could plop you down with Jen over at *SportsCenter* and the two of you could do a heartwarming human interest piece about it, which would get the fans rooting for you going into the Golden Palm. Right now Cutler's got all the sympathy, because of how much that little Russian scam artist is taking him for.

But I think this could help turn the tables in your favor, because everyone loves an underdog.

You know I think the name of that town of theirs is familiar to me for some reason, but I can't think why. I'm sure it will come to me soon.

Call me, if you ever remember to charge your phone.

XOXOX

Dolly
Dolly Vargas
Vargas Talent Management
Los Angeles, CA

Marshall　　　　　　　　　　　　　　　　　　4:45 PM
Dude I am going to kill you if you don't pick your fudging phone I meant fudge I meant fudge I'm going to kill MYSELF now MY LIFE IS OVER I can't believe you left me alone to deal with this shoot on my own I meant shoot I mean AHHHHHHHHHHHH

WHERE ARE YOU??????

Carly　　　　　　　　　　　　　　　　　　6:05 PM
Hi Reed, you've probably been playing golf all day and forgot to charge your phone or are out of range or something but if you can please call Marshall or me as soon as you get this text because there's a slight problem with your parents.

Nothing serious! No one is hurt. Except possibly Marshall, but only emotionally.

Please call. Thx!

Please Observe "Environmental Stakes." Green Tipped Stakes one stroke penalty. (Do Not Enter Area.)

HOLE	BLUE Rated 74.1/Slope 146	GOLD Rated 72.0/Slope 137	WHITE Rated 70.3/Slope 129	HANDICAP	PAR	REED		COBB			HANDICAP	RED Rated 72.3/Slope 129
1	500	495	461	9	5	4	−1	4	−1		5	434
2	307	300	265	13	4	3	−2	3	−2		13	224
3	407	340	334	5	4	4	−2	4	−2		11	305
4	190	176	160	15	3	2	−3	2	−2		15	127
5	451	411	385	1	4	5	−2	4	−2		3	342
6	400	390	345	11	4	4	−2	3	−3		9	306
7	418	412	382	3	4	4	−1	5	−2		1	341
8	158	152	146	17	3	2	−3	2	−3		17	127
9	394	367	357	7	4	4	−3	5	−2		7	326
OUT	3225	3043	2835		35	32		32				2532
	PLAYER										PLAYER	
10	520	477	467	8	5	4	−4	4	−3		10	401
11	365	353	318	14	4	4	−4	3	−4		14	285
12	432	421	406	6	4	4	−4	4	−4		4	341
13	126	119	99	18	3	3	−4	2	−5		18	76
14	576	546	541	2	5	4	−5	5	−5		2	475
15	390	372	342	12	4	3	−6	5	−5		12	296
16	200	191	157	16	3	3	−6	2	−6		16	129
17	413	376	368	4	4	4	−6	3	−7		8	321
18	574	524	510	10	5	5	−6	6	−6		6	476
In	3596	3379	3208		37	34		35				2800
Tot	6821	6422	6043		72	66		67				5332
HANDICAP												
NET SCORE												
DATE		SCORER					ATTEST					

SPECIAL NOTE: THE BEACH RESORT COURSES ARE IRRIGATED WITH RECLAIMED WATER.

PELICAN BEACH GOLF RESORT

Practice "Good Golf"

Date: March 13

Scorer: Reed Stewart

Attest: Enrique Alvarez

Please—Repair Ball Marks on Greens—Fill Divots With Sand
– USGA Rules Govern All Play –

Please Note: This course is proudly irrigated with reclaimed water.

Thank you for playing Pelican Beach Golf Resort!

| BECKY FLOWERS | 5:45PM | 98% |
| TODAY | ALL | MISSED |

Mom — 5:45 PM
Becky, Nicole just told me about the Stewarts! Bloomville hasn't been on the news in years. Not since that tornado over by the mall. And the Dumbbell Killer, of course.

Becky — 5:45 PM
Mom, where are you?

Mom — 5:46 PM
I'm at the park. I'd call but there's such terrible reception here. I could barely hear Nicole when she called to tell me Jackie Monroe from Channel 4 was talking about the judge. Can you imagine? Jackie was talking about OUR town!

Becky — 5:46 PM
Mom, it's going to get dark soon. Why are you at the park?

Mom — 5:46 PM
Sunset tonight isn't until after 7. And I found so many wonderful sticks here the other day when I was helping the Girl Scouts clean up after that storm.

Becky — 5:46 PM
You also found a drunk homeless man urinating near your car, remember?

Mom — 5:47 PM
Oh, he was harmless. I only called the police because I didn't want the girls to see him with his pants down. Although I'm sure some of them have seen worse.

Becky — 5:47 PM
Mom, they sell firewood at Home Depot.

Mom   5:47 PM
Not firewood, honey. Sticks. Didn't I show you my latest design? I'm spray-painting sticks white and then hanging little quilted letters from them that spell out the word BLESSED.

Becky   5:47 PM
Why exactly are you doing this?

Mom   5:47 PM
Because everyone uses the word BLESSED under the photos they post of themselves on vacation on Facebook. Or under their grandchildren's photos.

Becky   5:47 PM
I know what blessed means, Mom, and understand the connotation. I still use the Count Your Blessings Gratitude Journal that Grandma gave me for Christmas. I just don't get what the sticks are for.

Mom   5:48 PM
Oh, I'm so glad you still have the journal! Jackie Monroe says that journaling helps reduces stress.

But with my design, you can just hang the stick over your head and take your selfie. You don't have to write the word BLESSED underneath anymore. It already says BLESSED above. So it saves a step.

Becky   5:48 PM
It's called a hashtag, Mom.

Mom   5:48 PM
I'm calling them Blessie Sticks. You know like Selfie Sticks? I already made some Blessie Sticks for my craft booth at the farmers' market last Sunday, and they ended up being my bestseller! Dr. McLintock's wife bought 12 at $50 each to give to the nurses' aides at the hospital. I couldn't believe it!

Becky   5:48 PM
I can't believe it either.

Mom   5:49 PM

So I'm going to make a lot more for the craft show in South Bend next weekend. I have plenty of fabric so all I need are sticks. But they need to be NICE sticks, not too dirty or with any leaves on them. And no bugs, either, obviously.

So I wanted to know if you're going to call him?

Becky   5:49 PM

Who?

Mom   5:49 PM

Well, Reed of course. I'm sure he'll be coming back now that his poor parents are convicts. Are you going to call him?

Becky   5:49 PM

Why would I call Reed, Mom?

Mom   5:50 PM

Well, the two of you used to be so close.

Becky   5:50 PM

That was ten years ago, Mom. I'm an adult now and I'm in an adult relationship. Remember? My boyfriend, Graham?

Mom   5:50 PM

Oh, I know. Reed was just so special. Even in high school he stood out from the other boys, so tall and polite, and he got along so well with your dad. Remember how he used to take Dad to the country club to play golf?

Becky   5:51 PM

I remember, Mom.

Mom   5:51 PM

None of your other boyfriends ever did that.

Becky   5:52 PM

That's because Dad died, Mom.

Mom   5:52 PM

Well, I'm just saying, Reed was a very nice boy. And everyone makes mistakes, so you shouldn't hold that little thing that happened on prom night against him. He's obviously changed his ways. He'd have to, in order to win all those tournaments and endorsements! And maybe you could help those poor people.

Becky   5:52 PM

What people?

Mom   5:52 PM

His parents. They were so very kind to us when Dad got sick.

Becky   5:52 PM

Mom, I don't really have time for this now, I'm heading over to Authentic for the tasting tonight.

Mom   5:53 PM

Oh, well, give Graham my love. Tell him I simply adored his Blue Log.

Becky   5:53 PM

?!

Mom   5:53 PM

You know, that cheese he suggested for my quilting group. It was delicious.

Becky   5:54 PM

Oh. I'll be sure to let him know. Don't spend too long in the park, Mom.

Mom   5:54 PM

Oh, I won't. It looks like all the best sticks are gone anyway. I'll probably try the empty lot by the firehouse next. Have fun tonight! ♥

From: Trimble Stewart-Antonelli@Stewart&Stewart.com
Date: March 13 7:06:26 PM EST
To: Carly Stewart@StewartRealty.com; Marshall Stewart@StewartRealty
.com; Reed Stewart@reedstewart.com
Cc: Tony Antonelli@AntonelliPizza.com
Subject: Our Parents

Dear Marshall, Reed, and Carly (I am including you, Carly, because I know Marshall tells you everything anyway, and of course I'm including my own spouse, Tony):

I have bailed Mom and Dad out of jail.

No need to thank or repay me. As their eldest child (and executor of their Will) it was my obligation.

I'm writing to let you know, however, that this is the last time I will have anything to do with our parents. Their recent behavior is not only embarrassing, it is jeopardizing both my standing as an officer of the court, and Tony's standing in the community as a well-known restaurateur (for those of you who don't know, he's starting a sister restaurant to Antonelli's next month in Dearborn which he plans to call Antonelli's II).

I'm not sure if any of you are aware of the extent to which Mom and Dad have gone downhill. I found out this afternoon when I asked them to reimburse me for their bond ($1600.00), and they informed me that they have no money.

Not no money saved for retirement. They have NO MONEY AT ALL.

Not only have they taken out a second mortgage on the house, they've been taking out cash advances on their credit cards to pay (some of) their bills.

(I say "some of" their bills because when I dropped them off at the house, I found numerous "past due" notices in the mailbox, which they had clearly not checked in some time. They included bills from local businesses, such as Hayes Hardware, from which Daddy has evidently purchased a new pool liner.)

On the other hand, Mom has purchased over $5,000 worth of scratch-offs from Publishers Clearing House in the past three months. She paid for those by check.

When I confronted our parents about this, they laughed and told me not to worry because "It's all going to get straightened out."

Would you like to know how?

Apparently, our parents' entire financial plan for retirement is to make "millions" by selling more stamps like the one with which they tried to rip off Shenanigans last night, and winning the Publishers Clearing House Sweepstakes.

OUR PARENTS ARE COLLEGE EDUCATED. HOW CAN THIS BE HAPPENING?

I attempted to explain to both of them that even in the unlikely event they made a fortune off Daddy's stamp collection and Mom's scratch-offs, they'd still have to pay taxes on both the sales and winnings, and that even then there would certainly not be enough money left over to pay for:

1. The removal of over a dozen feral cats that currently live in and around the house.

2. The mortgage(s).

3. The two Mercedes (would anyone care to explain to me why our parents are currently leasing two brand-new Mercedes when they can't even afford one?), or

4. The US government, to which Daddy owes thousands in back taxes (which he does not feel he actually owes, because, he explained to me, his accountant died five years ago. According to Daddy, when your accountant dies, you do not have to pay taxes anymore. What a wonderful law of which I was not aware until now! Why don't we all start murdering our accountants? Then we'll never have to pay taxes again).

Thank God Daddy signed the office over to me outright as my graduation present from law school, or that would soon be foreclosed on as well.

When I told Daddy that he was deluded and it was clearly time for him and Mom to give me power of attorney over their finances so I could straighten out this mess (as executor, I can only arrange for payment of their debts after they are deceased), he told me to "Go suck an egg."

And when I suggested very nicely that he and Mommy might want to visit some doctor other than Dr. Jones to get an opinion on the state of their mental health, since it's very clear—to me, anyway—that the two of them are cuckoo, he told me on no uncertain terms to get out of the house.

Even my advice that they move to a nice senior living community in California like Uncle Lyle did, and sell the house (or at least put in the appearance of trying to sell it before the bank seizes it, not that anyone would ever want to buy that foul-smelling crumbling heap), was met with extreme harshness. Daddy informed me that the only way he'll ever leave Bloomville is "in a pine box."

So I'm writing this to say good luck. I have done my part today, and I won't be doing any more. My husband and I have our own businesses to run, as well as two teenagers to raise. I do not have the time or inclination to play games with those yo-yos who call themselves our parents.

In the unlikely event you ARE able to talk sense into those two, I hope you remember that Mom said I could have all the silver and Waterford crystal, and of course the Venetian glass chandelier from the dining room. You don't have a formal dining room, Carly, so the chandelier wouldn't fit, and your children are too young to appreciate stemware.

And none of those items would suit your lifestyle, Reed.

As executor of their Will—and what I've been through today—frankly, it's the least I deserve.

Sincerely,

Trimble Stewart-Antonelli
Attorney at Law
Stewart & Stewart, LLC
1911 South Moore Pike
Bloomville, IN 47401
(812) 555-9721
www.stewart&stewart.com

CARLY STEWART	8:00PM	92%
TODAY	ALL	MISSED

Carly — 7:37 PM
I hate your sister.

Marshall — 7:37 PM
Calm down. Remember what the therapist said.

Carly — 7:37 PM
I do. That's why I'm texting that I hate your sister instead of screaming it in front of the kids.

Marshall — 7:38 PM
No, not that part. About how Trimble can't help the way she is. She has self-esteem issues.

Carly — 7:38 PM
Well, maybe that is something your parents should have thought about before they named her Trimble.

Then she might not have felt the need to marry the first and only guy who ever asked her out, and who turned out to be so unlikable he could never get a job, so his own parents had to buy him a pizza parlor just so he'd have some form of employment.

Marshall — 7:39 PM
You think HER name is bad? I'm named after Thurgood Marshall.

And whoever heard of Supreme Court Justice Stanley Forman REED?

Carly — 7:40 PM
The supreme court justice your parents named your sister after died after serving only two years on the bench.

Plus people in high school called her TRIM for short.

Marshall   7:40 PM

Ergo why she has low self-esteem.

Carly   7:40 PM

I don't care. I still hate her. Almost as much as I hate Summer Hayes.

Marshall   7:41 PM

I hope you feel better now that you got that off your chest.

Carly   7:41 PM

I do a little. Thank you.

We still have to decide what we're going to do about your parents though.

Marshall   7:41 PM

Kill my sister?

Carly   7:41 PM

☺

FACEBOOK

Authentic Wine and Cheese Boutique
added an event

12 hrs

Wine and Cheese Tasting Tonight between 6pm and 10pm.
Sample wines and cheeses from around the world!

Tony Antonelli, Summer Hayes, Becky Flowers, and 54 others like this.

TOP COMMENTS

Becky Flowers–Can't wait!

Today at 1:10

Graham Tucker–☺ ♥

Henry De Santos–Save me some of that cabernet we had the other night!

Today at 1:16 PM

Nicole Flowers–And some of those ice wines!

Today at 2:45

Graham Tucker–On your special shelf, guys!

Today at 3:12 PM

Tony Antonelli–Totally going to see you there, bruh!

Today at 3:45 PM

Graham Tucker–Awesome!

Today at 3:52 PM

Trimble Stewart-Antonelli–We would love to come, but we have to put our little ones to bed after we make them a delicious, homemade, organic dinner with the whole family, like we do every night, because FAMILY comes first. Plus I get migraines when I drink wine.

Today at 5:30 PM

Graham Tucker—Next time, try stopping by to pick up a bottle of pinot noir to drink at home while you make your family dinner, Trimble. Pinots noirs are naturally low in tannins, as are white wines like pinot gris. The number one cause for wine headaches is dehydration, so be sure to drink plenty of water while enjoying my wines!

Today at 5:32 PM

Graham Tucker—I'd just like to say that I appreciate all of you supporting locally owned businesses, particularly Authentic, and that on St. Patrick's Day, there will be a 10% discount for any members of law enforcement or the Armed Forces who attend our Irish Cheddar tasting!

Today at 6:00 PM

Henry De Santos—Woo-hoo!

Today at 6:02 PM

Going (128)
Recent Guests (20+ new)
Maybe (47)
Invited (527)

Marshall Stewart Joined Chat 10:02 PM

Carly Stewart Joined Chat 10:02 PM

Marshall Stewart Wait, what are we doing here again?

Carly Stewart Instant messaging with Reed about your parents.

Marshall Stewart Why not Facetiming?

Carly Stewart I told you. Reed ran over his phone with a golf cart and broke the camera.

Marshall Stewart Again?

Carly Stewart Just be glad I finally reached him.

Marshall Stewart Why can't my family be normal for once?

Carly Stewart Oh, sweetie, if you think you or your family will ever be normal you are sadly mistaken.

Marshall Stewart What do you

Reed Stewart Joined Chat 10:04 PM

Reed Stewart Hey, hey, hey! How's my favorite pair of breeders?

Marshall Stewart Shut up. Our parents are felons.

Reed Stewart And a good day to you, too, big bro!

Carly Stewart Good evening. It's night here now, Reed.

Marshall Stewart What precisely is good about anything that has happened in the past 24 hours?

Carly Stewart Marshall isn't taking the news about your parents too well, Reed.

Reed Stewart So I see. But they're home now, right?

Marshall Stewart Oh, they're home. Didn't you get Trimble's email?

Reed Stewart Yeah, I got it, but I didn't read it. Trimble never sends me anything but hate mail ever since she found out I have access to a private plane and decided it would be an appropriate Christmas present from me to fly her, Tony, and their kids to Aspen. I thought a $25 iTunes gift card was a good enough Christmas present for each of the kids instead. Trimble called me a bad uncle. We agreed to disagree.

Carly Stewart YOU HAVE A PRIVATE PLANE????

Reed Stewart No. Trimble THINKS I do because she saw on some TV show that pro golfers fly private to their tournaments. And it's true sometimes we'll all chip in and rent a plane because we're not going to risk losing our clubs by flying commercial and having to check them. But that doesn't mean I'm dumb enough to buy my own plane. My finance guy would kill me. He says the two worst things a man can waste his money on are yachts and private planes. Both of them are just holes you end up throwing cash into because they're always broken.

Marshall Stewart Wow, Reed, it is so fascinating to sit here and read about the financial woes of a multimillionaire professional athlete. Please, tell us more.

Carly Stewart Marshall, come on. You know he didn't mean it like that. And I'm the one who asked about the plane.

Reed Stewart For your information, Marshall, the reason I have a financial advisor is so I can make sure I have enough money set aside to start a line of junior golf schools someday.

Marshall Stewart Junior golf school? Where'd you come up with *that* one?

Reed Stewart Come on, Marshall. You know what it was like in that house, especially between me and the Judge. Golf is the only thing that kept me sane—well, one of the things. In the end, it saved me—literally. I think more kids should be able to experience the game, and the only way that's going to happen is if it's made more accessible and less expensive. I want to start an after-school program that does just that. Plus I'm getting tired of always being on the road, living out of suitcases, laying my head down on a different pillow every night.

Carly Stewart   Oh, Reed. That's so sweet.

Marshall Stewart   Sweet? Are you kidding me? Are you actually falling for that cheesy line, Car?

Carly Stewart   What are you talking about?

Marshall Stewart   Reed, how often does that "tired of always being on the road, living out of suitcases" line work to get you laid?

Reed Stewart   Surprisingly often.

Marshall Stewart   I rest my case. My brother is a monster.

Reed Stewart   But a lovable one.

Carly Stewart   Would you two stop it? We're not here to talk about Reed's sex life. We're here to talk about your parents. Did you seriously not read Trimble's email, Reed?

Reed Stewart   I skimmed it.

Marshall Stewart   Skimmed it???? Our parents are apparently broke and possibly suffering from dementia, and you skimmed it.

Reed Stewart   Yeah, that's the part I'm not understanding. How the hell can they be broke? Trimble bragged in her Christmas e-newsletter about how proud she was to be pulling in over six figures a year in her private practice with The Judge.

Carly Stewart	Ew! I forgot she did that. And showed photos of her and Tony and their precious darlings on that ski trip to Aspen. Which she did manage to get to, despite Reed cruelly refusing to fly them there in his nonexistent private plane.
Marshall Stewart	Well, unfortunately, none of us thought to check what Mom and Dad were doing with their share of that money.
Reed Stewart	Evidently leasing new Mercedes and paying way too much for commemorative stamps of George Washington.
Carly Stewart	Don't forget playing Publishers Clearing House scratch-offs. That was my favorite part.
Reed Stewart	It sounds like some of this has been going on for a while. How is it that we're only finding out about it now?
Carly Stewart	We're not. *Some* of us have known about it for quite a while. But others of us have been in complete denial and refused to admit anything is wrong because he wants to avoid conflict at all cost, especially with your dad.
Marshall Stewart	That isn't fair. How were we supposed to know any of this was going on? Mom and Dad won't even let us into the house anymore since Carly dared to mention it wasn't smelling as fresh as it used to since they fired Rhonda.
Reed Stewart	THEY FIRED RHONDA?
Carly Stewart	I told you we should have waited to tell him in person, Marshall.
Marshall Stewart	How would we do that when he never COMES HERE? We only see him once a year—if that—when we go to LA to see him, or he plays at a course nearby.

Reed Stewart	How could they fire Rhonda? Rhonda's been working for them since we were kids! Where am I going to get baked chicken exactly the way I like it if they fired Rhonda?
Marshall Stewart	Yes, Reed, as always, this is all about you. And your stomach.
Carly Stewart	I know what you mean, Reed. And as far as we can tell, your parents fired Rhonda after 25 years of exemplary service because of your dad buying 800 antique judge's gavels from another collector of vintage courtroom memorabilia he met in Terre Haute.
Reed Stewart	Excuse me?
Marshall Stewart	Oh yes, you didn't know? Dad says he got a really great deal on them because the seller "had no idea what he was doing."
Reed Stewart	What is Dad going to do with *800* antique judges gavels?
Marshall Stewart	Dad says he plans to sell them for three times as much as he paid for them. He says between those and his stamp collection, which as you know he's been working on for years, he's going to be a MILLIONAIRE.
Reed Stewart	And it never occurred to you that this was slightly odd?
Carly Stewart	THANK YOU!!! You see, Reed? You see what I have to live with on a daily basis?
Marshall Stewart	Dad's always been a little bit eccentric! Remember when he and Mom used to let us ride our bikes to Dairy Queen when I was 11 and you were 7?
Reed Stewart	Yes. How was that eccentric?
Marshall Stewart	Reed, the nearest Dairy Queen was twelve miles away.

Reed Stewart   So you're saying they've always been this way, and firing Rhonda over a bunch of gavels makes perfect sense to you?

Carly Stewart   Your parents explained to me that they had to fire Rhonda because they didn't need a cook anymore once they got rid of the stove, which they did to make room for the washer and dryer, which they brought up from the basement to make space for all the gavels.

Reed Stewart   Was any of that supposed to make sense?

Marshall Stewart   It does when you think about it.

Reed Stewart   No. No, Marshall, it does not. Where is the stove now?

Carly Stewart   It WAS sitting out in the front yard with the turkey carcasses until Rhonda had her sons come and load it onto a truck and take it to their church. Rhonda said if the Judge wanted to act crazy, that was his business, but she knew of some non-crazy people who could still appreciate good home cooking.

Reed Stewart   Wait. What turkey carcasses?

Marshall Stewart   Carly, you know what the therapist said. 'Crazy' is a dehumanizing term. Mom and Dad, like Bailey, just do things a little bit differently than everyone else, and some people, such as our darling sister and maybe the Bloomville police, judge them a little too harshly for it.

Reed Stewart   What therapist? You guys are seeing a therapist???

Carly Stewart   Yes, because your older brother is living in complete denial, Reed. Your parents need help but refuse to get it because they don't see that there's a problem. And certain members of your family only see it's a problem when it's made public, like now. But even then they only want to sweep it under the rug to make it go away, not actually take steps to solve it.

Marshall Stewart	Exactly! Because now the *whole world* knows, thanks to what Mom and Dad did last night at Shenanigans, and the *NY Journal* publicizing it. That's why Trimble is so upset.
Carly Stewart	I wasn't actually talking about Trimble, Marshall, but that's besides the point. Although I'm still wondering who sent the article from the *Bloomville Herald* to the *NY Journal*.
Marshall Stewart	This isn't about your personal vendetta against Summer any more than it's about Reed's stomach.
Reed Stewart	Hey, can we all just take a breath here? And I can't believe Summer Walters is still around.
Carly Stewart	Of course she is. Every town needs its bitchy busybody, and ours is still Summer. Only it's Summer Hayes now. She married Bob Hayes. He inherited Hayes Hardware from his dad. That's where your dad bought the pool liner—well, not exactly, since he still hasn't paid for it.
Marshall Stewart	Can we FOCUS? I've made a list of the things we three need to get to work on since Trimble says she isn't going to help, and would be useless anyway.

1) Meet with a lawyer—not Trimble, obviously—to see what we can do about Mom and Dad's tax situation.

2) Start calling their credit card companies and see if we can negotiate some kind of payment plan.

3) Do the same with whatever local business people they owe money to—such as Hayes Hardware.

4) Start looking into retirement communities where Mom and Dad can go live where they'll be well taken care of. Because they sure aren't going to want to live with any of us after this, and none of us want them either—unless there's something you haven't told us, Reed.

5) Start sorting through their crap—if they'll even let us in the house—and see if there's anything that really is valuable that we can sell to pay off some of their debt.

6) List the house and sell it. Fire sale it if we need to. Just get them the hell out of there before reporters from around the world start descending on Bloomville to interview the couple who tried to defraud Shenanigans. Also because Dad slipped on the ice twice this past winter just trying to get to the garage, and Mom's thrown her back out three times falling in the bathtub.

Carly Stewart   How about Trimble's suggestion, getting them to see some doctor other than Dr. Jones? He's older than they are, *and* they're best friends. I highly doubt he's ever going to give your parents a diagnosis of dementia.

Marshall Stewart   Because my parents don't have dementia! Not unless they've had it they're whole lives. They're just weird. They've always been weird.

Carly Stewart   You see, Reed? You see what I have to put up with?

Marshall Stewart   What? Why do people automatically assume every person over the age of 60 who acts out of the ordinary has to have dementia? You know what that's called? Ageism.

Carly Stewart   I let your mother drive to Antonelli's the last time we had Ladies Lunch with her and the girls and she went through three red lights. When I pointed it out, she said red lights are for other people, not her, because she's such a good driver.

Reed Stewart   To be fair, she's always been that way. But, anyway, they aren't moving in with me. I'll take number four.

Marshall Stewart   Finding them a retirement home? That's the easiest one!

Reed Stewart   No, it's the hardest. Trimble says the Judge won't go.

Marshall Stewart Actually finding a place for them to move is easy. Getting them to go is the hard part. And all you're going to do is call Uncle Lyle to see if there's a spot for them at his place in Palm Springs.

Reed Stewart   For your information, Marshall, they wouldn't take Mom and the Judge at Uncle Lyle's place in Palm Springs, because it happens to be a retirement resort for members of the LGBT community only. Do you really think Richard and Connie Stewart would fit in there?

Marshall Stewart Oh. Well, okay maybe not. But you're still trying to do whatever you can to keep from having to come here. Don't pretend like you're not. And I know why, too. To keep from seeing HER.

Reed Stewart   I have no idea what you're talking about.

Marshall Stewart Well, I'm not talking about Rhonda, that's for sure.

Carly Stewart   Marshall, I think you're being a little unfair. Reed has a pretty good reason for not having visited Bloomville in so long.

Marshall Stewart Oh, please! It was a decade ago! He needs to get over it. And we've all got something a lot more embarrassing to worry about now, don't we?

Carly Stewart   Yes, but your father is the one who told him to get out and never come back.

Marshall Stewart Again, a decade ago. And Dad clearly wasn't serious.

Reed Stewart   Marshall, after I moved in with Uncle Lyle—the only family member who'd take me in after the Judge kicked me out—Dad sent me a letter by registered mail telling me to consider myself *persona non grata* in Bloomville. He said if I ever dared set foot in the state of Indiana, he'd have me arrested for trespassing, theft, assault, operating a motor vehicle while intoxicated, and underage drinking. And since he was the attorney general for the state of Indiana at the time, it seemed pretty serious to me.

Marshall Stewart   Fine. Maybe he overreacted. But as we all found out, you were going to move in with Lyle anyway. And Dad clearly regrets the things he said. The old man talks about you all the time, and watches every tournament you qualify for. I think he's really sorry about what happened. Only you've never had the balls to come back and let him apologize . . . All because of a GIRL.

Carly Stewart   Marshall, I think you're being a little harsh.

Reed Stewart   If you're talking about Becky, I was trying to do the right thing.

Carly Stewart   I think we should change the subject. Let's talk about how much we all hate Trimble. Or Summer Hayes.

Marshall Stewart   The right thing would have been for you to have come back here a long time ago, Reed, and face your demons. Then I wouldn't be the only sane person in this family here dealing with them now.

Carly Stewart   Marshall, STOP IT! Reed, I understand. Your dad used to be pretty scary. But he's gotten much more mellow with age. I think he's actually forgotten everything that happened between the two of you that night.

Marshall Stewart   It's not DAD that Reed is worried about facing again, Carly. Is it, Reed?

Carly Stewart   I said STOP IT, Marshall.

Reed Stewart   If Dad's so fine with me, why didn't he apologize to me at your wedding?

Carly Stewart	Well, possibly because you and Marshall were acting like such jackasses, remember? You made your sister's husband two hours late to the reception.
Marshall Stewart	Oh my God. I forgot about that.
Reed Stewart	How could Tony not have been able to figure out how to unlock the limo doors from the inside?
Marshall Stewart	Oh, Tony.
Reed Stewart	Too bad, Tony. Too Bad Tony.
Carly Stewart	You are both idiots. Look, Becky is fine, Reed. You don't need to worry about her. She owns her own business now. She took over her dad's moving company.
Reed Stewart	Oh, right. I saw that on Facebook.
Marshall Stewart	You stalk your ex on Facebook??? Creeper.
Carly Stewart	Marshall, leave him alone.
Reed Stewart	I'm not going to apologize for having a certain curiosity about what happened to the people we grew up with.
Marshall Stewart	Yeah. ONE person.
Reed Stewart	I find it interesting how the careers they have as adults match the personalities they had as kids. Like Bob Hayes being in hardware and Becky being in the moving business.
Marshall Stewart	Both their fathers died of cancer and left them the family business.
Reed Stewart	Yeah, but Becky always did like organizing things and bossing people around.
Carly Stewart	And Bob was always a tool.
Marshall Stewart	Too bad you didn't listen to Becky, Reed. You might actually have gotten a college education.

Reed Stewart	Instead of a six figure endorsement contract with Callaway Golf Clubs? Yes, I weep nightly into my pillow about that, Marshall.
Carly Stewart	Yes, I don't think your brother is doing too badly for himself, Marshall. So if you've been on Becky's Facebook page, Reed, you've probably seen that she has a great new boyfriend now. He owns that really nice wine and cheese shop on the courthouse square. He seems really great.
Reed Stewart	No. I must have missed that.
Marshall Stewart	HA HA HA! Creep fail.
Carly Stewart	Marshall, would you please grow up?
Reed Stewart	I've been seeing a really great woman too. She also owns her own business.
Marshall Stewart	Of course she does.
Carly Stewart	That's great, Reed.
Reed Stewart	She's a wine rep. I'm giving her golf lessons.
Marshall Stewart	Of course you are.
Carly Stewart	Stop it, Marshall. It's nice that you and your new girlfriend have similar interests, Reed.
Reed Stewart	Her name is Valery.
Carly Stewart	With a y. How unusual.
Marshall Stewart	OK great! So since the two of you are so close why don't you bring Valeryyyy here tomorrow with you to help us to clean up this mess of Mom and Dad's.
Reed Stewart	Tomorrow? Actually I can't tomorrow because I have the Golden Palm Invitational next week in Orlando. Valery and I were going to fly down there a little early

so I could look at investment properties and maybe get in a few practice rounds before the Golden Palm. My finance guy says if I live in Florida for six months of the year I could save a ton in taxes.

Marshall Stewart   Oh, yeah, buddy? Well guess what? I got a different invitation for you. It's an invitation to the game Carly and I have to play every single day while you're off looking at investment properties in the Florida sunshine with your new lady friend.

Carly Stewart   Marshall.

Marshall Stewart   Only in this game, you don't get any practice swings. Life just throws balls at you all the time, in the form of things like your parents getting arrested, or your seven-year-old kid deciding that she wants to dress like an Indian chief every day and do war dances at the halftime of her older sister's soccer games, which the other parents tell you is culturally insensitive. And you don't get days off, or even a choice. It's the same thing, day in and day out, until you want to stab yourself with the knives your mother gave to your wife for her birthday, because your mother thinks knives are an appropriate gift, and now she needs to have her maxed out credit cards taken away from her. Only in order to do THAT, you need the help of your brother, the brother who NEVER COMES HOME because of something that happened between him and some girl way back in HIGH SCHOOL.

Carly Stewart   Marshall!

Reed Stewart   All right. All right, I'm sorry. I understand. I'll book the first decent flight I can get for Indiana.

Carly Stewart   Great! See? That's the Reed I know.

Reed Stewart   It's going to be OK, Marshall.

Marshall Stewart   Is it? Is it really??? BECAUSE I DON'T THINK IT IS.
I THINK MY PARENTS ARE GOING TO BE LIVING
WITH ME AND I AM GOING TO BE SURROUNDED
BY CAT FIGURINES AND THEN I WILL GO INSANE.

Reed Stewart   No. No, Marshall. I will not let that happen. What cat
figurines?

Carly Stewart   I'm sorry, Reed. I saw them the last time your parents
let me in the house.

Reed Stewart   I don't want to know about this, do I?

Carly Stewart   No. Marshall didn't want to know, either. But I told him
anyway. Your mom has over 2,000 ceramic cat figurines,
many dressed in adorable period costumes or nursing
litters of equally cute ceramic kittens. She even has an
Amazon buyer's account under the name Not-So-Crazy
Cat Lady.

Reed Stewart   I knew I didn't want to know.

Carly Stewart   I'm so sorry.

Reed Stewart   Any chance we can hire back Rhonda?

Marshall Stewart   Seriously, dude? Is your stomach all you ever think
about?

Reed Stewart   I mean because Richard and Connie know and TRUST
her and might let her help with the sorting. Not
because her baked chicken is the best thing in the
world. Even though it is.

Carly Stewart   Reed, you don't understand. This is too big a job for
Rhonda. Not just the cleaning, but getting your parents
to part with their collections, and eventually getting
them out of there. They have to agree to downsize.
That's one thing I know Dr. Jones would agree with—
because I drove your dad to his office when he slipped
on the ice, and then when your mom got bronchitis.

We're going to need to get them into a new, smaller place, preferably in a warmer climate. I mean, this is all assuming they don't go to jail for the Shenanigans thing.

Reed Stewart   I see. Well, let me talk to my finance guy. I've got a bunch of cash squirrelled away. I was saving it for the golf school, but this is obviously more important. I can get you whatever you need.

Carly Stewart   Aw, Reed, thanks. That's really nice of you. Isn't it nice of Reed, Marshall?

Marshall Stewart   I guess.

Carly Stewart   Marshall, what's wrong with you?

Marshall Stewart   Money is not what we need at this point.

Carly Stewart   Money is EXACTLY WHAT WE NEED AT THIS POINT, Marshall.

Marshall Stewart   It's no use screaming at me in all caps Carly, or from upstairs, either. You'll only wake the girls.

Reed Stewart   So you're saying you DON'T want my money, Marshall? Because that's fine by me.

Marshall Stewart   THAT ISN'T WHAT I'M SAYING AT ALL. What we need is your body physically here to help for a change. Carly and I can't do it anymore. I literally cannot go over to 65 Country Club Road one more time for dinner and listen to Dad give me the provenance of every single one of his gavels while completely ignoring the fact that he owes tens of thousands of dollars in back taxes and credit card debt.

Carly Stewart   Yes, but we ALSO need your money, Reed. RIGHT, MARSHALL? The real estate business here hasn't been doing all that well, so we really don't have the money to lend your parents to get them out of the hole.

I don't know where your sister is getting all the money she's using to open up a new restaurant in Dearborn. I didn't think Antonelli's was doing that great. But Tony's parents are apparently loaded.

Marshall Stewart   Fine. OK, Reed. We need your money. But we want your body, too. Just not in the same way as those women who fall for your cheesy line about being tired of resting your head on a different pillow every night.

Carly Stewart   I think he gets that, Marshall.

Reed Stewart   Yes, Marshall, I get it. I said I'm coming. I'll get Richard and Connie back on their feet.

Marshall Stewart   STOP CALLING THEM THAT. You do realize we have to take this seriously, don't you? Because I'm afraid if we don't, the next thing that shows up in the paper about Mom and Dad is going to be their obituary. You get that, don't you?

Reed Stewart   OK, Marshall. Yes, I get it. I'm sorry I haven't been around in so long. I swear I'm going to do everything I can to help make it up to you. And to Connie and Richard, too.

Marshall Stewart   REED!!!!

Reed Stewart   Kidding! I'll text you with my flight info as soon as I have it.

Marshall Stewart   OK. Thanks.

Reed Stewart   Don't worry. I've got your back.

Reed Stewart Left chat 11:05 PM

Marshall Stewart   You still here, Car?

Carly Stewart   Have you seen me log off?

Marshall Stewart   No. Do you believe him? Do you really think he'll show up?

Carly Stewart   Of course. He said he would. He's never let us down when it's been important. He sent that check when we needed the loan to buy the house, remember?

Marshall Stewart   That was money. This is emotion—and conflict. Reed isn't good at emotion OR conflict. He runs from them both, as you might have noticed by the way he reacted on his prom night.

Carly Stewart   That was different.

Marshall Stewart   He could have killed her.

Carly Stewart   Marshall, don't be overdramatic. It was a golf cart.

Marshall Stewart   It was a moving vehicle, and he was drunk.

Carly Stewart   He'd had a few beers, and he's never been in trouble since.

Marshall Stewart   He's never been back *here* since.

Carly Stewart   He never forgets your daughters' birthdays.

Marshall Stewart   How hard is that? He has his assistant buy a card and tucks a $10 bill inside. Again, that's money. I know Reed can do money. What I'm asking is if you think he can do THIS.

Carly Stewart   I think Reed still cares about the people he left behind back here in Bloomville, no matter how much he might pretend not to.

Marshall Stewart   I'll believe it when I see it.

Carly Stewart   You've had a very bad day. Is there anything I can do to make it better?

Marshall Stewart   Do you have any strychnine?

Carly Stewart   No. But I'm wearing that red teddy you got me for Christmas.

Marshall Stewart   The one you said you were going to exchange for long underwear?

Carly Stewart   Yes.

Marshall Stewart   This has gone from the worst to the best day of my life.

Carly Stewart   ☺

Carly Stewart Left chat 11:10 PM

Marshall Stewart Left chat 11:10 PM

Blessings Journal

of

BECKY FLOWERS

Today I feel blessed because:

<u>My business is going well.</u>
<u>I have my health.</u>
<u>I have a great mom, sister, and boyfriend.</u>

No. You know what?

All of the above is lies.

Not that I'm not grateful for them. I am. I know how lucky I am. I have an amazing life, and so much to feel thankful for.

But I'm not going to pretend things are going 100 percent great when they're not. Yeah, things are going 100 percent better for me than they are for some other people—Judge Stewart and his wife, for instance—but it was really hard to remember that this evening at the wine and cheese tasting when that troll Summer Hayes came up to me and asked, right in front of Graham, "So Becky, did you hear about Reed Stewart? He's coming back, you know."

It's been ten years. Ten years! I've been in so many other relationships since Reed and I went out (well, okay—three, including Graham).

But I've had multiple hookups, if you count all the rebounding I did during freshman year, when I still thought I might hear from him.

I have very definitely moved on.

So why is it that everyone in this town still links our names together?

And why is it that whenever his name is mentioned, my heart still flips over in my chest, and I catch my breath—so much so that tonight I started choking on the mouthful of camembert I was chewing?

It was so hard to pass off an air of casual indifference in front of Summer and her bitchy friends (and I'm sorry, yes, I know it's anti-feminist to call other women bitches. But I still remember how catty she and her friends were back in high school. Especially since they were seniors when I was a freshman. They should have been supportive of us younger girls. Instead they were always snickering at us. Things have hardly changed).

"I highly doubt that," I said to her, after I'd finished choking.

I think—despite the coughing—I pulled off an air of cool indifference. The glass of pinot noir that Nicole thrust into my hand at the last second definitely helped because I took a long swig from it. That washed down most of the cheese.

"It's unlikely he'd come back after all these years for something that's obviously just a silly misunderstanding," I went on, still with my air of indifference. "I mean, he has siblings that still live in the area. I'm sure they're going to handle the situation."

Okay, I should add here that I was pretty drunk. Graham says the trick of wine tastings is to sip and spit. But I never spit because spitting is disgusting and wine is delicious. Who (besides Graham, and his wine-loving friends) is ever going to spit out something so lovely? Not me.

So I might have been slightly intoxicated at that point.

But not as drunk as Nicole, who of course was knocking back the ice wines Graham had put out as if they were shots. Nicole will not get it through her head that just because something is served in a small glass does NOT mean it's a shot.

"I know Reed has siblings in the area, Becky," Summer said, giving her girlfriends a smirky look. "Carly Stewart, who's married to Reed's older brother, just posted something about it on Facebook a few minutes ago. She's the one saying Reed's definitely coming back. He's got a flight booked for tomorrow. So I guess you're going to have an, uh, *interesting* week."

Then she and all her friends started laughing into their cold shoulder tunics, which I'm sure they got at Ross Dress for Less, because I saw them there last month marked down to twenty-nine ninety-five, which I thought was expensive for something that didn't even have material around the shoulders.

Before I could say anything, Nicole—who really was three sheets to the wind, because she'd already had four glasses of pinot and three ice wines, which she'd pounded, not sipped, and no dinner at all except for a couple mouthfuls of camembert and Wabash Cannonball on wheat-free crackers—slid off her barstool and yelled, "Hey! Hey, you bitches! You leave my sister alone! You can all go to—"

Fortunately at that point Henry stepped in, caught her by the waist before she hit the floor, and said, "Excuse me, ladies. I'm going to take Miss Flowers here outside for a breath of fresh air."

"I don't need any air!" Nicole slurred. "I need to kick those bitches' asses!"

Then Nicole did, indeed, try to kick Summer's ass, but fortunately all she ended up kicking was air, because Henry slung her fireman style over his shoulder and physically carried her from the bar, much to the delight of the other customers, most of whom were his fellow officers from the Bloomville Police Department, and who cheered Henry on.

"Well," Summer said, turning back towards me, her smile very snide. "I see that you still choose to keep charming company, don't you, Rebecca?"

I was so mad, I wanted to throw my glass of pinot in her pointy face.

But since I'm a local business owner in the area, and Nicole is a part-owner of that business as well, I could only say, "I apologize for my sister. She took a decongestant earlier for her allergies, and it appears to have hit her harder than usual."

Then I walked away with as much of my dignity as I could muster.

I wish it had been over after that, but it wasn't. Because Graham had seen the whole thing (of course, since he was behind the bar), and he kept asking, "Are you okay?" the rest of the night, which was totally humiliating (and slightly annoying), even more humiliating than the way Summer and her friends kept looking at me and smirking and then tapping things into their smartphones.

I shouldn't have been annoyed, since it was sweet of him to ask, and perfectly normal.

But it was still annoying.

And then of course on the way home—Graham had to drive me, which was ALSO humiliating, because after the incident with Summer, I may have had another glass or three of pinot, so I couldn't get behind the wheel, and of course Henry had left with Nicole, and there's no Uber in Bloomville, let alone a taxi company—Graham asked, "Who is this Reed guy everyone was talking about?"

And so then I had to tell him.

I didn't want to, but I felt I owed it to him. He was going to find out anyway.

I tried to keep it light, sticking only to the highlights: how Reed and I had dated our senior year. How he'd asked me to prom. How he'd come to pick me up that night not in a rented limo, like so many of the other girls' dates, or in the red convertible BMW he'd driven back then, but in a golf cart—his dad's golf cart, the one he and I used to cruise around on the country club golf course on which his parents lived and on which Reed, back then, had played nine holes every day before school and then the other nine every day after class, because all Reed Steward cared about—all he lived and breathed for back then—was golf.

And me.

At least that's what he'd said.

And how he'd decorated the golf cart in purple and white streamers and carnations—our school colors—and how hard I'd laughed when I'd seen it, and how hard our friends had laughed when we'd cruised up to Matsumori's Tiki Palace in it, and how much fun we'd had after dinner at the prom, dancing and drinking adult beverages that someone had acquired from their parents' liquor cabinet, the first time I'd ever done such a thing, and then how we'd driven the golf cart home, having the night of our lives . . .

Until the golf cart ended up in the country club's pool, with both of us still inside, enraging the club's aging security guard, who called the police, who in turn called Reed's father, who disowned his youngest son on the spot, not so much for the damage he'd caused the club, the injury done to me (I dislocated a shoulder), and embarrassment he'd inflicted upon the Stewart family (it made the local paper), but because Reed chose that moment—as I was being loaded into an ambulance—to blurt to the Judge that he had no intention of following in his father's footsteps and becoming a lawyer someday. He wasn't even going to college upon graduation (as his parents were expecting him to do: he'd received a four year athletic scholarship to Indiana University). Instead, he was going to move to California to live with his uncle, a professor of psychology, and become a professional golfer.

"Is that all?" Graham asked, as he made the turn towards the house in which I'd lived all my life. "My God, the way those girls were carrying on, I thought it was something much worse."

How could I tell Graham that it was . . . much, much worse?

I couldn't, not without explaining everything else . . . how I'd hated Reed Stewart, not after what he'd done to me, but before we'd ever even gone out, hated seeing his tanned, lanky body in the cafeteria, in those stupid Polo shirts and khaki pants, with those even stupider rich boy Ray-Bans tucked into that dark curly hair. Hated, hated, *hated* him, and the way he drove that BMW to school, instead of taking the bus like Nicole and me, because our dad had no money and wasn't a judge, he only owned a moving company and lifted boxes all day instead of making life-changing decisions.

Until the day Mrs. Leland forced us to split into pairs in government class to prepare oral presentations on the McCarthy era, and I got *Reed Stewart* as a partner.

I thought I would die of disdain until Reed looked at the book I was sneak-reading (because Government was so boring) and said, " 'There are few people whom I really love and still fewer of whom I think well.' "

I stared at him in shock. "*You've* read *Pride and Prejudice*?"

"Yes, Flowers." He smirked. "I can read, you know."

It was as if he'd peered into my brain. No, my *soul*.

"But . . ." I'd felt dismayed because all of my illusions about him being a stuck-up, ignorant rich boy jock were crumbling. "*Pride and Prejudice*?" How? How was this possible?

He'd shrugged. "Reading is important to my dad. He won't let us eat until we quote something literary. Kind of like how some families say grace? In our house, we have to prove we've spent ten minutes of every day in a rational manner . . . or that's how he puts it, anyway. I love our housekeeper's baked chicken more than anything in the world, so I memorized Austen pretty quick. I get why you like that one." He nodded at my copy of *Pride and Prejudice*. "But I prefer the other one—*Emma*. It's got a little more action. So, anyway." He lifted our textbook. "Joe McCarthy. What a dick, am I right?"

Falling in love with him was the biggest mistake I ever made in my life. I still hate myself sometimes for it.

Even as I was doing it, I knew it was a horrible idea, and tried to cling to my friends for safety, begging them to remind me of all the reasons to hate him. There were so many.

"He likes to party too much," said my best friend Leeanne, who is Japanese-American and can't metabolize alcohol (which is especially painful for her since her family owns Matsumori's Tiki Palace, the only restaurant with a tiki bar in a fifty-mile radius).

"He likes *golf*," said Nicole. "He wears belts with needlepoint *crocodiles* on them. He doesn't even have any tattoos because he says it's more unique *not* to. He's just so *weird*."

"I'm sorry, sweetie," my mother said. "I'd like to say bad things about him for you, but I think he's wonderful."

"Ew!" Nicole crowed. "Mom likes him! Kiss of death to any relationship."

We were sleeping together by Christmas break.

I told myself—and Leeanne and Nicole—that it was just sex. I wasn't going to let my heart get involved. I read *Cosmo*. I knew how to use birth control effectively and also what oxytocin does to a woman's brain. Therefore, I probably wasn't even really in love with him. It was just all the endorphins being released in my brain every time we made love.

I didn't have anything to measure it by, of course, never having been in a sexual relationship before. But it seemed to me that he was very, very good at lovemaking. So it was perfect. A brainless—well, mostly brainless—jock who enjoyed sex as much as I did? What could be better? He was the best guy from whom to learn these skills before I went to college.

We did it everywhere. His room. My room. His car. His parent's hot tub. The boathouse at the country club. Everywhere. It was so much fun.

Until it all came to a crashing—literally—halt at the country club. As the police showed up—and then the EMTs—and separated us, I was sure everything was going to be all right. Even when his father appeared, looking angrier than any human being I'd ever seen, I was certain it would all work out. Sure, I was in agonizing pain, my dress and hair soaking wet, the corsage Reed had made for me—from the pages of an old copy of *Pride and Prejudice* that he'd fashioned into a fairly recognizable floral shape—crushed and ruined.

But standing there with his head bent before his outraged father, his tux dripping, the flashing blue lights of the cop car reflecting off that thick dark hair I so adored, he'd looked exactly the way he always had—the boy I'd never meant to fall in love with.

It never once occurred to me as I was being loaded into the ambulance behind him that this would be the last time I'd see him.

But it was.

Once my shoulder was popped back into place and I got discharged from the hospital (and my parents were done lecturing me—they weren't angry, just "disappointed"), I called, surprised Reed hadn't left any messages.

It went straight to voicemail.

So did my next call.

And the next.

It was a week before I found out he'd left town, and that information didn't come from him, because he never spoke to me again. He never returned a single one of my phone calls, texts, or messages. He never even checked to see if I was all right after the accident (not that in a town the size of Bloomville it didn't quickly become common knowledge).

But still. For the Reed I knew, it would have been common courtesy.

"I told you he was weird," Nicole said. "Preppie freak."

"I'm so, so sorry," my friend Leeanne had said, over and over.

"I'm surprised," my mom had said. "A boy like that. I really expected better of him."

So had I . . . which was my own fault. I don't know why I'd been so naïve. Neither of us had made any promises—except the one I'd made to myself that I wasn't going to fall in love with him.

But not only had I broken that promise, I'd ended up breaking something else along the way—my heart.

It was a good lesson to learn. It had probably all been an act, because I never found another boy—or man—like him. I kept reading Austen—and *Cosmo*—and knew that part of it was that I kept comparing every guy to my first, which wasn't fair, to them . . . or to me.

But there it was: He'd broken my heart, and I was back to hating him again.

Which was why it was easy to laugh along with Graham in the car when I got done describing the incident with the golf cart in the pool.

"I know. It was ridiculous, right? But, you know. Small town. It was quite a scandal. Judge Stewart was so mad, he not only swore he'd never speak to Reed again, he told him never to set foot in this town again. And he never did."

"Never?" Graham was all astonishment.

"No. Both his siblings got married in places other than Bloomville, I think."

I didn't think, I *knew*. I totally cyber stalked the wedding of Reed's older brother, Marshall. Their sister had eloped to Hawaii—apparently there's no love lost between Trimble's family and her husband, Tony— before Reed and I started dating. But Marshall married his high school sweetheart, Carly Webb, in a fancy Chicago hotel on Valentine's Day the year after Reed and I broke up. Their wedding theme was hearts.

I'd stared for hours at those photos of Carly and Marshall, beaming at one another beneath an arch of dangling paper hearts, then hated myself for doing so.

"But you're cool with this guy, right?" Graham asked me from the driver's seat of his SUV. (He likes to go camping on weekends. I make sure to tell him I have to work. I don't understand camping. It's organized inconvenience.) "If he really is coming back to town, there aren't any bad vibes between you two or anything?"

"Oh, God, no," I said with a huge smile. "Nothing like that."

"Right," he said. "That's what I thought. Because that doesn't seem like you. You're so kind."

That's me. "So kind."

"I don't have any bad vibes with any of my exes," Graham said. "We're all still friends."

"Completely," I said. "Same here. I'm completely still friends with all my exes. Especially Reed."

"Right," he said. "Because sometimes when there are bad feelings between exes, it means there are still—you know. Feelings of another kind."

"Well," I said. "There are no feelings of any kind whatsoever between me and Reed except friendship."

I can't believe that Graham fell for this, but he did, because the next thing I knew, he was saying, "Great!" and looking expectantly at the basement windows of the house.

That's when I told him I had an early appointment tomorrow, and also that I didn't want to wake up my mom.

He seemed surprised—and slightly horrified.

"But I thought your apartment was totally separate from the rest of the house. You've never said it was a problem before. Can your mom *hear* us?"

"Oh, no," I said, feeling as horrified as he looked. "It's not that. It's just that I . . . I have a headache. All the wine, maybe. And the cheese."

"Oh." He looked disappointed. "You're usually fine with pinot noirs. And I wasn't serving any blues tonight. You shouldn't have a headache."

"I know." What was wrong with me? "I must have forgotten to hydrate."

I did know what was wrong with me, actually. It was Reed Stewart, back (in spirit, anyway) to ruin my whole life. AGAIN.

"I spent a lot of time stuck in traffic today, though," I went on. "I think I inhaled a bunch of diesel fumes. Can I get a rain check until tomorrow, maybe?"

"Of course." He tenderly tucked a curl of my hair behind one ear. I hate it when guys do this. Well, any guy except Reed. UGH, no, why did I write that? "See you tomorrow, baby."

Seriously. I have this amazing guy who is completely into me, and I'm still obsessed with a guy I haven't seen since high school.

I have GOT to get a hold of myself.

I'm cool. I really am. I'm a completely different person than that dumb high school girl who fell for Reed Stewart's quirky Jane Austen quoting, BMW driving, Ray-Ban wearing golfer dude act. I own my own business now. I have a wonderful boyfriend. I have a condo. (Admittedly it's in my mom's basement, but whatever. Real estate prices are beyond absurd around here, and there's no reason for me to plunk down a chunk of cash on a place when I can invest it back into the business.) I drink pinot noir.

I'm over Reed Stewart. I am over Reed Stewart.

I AM GRATEFUL FOR BEING OVER REED STEWART.

It doesn't matter that Leeanne is in Tokyo for six months trying to learn her grandmother's secret recipes in order to make the food at Matsumori's Tiki Palace more "authentic"—Nicole's least favorite word, though in this era of chain restaurants, when everyone is craving authenticity, it should also make the Palace more profitable.

But which also means Leeanne's in a time zone fourteen hours ahead of me, making it very difficult for us to catch up with one another on Chat App like we used to, at a time when we're both actually awake.

I can handle all of this without the advice of my best friend since kindergarten. I can.

Because it's likely I won't even see Reed when he comes to town. *If* he comes to town. Why would I? None of this has anything to do with me. As far as I'm concerned, Reed Stewart can continue living his life, and I'll continue living mine, and we'll both continue being the happy, well-adjusted adults we've grown into.

Okay, well, I better finish up the last of this pinot noir that Graham gave me because there's no point leaving this tiny bit in the bottle. It will just go bad.

But then I had better go to sleep, because tomorrow is a big day. I've got the Blumenthals to deal with. Plus I promised Mom I'd help her find more sticks.

See? I'm grateful that I'm an adult woman who is so over Reed Stewart that I can just forget about him after journaling and fall right to sleep.

Right. After I finish this wine.

And maybe take a Tylenol PM.

And watch one more episode of *Emergency Guest Room Makeover*.

From: Reed Stewart@reedstewart.com
Date: March 13 9:07:21 PM PST
To: Lyle Stewart@FountainHill.org
Subject: Richard and Connie

Hi, Uncle Lyle, just a quick note to let you know I'm not going to be able to have lunch with you this week like we planned.

I'm assuming by now you've heard about the Judge's run-in with "the fuzz" (as you like to call them).

So I'm flying to Bloomville tomorrow.

You can wipe the smirk off your face now. I know I said I'd never go back there unless Dad begged me, and I meant it.

But I consider Dad getting arrested for fraud at a casual family-style eatery begging.

Also, when Carly asks for help, I know it's serious. She's only five feet tall and can't weigh more than ninety pounds, but I've never met anyone tougher. Last time she was in LA, I saw her sling both her kids over her shoulders—while wearing the third in a BabyBjörn—and run a hundred yards in ten seconds flat because Marshall accidentally knocked a hornet's nest out of a tree with the pool skimmer.

So if Carly says things are bad, they probably are. Or she's at least come to the end of her rope, and needs a helping hand.

And yes, I know exactly what you're going to say next:

My true motivation for going there is Becky, because I've found out she finally has a serious boyfriend.

If that's what you think, you don't know me at all.

Even if I wanted to see for myself—which I don't—if there was some small chance the two of us could get back together after everything I've done, some way I could patch things up before it's too late and she marries the guy, I am not that person.

I wish her all the best in the world. I want her to be happy. She deserves to be happy.

And why would she even want to be with me anyway, after what I did?

And this doesn't have anything to do with that thing you said the last time I saw you, either, about my needing closure. I do not need closure. I don't even believe in closure.

The reason I lost at Augusta last year—and at Pebble Beach or Doral—isn't because of what happened between me and the Judge ten years ago. And it *especially* isn't because of my having anything I need to resolve with Becky. I know you were a psychology professor, but as I've told you before, please don't try to shrink me.

My problem at Augusta (and Pebble Beach and Doral) doesn't have anything to do with the past, but my future.

I'm simply ready to focus on it, and according to my real shrink—aha! You didn't know I got one, did you? Yeah, I did. Cutler gave me the number for his—what I see in it isn't more trophies.

He also said that if you want to eat an elephant, you have to start with the tail.

He didn't really explain what that means, but I think it means if you want to make changes in your life, you have to start small.

So the first one I'm going to make is that I'm going to go back to Bloomville to help out Marshall and Carly. I'm sure things there can't be as bad as they're making them out to be.

Then after that maybe some other stuff will fall into place for me. Who knows?

Okay, well, I gotta pack. I expect it's going to be cold in Indiana. I wonder where I put my coat. I haven't been any place where it was actually cold in ages!

Anyway, I'm sure Mom and Dad are fine, and you and I will be back to brunching soon.

Can't wait to hear all about the Orchid Expo. I'm positive your entry is going to take first prize, as usual.

Love,

Your Favorite Nephew,
Reed

Not-So-Crazy Cat Lady

Reviewer ranking: #2,350

92% helpful

votes received on reviews

Reviewed

Pretty Kitty Play Time Figurine

$59.00 + Shipping

As pictured

March 13

This is an exquisitely detailed hand-painted ceramic figurine of three kitties playing with one another. I bought it because I'm a collector (and licensed reseller) but also because the kitties reminded me of my own three "kiddies" when they were younger—Marshall, Reed, and my sweet, beautiful Trimble—who would get up to all sorts of mischief when we left them alone in the house, just like these naughty kitties!

This item arrived today in perfect condition, and just when I needed a little pick-me-up, as the children are a bit angry with me. I suppose their father and I were the ones who were a little naughty last night! Goodness, it's strange how things change over the years. One moment they're the ones in diapers, and the next moment, it's you! Pardon me if that offends anyone—a little senior humor!

Ooh, dear, I suppose I've strayed from my review a bit. Oh, well, in any case, I highly recommend these beautiful, playful kitties. They will liven up your home, and your heart . . . and hopefully the hearts of anyone who might be a bit angry with you, even though of course you didn't mean to hurt anyone!

10 of 10 people found this review helpful

The Bloomville Herald

The Tri-County Area's Only
Daily Newspaper
• Tuesday, March 14 • Vol. 140 •
Still Only 50 Cents!

JUDGE STEWART ARRESTED

BY CHRISTINA MARTINEZ Herald Staff

Bloomville, Ind.—A retired judge has admitted that he attempted to defraud a local full-service chain restaurant.

The Honorable Richard P. Stewart, 75, was arrested Monday along with his wife of 50 years, Constance Stewart, for allegedly trying to pay for a $59 meal at Shenanigans Neighborhood Bar and Grill with a two-cent George Washington stamp, reportedly worth over $400.

"At first I was excited," said server Tiffany Gosling, 24, upon finding the stamp attached to the bill for the couple's meal. "I thought I'd gotten a really big tip."

But excitement turned to dismay when Gosling did an Internet search of the stamp's true value and discovered it was worth only $4.

"That wasn't enough to cover their mozzarella sticks," said Gosling. "Let alone their potato twisters."

Gosling was not in favor of notifying the police. That was night manager Randy Grubb's decision.

"Yes, I called the cops," Grubb, 35, told the Herald. "This has been an ongoing problem with older people in the area thinking they can eat without paying due to something being wrong with the food or whatnot. It has got to stop. At the end of the night, I'm still accountable to corporate headquarters if the register comes up short."

Attempts to clear up the misunderstanding did not satisfy Grubb, who insisted the couple be taken into custody.

"I know the Stewarts," said Bloomville officer Corrine Jeffries. "I truly believe they thought the stamp was worth a lot more than it was. I don't think they meant any harm. But ultimately what they did constituted fraud."

Grubb insists he was only following corporate orders in notifying the police and insisting on the elderly couple's arrest.

"Here at Shenanigans Neighborhood Bar and Grill, we don't put up with actual shenanigans."

When reached at home after Monday's arrest, Stewart told reporters he was not aware the stamp had such little value.

"Of course I didn't know. Obviously, I was scammed by the seller. I paid over $100 for that stamp."

Stewart—who served two terms as Indiana state attorney general and thirty years as a criminal court judge in Bloomville—is now retired, but still represents occasional local clients in private practice along with his daughter, Trimble Stewart-Antonelli, 36.

Stewart's eldest son, Marshall Stewart, 32, owns Stewart Realty Company. Another son, Reed Stewart, 28, is a well known professional golfer, and one of the youngest players in history ever to win the US Open.

Judge Stewart presided over a number of high

profile cases during his tenure, including the well-known "Dumbbell Killer."

In addition to state charges, Judge Stewart and his wife may face federal prosecution, as it is against federal law to use or attempt to use postage stamps in the pursuance of a crime.

From: Trimble Stewart-Antonelli@Stewart&Stewart.com
Date: March 14 9:07:28 AM EST
To: Carly Stewart@StewartRealty.com; Marshall Stewart@StewartRealty
.com; Reed Stewart@reedstewart.com
Subject: This morning's paper

Have you seen the paper this morning? What is going on? I thought you said you were going to take care of the situation.

But as usual, you haven't taken care of ANYTHING!

Well, don't expect any help from me. As I already told you, I'm out of this.

Trimble Stewart-Antonelli
Attorney at Law
Stewart & Stewart, LLC
1911 South Moore Pike
Bloomville, IN 47401
(812) 555-9721
www.stewart&stewart.com

From: Marshall Stewart@StewartRealty.com
Date: March 14 9:10:08 AM EST
To: Trimble Stewart-Antonelli@Stewart&Stewart.com; Carly Stewart
@StewartRealty.com; Tony Antonelli@AntonelliPizza.com
Subject: Re: This morning's paper

Trimble, calm down. We ARE taking care of it. Reed's flying in today. We've got it all under control.

From: Trimble Stewart-Antonelli@Stewart&Stewart.com
Date: March 14 9:13:28 AM EST
To: Carly Stewart@StewartRealty.com; Marshall Stewart@StewartRealty
.com; Tony Antonelli@AntonelliPizza.com
Subject: Re: This morning's paper

Oh, Reed is flying in today? That's your solution? REED is flying in?

What possible good is THAT going to do? Dad hasn't spoken to Reed in ten years! He's certainly not going to start listening to anything Reed, a professional GOLF player, has to say now.

I thought you were actually going to DO something to solve this problem. I should have known better than to count on you, Marshall. You were useless when you were a kid, and you've grown into a useless man.

Trimble Stewart-Antonelli
Attorney at Law
Stewart & Stewart, LLC
1911 South Moore Pike
Bloomville, IN 47401
(812) 555-9721
www.stewart&stewart.com

From: Tony Antonelli@AntonelliPizza.com
Date: March 14 9:17:28 AM EST
To: Carly Stewart@StewartRealty.com; Marshall Stewart@StewartRealty
.com; Trimble Stewart-Antonelli@Stewart&Stewart.com
Subject: Re: This morning's paper

Uh, if I might interject here, I actually think I might have a solution to all your problems.

I watched a show last night on TV about these people who will come to your house and move out all your stuff and then fix the house up and put in new stuff to make it look better, then hold a big open house to attract buyers.

Then they sell the house for you for twice as much as it's worth, and then the sellers take that cash to move to a new, much bigger place.

I think that's what you should do for your mom and dad. Just sign them up to be on that show!

Cheers.

Anthony Antonelli III
Antonelli's Pizza
1371 South Moore Pike
Bloomville, IN 47401
(812) 555-PZZA
www.Antonellis.com

From: Marshall Stewart@StewartRealty.com
Date: March 14 9:20:08 AM EST
To: Trimble Stewart-Antonelli@Stewart&Stewart.com; Carly Stewart
@StewartRealty.com; Tony Antonelli@AntonelliPizza.com
Subject: Re: This morning's paper

Thank you, Tony, for that enlightening piece of advice. As realtors, Carly and I never thought of it. How fortunate we are to have you in our lives. We are truly blessed.

Sadly, however, your plan won't work, seeing as how Mom and Dad have neglected to pay their mortgage for so long that their home is ABOUT TO BE SEIZED BY THE BANK.

We need to sell the place NOW, immediately, so Mom and Dad can downsize to a smaller, much less expensive place (hopefully not a cell in the local jail) so we can pay off some of their debt and keep them from going to FEDERAL prison.

We can't wait for some television casting agent from Hollywood or Toronto or wherever to come here and decide whether or not Mom and Dad are telegenic enough to be on their show.

(Here's a hint: They are not. Would you like to watch a show during which one of the homeowners begins to lecture the viewer about the historic significance of his stamp collection? I'm guessing not.)

But thanks for the help, Tony. Carly and Reed and I are handling the situation.

From: Trimble Stewart-Antonelli@Stewart&Stewart.com
Date: March 14 9:25:48 AM EST
To: Carly Stewart@StewartRealty.com; Marshall Stewart@StewartRealty.com
Subject: Re: This morning's paper

STOP making fun of Tony. You know he was only trying to help. Unlike us, he came from a loving home where they didn't force the children to quote from classic fiction at mealtimes, and they never used sarcasm.

Now you've hurt his feelings and he doesn't want to get together with you for Easter. He wants us to go to his parents' in Muncie.

If you fail to comply with my demand to stop harassing my husband, you could risk incurring severe legal consequences.

So watch it!

Trimble Stewart-Antonelli
Attorney at Law
Stewart & Stewart, LLC
1911 South Moore Pike
Bloomville, IN 47401
(812) 555-9721
www.stewart&stewart.com

From: Marshall Stewart@StewartRealty.com
Date: March 14 9:26:02 AM EST
To: Carly Stewart@StewartRealty.com
Subject: Re: This morning's paper

Aw, Tony! Too Bad Tony.

From: Carly Stewart@StewartRealty.com
Date: March 14 9:28:03 AM EST
To: Marshall Stewart@StewartRealty.com
Subject: Re: This morning's paper

We really are terrible people.

But your sister is even more annoying than Summer Hayes, which I didn't think possible.

Carly R. Stewart | Accountant | Stewart Realty | 801 South Moore Pike, Bloomville, IN 47401 | phone (812) 555-8722 | Please visit StewartRealty.com for all your realty needs

| MARSHALL STEWART | 9:55AM | 95% |
| TODAY | ALL | MISSED |

Marshall — 9:32 AM
So what are we doing to handle the situation?

Carly — 9:32 AM
I got us a meeting with Jimmy Abrams this afternoon.

Marshall — 9:32 AM
Jimmy Abrams isn't a real lawyer! We went to high school with him.

Carly — 9:33 AM
He is, in fact, a real lawyer, working for one of the best firms in the state specializing in bankruptcy.

Marshall — 9:33 AM
My parents don't need a bankruptcy lawyer. If Shenanigans doesn't drop the charges, they're going to need a criminal lawyer.

Carly — 9:33 AM
Sweetheart, your parents need all the legal help they can get, but a bankruptcy lawyer is as good a place as any to start since they owe so much in back taxes. And Jimmy Abrams owes me a favor.

Marshall — 9:34 AM
What kind of favor?

Carly — 9:34 AM
Let's just say I did him a solid back in 9th grade. So when you're at your parents' this morning, tell them they have a meeting with Jimmy this afternoon at 2:15PM.

Marshall   9:34 AM
Why am I going to my parents' this morning?

Carly   9:34 AM
Oh, didn't I tell you? Your mother called earlier, and she needs someone to bring in the trash cans.

Marshall   9:35 AM
Are you kidding me?

Carly   9:35 AM
No, I am not kidding you. Your dad's complaining that he strained his back while getting arrested the other night.

Marshall   9:35 AM
I swear to God if he tries to file a claim of police brutality, I will go over there and give him something real to complain about.

Carly   9:35 AM
Nice. But someone does need to go over there and wheel in the trash cans or your parents will get another fine from the country club. Your mom can't do it. She says her sciatica is acting up.

Marshall   9:35 AM
Why can't Too Bad Tony do it? They live down the street!

Carly   9:36 AM
Your sister and executor of your parents' will isn't speaking to your parents anymore, remember?

Marshall   9:36 AM
Oh, for Crisis sakes. I mean Cross sakes. Whatever. I'll do it. Should I take my dad to see Dr. Jones?

Carly   9:36 AM

You can try. But you know your dad doesn't trust hospitals or doctors, not even Dr. Jones. He only willingly goes to see Dr. Jones when there is bone actually piercing his skin, like this past winter when he fell on the ice outside the garage.

Marshall   9:37 AM

Why do you have to remind me of these things?

Carly   9:37 AM

Sorry. Anyway, I did some research. Did you know there are people you can hire who do this kind of thing professionally?

Marshall   9:37 AM

What, bring in my parents' trash cans?

Carly   9:38 AM

Well, that, too, but I meant help "seniors" transition into new living situations. They've been trained in exactly this kind of thing—convincing older people like your parents who need to downsize, relocate, or even stay where they are, but in a safer home environment, that it's time to do so.

Marshall   9:38 AM

How do they do that, Carly? Magic? Hypnosis? Do they shoot them with tranquilizer darts? Because that's what it's going to take in my parents' case.

Carly   9:39 AM

I told you, Marshall. They've got specialized training. They're part social workers, part psychologists, and part organizing consultants who also know how to arrange short and long distance moves, declutter and clean houses, coordinate estate sales, and put families in touch with representatives from social services who can assess the wellness of their elderly loved one.

Marshall   9:40 AM
Did you just cut and paste that from a website?

Carly   9:40 AM
Yes.

Sometimes having someone from *outside* the family point out how much better their life could be is all it takes to convince an elderly person to pursue that life.

Marshall   9:40 AM
You're kind of sexy when you're resourceful.

Carly   9:41 AM
Thanks.

So can we hire someone from outside the family to get your parents to open up about their needs since they won't listen to us, and you're in denial about the whole thing?

Marshall   9:41 AM
For the last time, I am not in denial.

Carly   9:41 AM
Okay, you're not in denial. Can we?

Marshall   9:42 AM
I don't care what you do, so long as Reed pays for it.

Carly   9:42 AM
Great. That's what I was hoping you'd say. There's just one little problem.

Marshall   9:42 AM
What? The fact that my parents are going to jail so this whole thing isn't going to matter anyway?

Carly   9:42 AM
No. The only senior moving consultant within a 100 mile radius is Becky Flowers.

Marshall   9:43 AM
NO.

Carly   9:43 AM
Marshall. We have to.

Marshall   9:43 AM
No, Carly, we don't HAVE to. You're only doing this to play matchmaker. I know you.

Carly   9:43 AM
No! Of course not. She seriously is the only one.

Marshall   9:44 AM
Carly, leave it alone.

Carly   9:45 AM
Honestly, Marshall, I don't know what you're talking about. She comes very highly recommended. She's got about a million five star reviews on Yelp.

Marshall   9:45 AM
I'm telling you not to contact her. We can do this on our own.

Carly   9:46 AM
Marshall, no, we can't, or your parents wouldn't be the laughingstock of the Internet right now.

And your brother said that thing about how he's getting tired of putting his head down on a different pillow every night. I think he's finally ready to settle down.

Marshall   9:46 AM
But why HER? My brother practically ruined her life.

Carly   9:46 AM
Yes, but before that I'd never seen him happier. He really loved her.

Marshall   9:46 AM
He was 18 years old. He didn't know what love was.

Carly   9:47 AM
You were in love with me at 18.

Marshall   9:47 AM
Leave her alone. Don't you think my family has made enough people miserable lately?

Carly   9:47 AM
Don't YOU think this is fate, Marshall? Your parents needing help and Becky Flowers turning out to be the only person in the area who can offer that kind of help?

Marshall   9:48 AM
No, I don't. Do NOT contact her. It's embarrassing enough that the entire world thinks that my parents tried to pull a fast one at our local Shenanigans. You don't need to let the one girl my brother ever loved know the rest of our embarrassing family secrets.

Carly   9:48 AM
So you admit it! He DID love her!

Marshall   9:48 AM
Maybe he did, Carly. But if he was still in love with her, don't you think he'd have contacted her on his own sometime in the past decade?

Carly   9:49 AM

No, because he's a big stupid baby, just like his big brother. If I hadn't actively pursued you all through high school, then TOLD you during college that you were in love with me and that we were going to get married, would we have? No, because you are an insecure idiot who can't make up his mind or take a stand about anything.

Marshall   9:49 AM

I can't tell you how little this is helping your case.

Carly   9:49 AM

Jackie Monroe says it's the duty of every person in a committed, happy romantic relationship to try to help at least one other person find romantic happiness too. And I haven't managed to help any!

Marshall   9:50 AM

Well, my baby brother is not going to be the first. Swear on Blinky's life that you'll stay out of this.

Carly   9:50 AM

I'm not swearing on the life of the dog, Marshall.

Marshall   9:50 AM

DO IT.

Carly   9:51 AM

Fine. I swear on Blinky's life.

Marshall   9:51 AM

Good. I'm going to my parents' now to move their gosh darn trash cans.

I did not write that. I did not write gosh darn!

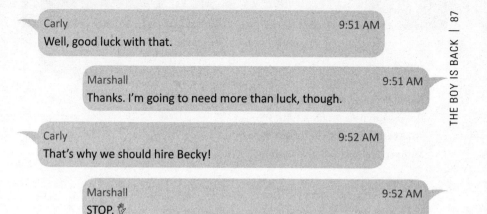

Carly   9:51 AM
Well, good luck with that.

Marshall   9:51 AM
Thanks. I'm going to need more than luck, though.

Carly   9:52 AM
That's why we should hire Becky!

Marshall   9:52 AM
STOP. ✋

PHONE SCREEN OF REED STEWART

From: Lyle Stewart@FountainHill.org
Date: March 14 12:08:22 AM PST
To: Reed Stewart@reedstewart.com
Subject: Re: Richard and Connie

Dear Reed,

I'm sorry I won't be seeing you this week (and even more sorry you won't be seeing how my *Phalaenopsis amabilis* has blossomed. It is truly a magnificent specimen, if I do say so myself).

But I'm beyond glad of the reason for it.

I've been worried about your parents for some time now, though I didn't like to burden you with my fears, knowing, as I do, of your own challenging relationship with them.

Your father and I did not see eye to eye on many things—though I must say, out of all the family (the older generation, at least), he was always the staunchest defender of gay rights.

But the one thing on which we could never agree was his treatment of you.

I do not think it was so much the foolishness of what happened that night with Miss Flowers that angered him as much as it was your refusal to go to college and take the life route that he'd laid out for you, as your sister and brother did.

It was not in the Honorable Judge Stewart's plan to have a professional athlete—particularly a golfer—in the family, and when you upset that plan, I believe it was the straw that broke the proverbial camel's back.

Because it was right after that that I began to notice your father's "collecting" behavior—which before had simply been a hobby—begin to become an obsession.

When an activity that was once rewarding becomes a compulsion, an act which no longer gives pleasure, but only reduces anxiety, we in the mental health profession call it a disorder.

It did not help, of course, that Connie encouraged it. Your mother and father were always very close. A couple more in love I've never known.

But now, with the collecting, a less generous person might call Connie's encouragement "enabling." Their constant need to shop has turned unhealthy, and they are co-dependent upon one another, each finding excuses for the other's increasingly compulsive behavior.

Not that I am blaming you for anything that has happened. We are all responsible solely for our own behavior.

And while I concur with Richard that education is important, and that one must never stop learning, academia is not for everyone. Your decision to attend golf academy instead of a four year college was the right one for you—at the time.

It is never too late, however, to go back—to go back home, and to go back to decisions made when one was in one's youth, and reexamine them. It is never too late, in other words, to change one's mind . . . just as it is never too late to change one's behavior, though the older one is, the more difficult it becomes.

The only thing it might be too late to do is win the heart of the object of one's affections . . . especially when she has already given it to another.

Then—*then*, my boy—it might be too late. Act soon, Reed, if you decide to act at all.

In any case, do let me know how my brother and Connie are doing, and if there is anything I can do to help. The Hoosier heartland has never, of course, been my favorite place, and certainly not in early spring, when it is often still snow-covered.

But if you need me to travel there to lend a hand, I suppose I could—though they will miss me at the Expo, and I don't know how my orchids will fare if I'm not there to supervise their transport and care.

But family are more important than flowers. So call me if you need me.

Yours very sincerely,

Uncle Lyle

_____**AMERICAN AIRLINES**_____
BOARDING PASS

TSA PRECHK
Name: Stewart, Reed

FROM:	CARRIER:	FLIGHT:	CLASS:	DATE:
Los Angeles LAX	AA	1556	FIRST	14MAR

TO:	GATE:	BOARDING TIME:	SEAT:
Indianapolis IND	57G	6:55AM	2D

_____**PRIORITY ACCESS**_____

Reed Stewart   6:37 AM

Hey, Val, sorry, I forgot to call you earlier. Can we take a rain check on Orlando? I'll make it up to you.

Val King   6:38 AM

Reed. You woke me up.

Reed Stewart   6:39 AM

Oops, sorry. But I'm leaving on a 7AM flight. I have to go see my parents for a few days.

Val King   6:40 AM

Oh God, is it true? You really are the son of those postage stamp people—the Dumbasses of the Week? LOL JK ♥♥♥

Reed Stewart   6:41 AM

Who's been saying that?

Val King   6:42 AM

LOL literally everyone.

Why? Believe me, they've been saying far worse stuff about you—especially your chances at ever winning another Major.

JK! You know I love you. ♥

Reed Stewart   6:45 AM

As a matter of fact, those are my parents.

Val King   6:50 AM

LOL! Oh, Reed! I had no idea. I'm so sorry, baby! ♥

Reed Stewart   6:55 AM

It's okay. That's why I have to go back home. I've got to see what I can do to help. Anyway, I'm boarding now.

Val King   6:56 AM
Of course, baby. Take care! Say hi to your parents for me! ♥

Reed Stewart   6:59 AM
Sure. Maybe I'll see you again someday.

Val King   7:00 AM
???? Maybe you'll see me again someday? What the F does that mean????

Reed Stewart   7:05 AM
Alvarez, I know this is last minute, but I'm not going to make it to Orlando until next week. I've got some family stuff I need to straighten out. I'll see you there Monday.

Enrique Alvarez   7:07 AM
You don't think Monday's cutting it a little short, boudro? Cutler's already there.

He and his caddy walked the course yesterday. He signed up for nine holes today. He's doing a full practice tomorrow—and I'm guessing with this divorce, he's got more family stuff going on than you do.

Reed Stewart   7:07 AM
Cutler's an ass.

Enrique Alvarez   7:07 AM
An ass who just made World Number 1. MacKenzie dropped out, citing back problems.

Cutler's an animal.

Reed Stewart   7:08 AM
Yeah, well, I'm an animal, too.

Enrique Alvarez   7:08 AM

Animals don't go home to their mommies the week before a tournament.

Reed Stewart   7:09 AM

Fine. You go now, check out the greens, and while you're there, meet with local realtors and pick out a house for me to buy.

Enrique Alvarez   7:09 AM

Pick out a house for you to buy? I'm your caddy, not your girlfriend.

What happened to Valerie?

Reed Stewart   7:10 AM

It's Valery and we broke up.

Enrique Alvarez   7:10 AM

Oh, big surprise. You never stay with a woman for more than 3 months. You know that Chan says you got the 3 month itch. I tried to tell him it's not true, but you make it hard.

Reed Stewart   7:11 AM

Just find me a house. Nothing too big. Two bedroom, two bath would be great. With a pool, or at least access to a pool. A condo would be best. No yard to mow.

Enrique Alvarez   7:11 AM

What? Where's the hot tub, home theater system, and dedicated game room? This place don't sound like you, boudro.

Reed Stewart   7:12 AM

It's not for me. It's for my parents.

Enrique Alvarez   7:12 AM

Now I know you've lost it.

You haven't spoken to your parents in all the years I've known you.

They've never been to one of your games, not even when we played Crooked Stick, and that was only 50 miles from where they live.

And now you're not only going home to see them, you're buying them a house?

What is going on with you, boudro?

Reed Stewart   7:12 AM

It's a long story.

Enrique Alvarez   7:13 AM

I can't wait to hear it.

Fine, I'll look for a house for your parents.

But I think you should know that none of the other players ask their caddy to look for houses for their parents.

Reed Stewart   7:13 AM

None of the other players pay their caddy as much as I pay you.

Enrique Alvarez   7:14 AM

Not lately, boudro. 10% of nothing is nothing.

Reed Stewart   7:14 AM

I pay you $1700 a week on top of that 10% cut of my winnings, but thanks for the tender reminder.

Enrique Alvarez   7:14 AM

Like I said, I ain't your girlfriend.

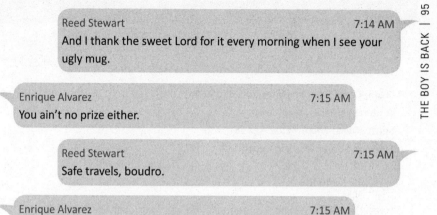

Reed Stewart   7:14 AM
And I thank the sweet Lord for it every morning when I see your ugly mug.

Enrique Alvarez   7:15 AM
You ain't no prize either.

Reed Stewart   7:15 AM
Safe travels, boudro.

Enrique Alvarez   7:15 AM
Same to you, boudro.

BECKY FLOWERS	2:43PM	98%
TODAY	ALL	MISSED

From: Carly Stewart@StewartRealty.com
To: Becky@MovingUp.com
Sent: March 14 10:46:09 AM EST
Subject: Senior Moving Consultant

Dear Ms. Flowers,

I was referred to you by the American Association of Senior Move Management website. I hope you can help.

I'm looking for a caring, experienced individual who can assist my in-laws, the Honorable Judge and Mrs. Richard Stewart, in transitioning to an as-yet-to-be-determined retirement community.

They have a large home here in Bloomville, which they are somewhat reluctant to leave, but I know it will be for the best considering recent developments. Perhaps you've read about them in the newspaper.

Is there any possible way you'd be interested in helping us? We'd be eternally grateful.

Please call me any time at your earliest opportunity. My cell number is 812-555-8722.

Carly Stewart
P.S.: I think you might know my brother-in-law, Reed Stewart? These are his parents. I hope this won't be a problem. We would really, really be so grateful.

Carly R. Stewart | Accountant | Stewart Realty | 801 South Moore Pike, Bloomville, IN 47401 | phone (812) 555-8722 | Please visit StewartRealty.com for all your realty needs

From: Beverly@MovingUp.com
Date: March 14 11:09:09 AM EST
To: Becky@MovingUp.com
Subject: Re: Senior Moving Consultant

Becky, honey, have you seen this? It just came in for you. What would you like me to do?

P.S. I really think you should say yes. Did you see the article in the paper today? I think it was just disgraceful. I know they have to report the news, but there's no reason they have to put stories like this on the front page.

And that Randy Grubb has always been trouble.

I believe the Stewarts should take Shenanigans to court. That's elder abuse, if you ask me. I'm going to write a letter to the editor to say so.

From: Becky@MovingUp.com
Date: March 14 11:13:02 PM EST
To: Beverly@MovingUp.com
Subject: Re: Senior Moving Consultant

Mom. Stop reading my email.

Becky Flowers, CSMM
Moving Up! Consulting LLC, President

Nicole F   11:14 AM
OMG I can't believe he had the nerve to ask you for help with his parents.

Becky F   11:14 AM
He didn't. His sister-in-law did.

Nicole F   11:14 AM
Yeah, but that's basically like him asking. He has to know about it. I bet he's still in love with you.

Becky F   11:15 AM

Are you still drunk from last night?

Nicole F   11:15 AM

No. Shut up. I'm totally hydrating with vitamin water.

So what are you going to say in your reply? Are you going to tell her to go to hell? Do you even know her? I think I remember her. Carly Webb, right? She was on the volleyball team with that stuck-up Summer Walters.

Becky F   11:16 AM

It's Summer Hayes now. Remember? You should, you tried to kick her last night.

Nicole F   11:16 AM

NOOOOOOO!!!! I tried to kick Summer Walters?

Becky F   11:16 AM

Hayes. How many times have I told you? Ice wines are for sipping, Nicole, not chugging.

Nicole F   11:17 AM

OMG. Henry's right, I really shouldn't be allowed anywhere classy like a wine boutique, only biker bars.

So how are you going to break the news that you're not taking the job? Do you want me to do it? I'm an expert at rejecting people.

Becky F   11:17 AM

I haven't decided yet whether or not to turn down the job.

Nicole F   11:17 AM

ARE YOU KIDDING ME???? You're actually thinking about saying YES???

Becky F   11:18 AM

We need the money, Nicole.

Nicole F   11:18 AM

No, we don't. I mean we do, but not that much. I can't even believe you're suggesting it. We do NOT need any of Reed Stewart's money. He hurt you, Becky! I was the one who had to mop up your tears all those nights you cried after he went away and never called you again! I will never let you accept a dime of his gross preppie golf money.

Becky F   11:19 AM

Nicole, please don't be dramatic.

Nicole F   11:19 AM

I'm not being dramatic! I will not let you accept this job!

Becky F   11:19 AM

Have you ever been inside the Stewarts' house? It's massive.

Nicole F   11:20 AM

Uh, no, I've never been invited inside the Stewart manor house because I'm just a lowly little scullery maid, not a stunningly beautiful princess like you, who got courted by the handsomest prince in the kingdom and then summarily dumped by him so he could go off and win all that tournament money while you toiled away at college, then your father's business after he died, building it into this empire the prince now wants to take advantage of, which I will not allow.

Becky F   11:22 AM

Stop being insane.

The Stewarts' place is huge. Three stories, not including the attic, basement, and detached garage. It's historic. And Reed's parents loved antiquing.

Nicole F 11:22 AM

So Reed Stewart's parents are now hoarders. Is that what you're saying? You want to take on hoarders in addition to the ex who ruined your life? You're the one who's insane. I thought we agreed after the Mayhews, no more hoarders.

Becky F 11:23 AM

He did not ruin my life. I'm with Graham now.

Nicole F 11:23 AM

A lumbersexual whose favorite subjects are locally sourced goat cheese and how to avoid tannins?

Becky F 11:24 AM

And the Stewarts are not hoarders. They're lovely, sophisticated people. I think I recall a suit of armor and a Venetian glass chandelier. We're not talking Princess Diana memorial plates here.

Nicole F 11:25 AM

I've never seen a Venetian glass chandelier before. Except on PBS.

Becky F 11:26 AM

Nicole, this could be the biggest job of our lives.

Nicole F 11:28 AM

It's not about the money, though, Becky. You always told me that what we do has never been about the money. It's about helping people during the time in their lives when they most desperately need it.

Becky F 11:30 AM

And we *will* be helping a member of the community who was extremely kind and generous to me when *I* needed help, and when many other members of the community needed help. Remember the Dumbbell Killer?

Nicole F   11:34 AM

For heaven's sake, Becky, that had nothing to do with you. Or me. Or any of us except that poor, crazy lady.

Becky F   11:34 AM

She wasn't crazy.

Nicole F   11:35 AM

She dropped a spinlock adjustable dumbbell on her husband's head 57 times while he was asleep.

But oh yes, you're right. That is the action of a sane person.

Becky F   11:36 AM

It was while her husband was passed out drunk and she only dropped it 12 times and it was because he'd just beat her and their three children nearly to death.

That's why Judge Stewart instructed the jury to consider a verdict of justifiable homicide.

The judge had seen her—and her children—in court many times before, bailing the husband out of jail, always with black eyes and their arms in slings.

I think the jury did the right thing, finding her guilty of justifiable homicide.

Nicole F   11:37 AM

Okay so because Reed Stewart's dad was a social justice warrior while in his prime, you want to take this job?

Becky F   11:38 AM

It's more complicated than that, but yes, I think because he served this community well, we owe it to him and his wife and family to help him now that he's the one in need.

Nicole F   11:38 AM

You are a complete sap. I totally get why you're dating a guy who looks like he just walked in off a Civil War battlefield and knows fifteen different ways to describe cheddar.

I have just one question for you:

Is the real reason you're doing this because of some kind of need for closure with Reed?

Becky F   11:38 AM

Absolutely not.

Nicole F   11:38 AM

Do you swear on Dad's urn?

Becky F   11:40 AM

Nicole!

Nicole F   11:40 AM

Do you?

Becky F   11:41 AM

Fine, yes, if I must. We need to find a place to bury that, by the way. Or sprinkle the ashes. Maybe over Lake Bloomville. Dad liked to go fishing, remember?

Nicole F   11:41 AM

Mom likes talking to it at night. Haven't you heard her?

Becky F   11:41 AM

I thought she was on the phone. That's kind of sweet, I guess.

Are we good now?

Nicole F   11:42 AM

Only if you promise there'll be Dumpsters. I know how you love a Dumpster.

Becky F   11:42 AM

I'm envisioning Dumpsters AND a couple of portable on demand storage units at the very least, since the Stewarts don't know where they're going yet.

Nicole F   11:43 AM

Things are becoming clearer to me. And didn't you say they live on the golf course?

Becky F   11:43 AM

Near the country club. Yes.

Nicole F   11:43 AM

Now I get it. This IS about closure after all.

What would be more satisfying revenge than plopping down a bunch of PODs and a Dumpster or two in front of Reed Stewart's parents' magnificent mansion RIGHT IN FRONT of all of his rich friends at the country club where he humiliated you in 12th grade?

And then ripping his parents' house apart, and throwing all their nice stuff into those Dumpsters?

Like that chandelier.

Becky F   11:44 AM

No, Nicole. That is not it at all. There will be no throwing of Venetian glass chandeliers into Dumpsters.

Nicole F   11:45 AM

Sure. Sure.

But I like where this is going.

Especially since we have that six week credit with Hoosier Disposal.

Becky F   11:47 AM

Seriously. Do not start scheduling Dumpsters yet. Let me contact
Carly Stewart to find out more about what's going on. She may
not even end up hiring us.

Nicole F   11:48 AM

Oh, right. Who else are they going to hire?

Becky F   11:48 AM

Well, you never know. Maybe she'll talk to Reed and he'll say
booking me is a conflict of interest. It would be kind of a weird
thing, you know, to have your ex clean out your childhood home.

Nicole F   11:49 AM

That he hasn't visited in a decade? Like he should be allowed any
say in the matter.

Becky F   11:50 AM

Nicole, I know it's hard, but let's try to be professional where
Reed is concerned, just in case we do end up having to work
with him.

Nicole F   11:52 AM

Fine. I'll try. But you can't make me like him.

Becky F   11:53 AM

Trust me, I would never dream of asking you to.

From: Becky@MovingUp.com
To: Carly Stewart@StewartRealty.com
Sent: March 14 12:16:07 PM
Subject: Re: Senior Moving Consultant

Dear Carly,

I do remember Reed, and of course his parents. The Judge and Mrs.
Stewart were very generous to me when my father was first diagnosed

with cancer. Of course I'll try to help them through their current difficulty as best I can.

Normally in cases like this the first step is to meet at the clients' home so that I can do an assessment. I'm sure you'd probably like an estimate of the cost of the packing and removal of your in-laws' belongings (although since we don't yet know where they're going, it will not be possible to give you an estimate for shipping).

If you could let me know the earliest dates when it would be convenient to meet with you and your in-laws at their home, so I could begin my assessment, that would be great, as right now our spring calendar is very full.

Looking forward to working with you, and of course the Stewarts, whom I've always very much admired.

Sincerely,

Becky Flowers
Becky Flowers, Certified Senior Move Manager
Moving Up! Consulting LLC, President

From: Carly Stewart@StewartRealty.com
To: Becky@MovingUp.com
Sent: March 14 1:01:17 PM
Subject: Senior Moving Consultant

Dear Becky,

Thanks so much for agreeing to take on our case!

Would it be possible for us to meet at my in-laws' tomorrow at noon? Since my father-in-law hasn't yet entirely accepted the idea of relocating, I think it might be nice to meet with him over lunch, which I'll bring with me as a way to "sweeten" him up. He and my mother-in-law, Connie, don't cook much at home anymore, as you'll see for yourself.

If that time works for you, do you have a favorite dish I could pick up for you from Shenanigans? My treat!

Their home, in case you don't remember, is at 65 Country Club Road. You can't miss it, it's the oldest home in the area, and looks it.

Thank you so much for agreeing to this! You have no idea how grateful I am.

Carly R. Stewart | Accountant | Stewart Realty | 801 South Moore Pike, Bloomville, IN 47401 | phone (812) 555-8722 | Please visit StewartRealty.com for all your realty needs

---

From: Becky@MovingUp.com
To: Carly Stewart@StewartRealty.com
Sent: March 14 2:06:17 PM
Subject: Re: Senior Moving Consultant

Noon tomorrow sounds great. I do know where the house is. And a Shenanigans Fiesta Chicken Chopped Salad would be great.

Sincerely,

Becky Flowers, Certified Senior Move Manager
Moving Up! Consulting LLC, President

MARSHALL STEWART	4:45PM	45%
TODAY	ALL	MISSED

Carly 10:45 AM

No, I did not have my fingers crossed when I swore on Blinky's life that I wouldn't contact Becky Flowers. That would be childish.

How's it going with your parents? I take it from the fact that you keep leaving voice messages from their landline instead of texting from your own phone that you either forgot to charge your cell this morning or you're in their basement where there's no service.

I hope you're having fun down there with all the judge's gavels and your mom's cat figurines.

Carly 11:05 AM

Well, I don't know what to tell you, but personally I think the fact that your dad is giving you such a detailed history of each of his gavels is a good sign. It means he might be ready to part with them.

Carly 11:37 AM

No, Marshall, I'm not going to look up the value of a box of Stayfree Maxi Pads from 1982 for you. I don't think they're worth anything at all. I'm actually working right now.

You remember work, don't you? A place we both used to go.

Carly 11:42 AM

You're not going to believe this, but I actually got us a listing.

It's the old Bloomville Elementary School on the west side. And yes, I know it's filled with asbestos, and that's the reason no one else wants it.

But it's a listing, and it's ours. So you were wrong: We are NOT the least popular realty company in Bloomville.

Carly   12:45 PM

What do you mean, your parents won't agree to meet with Jimmy? That is ridiculous. Call me. And not from their landline!

Carly   1:23 PM

Tell your Mom and Dad that they most definitely DO need a lawyer, and that no, writing a letter to the President of the United States is not going to help.

Carly   1:45 PM

Because the President of the United States does not have jurisdiction in this matter.

Also I'm fairly certain the President of the United States has more important things to do.

Reed Stewart   3:30 PM

Hi. I'm at the airport. Was anybody planning on picking me up? I'm pretty sure I forwarded you the time of my arrival.

Oh, well. It's fine. I know seeing Uncle Reed is pretty underwhelming these days.

Reed Stewart   4:07 PM

Seriously, it's okay. It's better for me to rent a car.

Did you know there's a Kiwanis convention in town? Neither did I.

It's fine, though. I enjoy the all-you-can-eat breakfasts at the Hampton Inn. I find them quite filling.

So that's where you'll find me, if anyone cares to look.

Carly   4:45 PM

OMG, Marshall, did you remember to pick up your brother at the airport???

Sweetie Ty

Reviewer ranking: #1,162,358
12% helpful
votes received on reviews

Reviewed
Women's Silver and Diamond Dress Watch
$475

As pictured
March 14

This is a totally hot "everyday" watch because it goes with everything thanks to the silver tone. It's an excellent choice in this price range, which of course not many can afford, but sometimes a girl needs a little pick-me-up.

I received many compliments while wearing this watch to school yesterday. The links are adjustable to fit any size wrist, even a very slim one like mine (I wear size 00, so finding clothes/jewelry that fits is nearly impossible).

One potential problem with this watch might be that it's TOO sparkly. Because even my homeroom teacher noticed me wearing it!

And that four-eyed troll never notices anything.

She went, "Where'd you get that watch, Ty?" and I was like, "None of your business," because I didn't want her to know I borrowed my mom's credit card out of her wallet to buy it off this site.

But of course she must have fully suspected something was amiss since she told the principal who called my mom (everyone in this school, for which my parents pay $20,000 a year in tuition *each* for me and my brother, is a narc).

So then my mom came to school—my dad couldn't because he owns a restaurant and he's always really busy. My mom's just a lawyer—and asked where I got the watch.

Since I couldn't tell her the truth, she decided I must have shoplifted it.

LOL can you believe it? My own mom thinks I'm a full on thief.

If only she knew the kind of crap my brother Tony Jr. does on a daily basis. She'd completely freak. Tony Jr.'s only goal is to be OG—original gangster.

I've told Tony Jr. that that isn't a very practical goal. At the very least he should learn a skill that will enable him to get a job that pays him enough money to live in a climate where the sun shines over 300 days a year. Seasonal Affective Disorder and lack of Vitamin D due to our harsh winters are at nearly epidemic proportions in this part of the Midwest.

But Tony Jr. never listens to me, which is sad because I'm in almost all AP classes and got a 1600 once when I took a practice SAT for fun.

Anyway, now I'm grounded, and Mom took my phone.

Thank God she didn't think of taking my tablet, though, because then I wouldn't be able to write this, or follow the Instagram feed of my perfect bae, Harry Styles.

But Mom's got way bigger problems now than me. I'm not talking about my brother Tony Jr., either.

No, it turns out my grandma and grandpa, of all people, went to jail for dining and ditching. LOL!

So now my uncle Reed is here in town because of the "incident," which kind of sucks because he's never visited before and I'm grounded, and he's a way famous professional golfer.

No one famous ever comes to this town, except this super old rock 'n roll star named John Cougar Mellencamp, who no one has ever even heard of and who has never even set foot on stage with my bae, Harry

Styles. He got a flat tire here once, and bought a bottled water from the Mobil gas station.

I've never gotten to meet anyone famous, including my uncle Reed, since my mom wouldn't let me be a flower girl at Uncle Marshall and Aunt Carly's wedding.

And now I won't get to meet him because not only am I being punished for allegedly stealing a bracelet, but my mom won't let us go to my uncle Marshall's house where my uncle Reed is staying, since she says my cousins are weird, just because one of them dresses like an Indian chief all the time, which I actually think is kind of cute, but my mom says is a sign of bad parenting.

My mom also thinks we might get lice because my cousins go to public school, which isn't exactly fair, since my friend Sundae's brother got lice, and he goes to our school, which is private. He got lice from taking a selfie with a girl in the mall who had lice.

But when I told my mom that, she said the girl at the mall probably went to public school.

The whole thing is totally unfair because I saw on a gossip site that one time Uncle Reed was at a party with Ava Kuznetsov, the famous model.

Well, maybe not WITH with her, but she was there with her husband, this other golfer.

And once Ava Kuznetsov was at *another* party where my perfect bae, Harry Styles, was photographed leaving by the backdoor.

So that means in a way, my uncle Reed KNOWS Harry Styles.

But when I tried to tell my mom that, and that I HAD to go over to Uncle Marshall's tonight, my mom said that she didn't care, and that Uncle Reed is a "bad influence."

Which is kind of hilaire, because look at me! I'm a total juvenile delinquent.

And it's clear from whom I inherited my criminal tendencies:

Grandma, Grandpa and Uncle Reed!

Which basically means nothing I do is my fault. It's in my genes.

Oh well. I'd sneak out later, but if I get caught, Mom says she'll take away my door. That's her new thing. She saw it on Dr. Phil. When parents have taken everything else from their kids, like all their electronics and their freedom and stuff, and they STILL do bad stuff, then they should take away their door, so they don't have privacy, either.

LOL! Whatever, Dr. Phil. I'm sure that will work. How about having parents try not being such total a**holes who are on their Facebook pages all the time and only think about themselves and how many likes they have and never spend any quality time with their kids? Did you ever think of that?

Oh, I guess not.

Anyway, I hope you all enjoy this review as much as I enjoy this watch, b*tches!

2 of 10 people found this review helpful

Leeanne Matsumori created chat "Reed Stewart"

Leeanne Matsumori 19:17

Becky, why did I just get a text from my mom that she saw REED STEWART at Antonelli's Pizza picking up two extra large pies with his brother Marshall?

Is Reed Stewart back? And if so, why am I only hearing about this now and from my MOTHER of all people?

Becky Flowers 19:17

Okay, it's frightening that someone who is living in Japan has more information about the situation than I do. I didn't know Reed was back. I heard he MIGHT be coming back, but I didn't know he was back back. Thanks for the heads-up. I will definitely not be going to Antonelli's tonight.

Leeanne Matsumori 19:17

Well, actually tonight's probably the only safe night to go to Antonelli's, because he was already there and left.

Becky Flowers 19:18

True. I should probably head over there now and order ten pies, then cram them all into my freezer so I can avoid running into him for the rest of the week.

Leeanne Matsumori 19:18

That sounds 100% normal. Definitely something a healthy 28 yr old woman would do:

Hide in her mom's basement for the rest of the time her ex is visiting his family in their hometown in order to avoid seeing him.

Becky Flowers   19:19

Yeah, OK, you're right. I'll just never go out again in anything less than full makeup and my most flattering outfits.

Ha ha, just kidding.

No, seriously, I'm fine.

Leeanne Matsumori   19:19

Sure. You sound fine. When I left you were hot and heavy with Graham. What do you even care what Reed Stewart thinks?

Becky Flowers   19:20

I don't. In fact, Graham and I are going out tonight. Well, we were. I actually just had to call him and cancel. I got a new gig and I have a lot of organizing to do to get ready for it.

Leeanne Matsumori   19:21

God, you haven't changed at all. You are still such a geek! You used to do the same thing in high school, remember? A hot guy asks you out, but you prefer to stay home and create a spreadsheet for your homework. Or is it a binder?

Becky Flowers   19:21

Both. And what's wrong with it? Organization is the key to happiness in life.

Leeanne Matsumori   19:21

Uh, I thought it was love. Meanwhile, I bet you still think Reed Stewart was the best you ever had, even though he drove a golf cart drunk with you in it into a swimming pool and dislocated your shoulder, then never spoke to you again.

Becky Flowers   19:21

Actually, I was the one who did that.

Leeanne Matsumori   19:22
What?

Becky Flowers   19:22
I was driving the golf cart drunk. I dislocated my own shoulder.

Leeanne Matsumori   19:22
What the hell are you talking about?

Becky Flowers   19:22
I'm the one who was driving. God, it feels so good to finally tell someone!

But don't tell anyone else. And please delete this chat when we're done.

Leeanne Matsumori   19:23
I'm living in Tokyo with a bunch of old people who don't know you and barely speak English. Who am I going to tell?

But can we please go back to WHAT? We have been friends for HOW long and you're only choosing to tell me this NOW?

Becky Flowers   19:23
Ugh, I know. Don't kill me. Maybe it's BECAUSE you're so far away that I feel like it's finally okay to tell you.

But you remember that night at dinner at your parents' restaurant, your brother served us all those mai tais?

Leeanne Matsumori   19:23
You mean at Prom. They barely had any alcohol in them, Becky. You know Raymond.

Becky Flowers   19:23

Well, it was enough to get me feeling tipsy.

And then afterwards I begged Reed to let me drive the golf cart because
it looked like so much fun. I shouldn't have because I'd had a mai tai.
Well, two.

But anyway, it was his dad's golf cart and I had no idea what I was doing.
That's how it ended up in the pool.

Leeanne Matsumori   19:23

You drove Reed's dad's golf cart into the pool. After two watery mai tais.
On prom night. And let Reed take the blame.

Becky Flowers   19:24

Reed wouldn't let me take the blame! He took responsibility for
everything. Even my shoulder.

Leeanne Matsumori   19:24

That. Is. So. Hot.

Becky Flowers   19:24

At the time I was glad because when his dad showed up, he was so mad.
I'd never seen anyone so angry!

And the cops were there, too. Something like that on my record, I'd
have lost my scholarship to IU. Reed didn't have anything to lose. Well,
I mean, he could have lost his scholarship, but it turned out he didn't
even want to go. He'd lied to everyone about his real plans for the
future. Even me.

Then afterwards, he lied to everyone FOR me.

Leeanne Matsumori   19:25

That is basically the hottest thing I've ever heard.

Tell me more.

Becky Flowers   19:25
Leeanne, I'm serious.

Leeanne Matsumori   19:26
So am I. Do you know how long it's been since I've been on a date? I'm half-Hoosier, half-Japanese. The only guys who ask me out here are the ones with fetishes. And not the sexy kind.

Becky Flowers   19:26
Well, you could always come home. I miss you.

Leeanne Matsumori   19:26
No. I'm staying until Obaasan Matsumori tells me the secret of her agedashi tofu. Anyway, more please about all the hot lying.

Becky Flowers   19:27
There's nothing more to say except that I shouldn't have let him do it. I've regretted it every day since. His dad threw him out, he went to California, and I never heard from him again. I sent him a million texts, emails, and even letters, apologizing. He never replied to a single one.

Leeanne Matsumori   19:27
Well, THAT I knew. The rest of it, though—you just blew my mind. Becky Flowers, little miss goody two shoes, a criminal!

Becky Flowers   19:27
It's not funny.

Leeanne Matsumori   19:27
It's kind of funny.

Becky Flowers   19:28
No, it's not. It's no wonder he never contacted me again: He must hate me.

And I don't blame him.

Leeanne Matsumori   19:28

Why should he hate you? You didn't ask him to do what he did. It was his own choice.

And things turned out pretty great for him. He's a star athlete now with several multimillion endorsement deals. I mean, what makes you think he even remembers you?

Becky Flowers   19:28

Thanks.

Leeanne Matsumori   19:29

Sorry! But no offense, he probably has models crawling all over him. Not that you're not hot, but you're no model.

Becky Flowers   19:29

No, really, thanks.

Leeanne Matsumori   19:29

I can see why you haven't gotten over him, though. That was so amazing, him taking the blame like that.

Plus he liked the same books you liked.

And there was the thing you mentioned about the sex. Tell me again about the hot sex. What was that trick he did with his pubic bone? Maybe that's a thing only golfers can do.

Becky Flowers   19:30

No. I'm over him. I'm so over him that the job I have tomorrow is at his parents' house, helping them downsize.

Leeanne Matsumori   19:30

WHAT.

Becky Flowers   19:30

His sister-in-law hired me.

Leeanne Matsumori   19:31
ARE YOU INSANE?

Becky Flowers   19:31
No. Look, it's going to be fine.

Leeanne Matsumori   19:31
Aren't you and the cheese guy engaged???

Becky Flowers   19:32
We've talked about marriage, nothing formal.

Well, unless you mean the outdoor ceremony we plan to have someday on the courthouse square, which of course will be catered by Authentic. And please stop calling him the cheese guy, he has a name.

Leeanne Matsumori   19:32
I can't believe you're using Authentic as the caterer of your fake wedding, and not Matsumori's Tiki Palace. We could do sushi boats, pupu platters, and even daiquiris for your guests.

Becky Flowers   19:32
I don't think serving raw fish at an outdoor ceremony is a good idea. And think about the spicy mayo on your dad's Atomic Tuna rolls.

Leeanne Matsumori   19:32
And will Judge Stewart be presiding over this fake ceremony?

Becky Flowers   19:32
Look, just remember not to tell anybody what I told you about Reed, okay? No one knows—not even Nicole. I never even admitted it to my blessings journal.

Leeanne Matsumori   19:33
Of course you have a blessings journal. Whatever you say, Miss Demeanor.

Becky Flowers   19:33

Stop.

Leeanne Matsumori   19:34

I can understand now why you don't want to run into Reed. What I don't get is how you expect to avoid it while you're working in his parents' house.

Becky Flowers   19:34

Well, until this moment, I didn't know he was actually coming back.

Leeanne Matsumori   19:34

Oh, he's back all right.

But maybe he and his dad still aren't speaking, so you won't run into him over there.

And from the other stuff my mom told me—like about Judge Stewart getting arrested—those people sound like a hot mess.

Becky Flowers   19:35

Cleaning up hot messes is my specialty.

Leeanne Matsumori   19:35

Oh, right! I'm 6500 miles away, and even I can see that *YOU* are a hot mess.

Becky Flowers   19:36

Thanks. Thanks for that.

Leeanne Matsumori   19:36

Douitashimashite (that's "You're Welcome"—formal—in Japanese) ☺

From: Dolly Vargas D.Vargas@VTM.com
Date: March 14 9:45:37 PM EST
To: Reed Stewart@reedstewart.com
Subject: Lyrexica Offer

Darling, normally when a major pharmaceutical company offers one of my clients low-to-mid six figures to endorse one of their products, I at least get a return phone call.

And when that company ups their offer from low-to-mid six figures to high six figures, I often get flowers, or even a box of chocolates, which of course I can't eat, due to my acid reflux, which my physician tells me is entirely stress-related, and thanks to my career.

But no. Reed Stewart is much, much too busy to think of his poor, stressed-out, hardworking agent.

CALL ME.

XOXO

Dolly
Dolly Vargas
Vargas Talent Management
Los Angeles, CA

Val King 9:45PM EST

I can't believe what we had meant so little to you. Why am I hearing that you sent Enrique to look for condos for your parents??? It's like you don't even remember that I have a realtor's license.

Maybe it's not valid in the state of Florida, but you know I have an eye for a good piece of property.

I can see now exactly why your game has been suffering. Your lack of confidence in those who should mean the most to you directly reflects your lack of confidence in yourself.

From: Reed Stewart@reedstewart.com
Date: March 14 11:37:22 PM EST
To: Lyle Stewart@FountainHill.org
Subject: Richard and Connie

Dear Uncle Lyle,

Thanks for your email. I'm sure your *Phalaenopsis amabilis* is extraordinary. If it doesn't win or at least place, the Expo is probably rigged. Send me a photo if you get a chance.

It's weird to be back here . . . weirder than I thought it would be. The town has changed a *lot*. There's a CVS drugstore where the Jiffy Lube used to be, and a Target where the old football stadium was.

And even more buildings have been abandoned, especially since they shut down the limestone quarries. The old Bloomville Elementary building is sitting empty since they built a new, state-of-the-art one a few years ago.

The good news is, apparently I can buy my old school!

The bad news is, it's full of asbestos.

So reassuring to know we were educated in such a safe, healthy environment.

Anyway, it's good to see Marshall and Carly and the kids. You'd like the kids. One of them—the middle one, Bailey—refuses to take off the Chief Massasoit costume Carly made her for the school's Thanksgiving play.

I don't really blame her. If someone cast me as Chief Massasoit in the school play, I'd probably never take the costume off, either.

I haven't seen Mom and Dad yet. Marshall drove me by the house on our way to pick up pizza for dinner—at Antonelli's, of course, which was better than I expected it to be, but not great—and I have to say, I was pretty shocked.

Dad used to keep the place in tip-top shape—or at least always hired people to keep it that way for him—and you definitely can't say that about the house now.

It's kind of hard to see with all the snow—March in Indiana, of course there's going to be one last snow before spring—but there appear to be a lot of shingles missing, shutters askew, the lawn and hedges look like hell, and there are stray cats *everywhere*.

I asked Marshall what was going on with the cats, and he only muttered darkly, "Don't."

Marshall hasn't changed a bit.

No one's mentioned my going by to see Mom and the Judge. I'm sure I'll have to eventually, but Marshall seems to think it might be too much of a shock for the old man all at once, and we should ease into it slowly, maybe by giving him a call tomorrow morning and dropping him a hint that I'm around. I guess his ticker isn't what it used to be?

Carly disagrees. What else is new.

I haven't seen Trimble. Something appears to be going on with one of her kids. No one knows what. She's enrolled them in the private school— Marshall and Carly's kids go to the new public elementary school— because Trimble doesn't trust public education, which is odd because it was good enough for all of us when we were kids.

I haven't seen Becky. I'm certainly not going to contact her. I know it would be the gentlemanly thing to do, but what am I going to say to her after all these years? "I'm sorry" doesn't seem adequate.

Also, you might not be aware of it, but my family has become the laughingstock of this town. I'm sure she doesn't want to have anything to do with us. Carly showed me the local paper. Dad is all over the front page.

And where would this meeting between us take place, anyway, Antonelli's Pizza? The café in the bookstore? It isn't like there's fine dining in this town. Well, except for Matsumori's Tiki Palace, but her best friend's parents own that.

And that's where we went the night everything fell apart in the first place, so it doesn't exactly hold the best memories.

I guess I could take her to Shenanigans.

Ha, ha, that was a joke. A bad one, but at least I still have my sense of humor. Or some of it, anyway.

I'm not trying to be pessimistic, I'm just saying, maybe it's better for both of us that I conduct the business I came to conduct and get out without stirring up old emotions that are maybe better off left alone anyway.

In other news, Carly keeps hinting darkly that she has something to tell me. Knowing her, it's probably that she's pregnant again.

I can see why she wants to keep it from Marshall. I know he's always wanted a son, but Marshall will probably kill himself if Carly has a fourth kid. As it is, they had to double up two of the girls so I could stay with them instead of the hotel room I reserved, since they don't have a guest room, and the hotel is practically in Dearborn.

So now I'm sleeping in a pink canopy bed with a unicorn mobile dangling over my head.

I kind of like it. The unicorns dance to "Somewhere Over the Rainbow" when you wind it up.

Maybe there is a place somewhere that dreams really do come true. I hope so.

Well, that's it for now. I really hope your *Phalaenopsis amabilis* wins. It should, if there's any justice in the world.

Love,

Your Favorite Nephew,
Reed

The Bloomville Herald

The Tri-County Area's Only
Daily Newspaper
• Wednesday, March 15 • Vol. 141 •
Still Only 50 Cents!

BLOOMVILLE HERALD
LETTERS TO THE EDITOR

Bloomville Herald Letters to the Editor Policy:

All letters to the editor are welcome as long as they follow these submission guidelines:

- Only original letters addressed to The Herald that include the writer's name, address and a daytime telephone number will be published. Anonymous letters and letters written under pseudonyms are not knowingly accepted.
- Maximum length for letters is 350 words.
- The Herald does not publish poetry, fiction, or political endorsement letters.
- Writers are limited to one letter every two weeks.

To the Editor,

It is with great sadness that I read the front page story of Tuesday, March 14, concerning Judge and Mrs. Stewart and their arrest at a certain local casual eatery.

I find it shocking that any resident of this town would support the pressing of charges against a man

who has served Bloomville for as long and as faith-
fully as Judge Richard Stewart, especially for what was
clearly a misunderstanding.

I can appreciate that the night manager of Shenanigans feels pressure from his corporate supervisors to
balance his register.

But surely there is such a thing as a moral balance,
as well?

In this case, I believe the morally balanced thing to
do would be to drop all charges against the Stewarts,
who clearly did not mean to cheat the restaurant out of
a meal, or Miss Gosling of her tip.

I'm equally sure there are many of us in this community who can find it in our hearts (and wallets) to
contribute the $59 the judge and his wife owe (plus a
15 percent tip for Miss Gosling) in order to make this
right.

If paying the Stewarts' bill ourselves does not cause
the restaurant to drop the charges, then I personally
call for a boycott against Shenanigans Neighborhood Bar and Grill, particularly this coming Friday,
when I see that the restaurant is having its annual
All-You-Can-Eat Irish Blarney Burger and Shamrock
Fries special in honor of St. Patrick's Day. Traditionally,
I know that many locals have attended this event to
enjoy the eatery's green beer and darts contest.

I am asking all Bloomville residents to join me in
boycotting Shenanigans Neighborhood Bar and Grill
until they drop the charges against Judge Stewart!

Perhaps if morality isn't something corporate
America—or Mr. Grubb—understands, money is.

Sincerely,
Beverly T. Flowers

REAL ESTATE SECTION

Looking for your dream home in the Bloomville area?

Make sure your first stop is the Bloomville Herald Real Estate Section . . . It's Where Buyers and Sellers Meet!

BLOOMVILLE

STEWART MANSION
65 Country Club Road

A once-in-a-lifetime listing, this is the first time this home has been on the market in 35 years. The Stewart Mansion—recorded in the National Register of Historic Places—was built in the late 1800s in the French Second Empire style. Made of limestone blocks laid without mortar, these 22-inch walls have stood strong against over a century and a half of midwestern flooding, tornadoes, and blizzards.

The distinctive slate mansard roof and ornate

ironwork are thought to have been inspired by the work of the architect who designed many of the great casinos of Europe.

At over 6,000 square feet and three floors, with a full attic and basement, this home has enough room for the largest of families, particularly when the detached 4-car garage and large acreage (three) are taken into consideration. The house comes complete with a large outdoor pool; 6 bedrooms; 7 full baths; 12-foot ceilings; 7 fireplaces; newly renovated kitchen with easy access to laundry; and a Venetian glass prism chandelier in the formal dining room.

All city utilities. Mixed use zoning and fiber optic internet. Full access to golf course; country club amenities with membership only.

$395,000
Shown by appointment only.
Contact: Marshall Stewart, REALTOR
812-555-2863
marshall@Stewart&Stewart.com

REED STEWART	8:37AM	100%
TODAY	ALL	MISSED

Marshall — 8:40 AM
Where are you?

Reed — 8:41 AM
Breakfasting at Bloomville Books. Not to malign your daughters' choice of cereal, but I'm more of a bacon and eggs than Fruity Pebbles man myself.

Marshall — 8:41 AM
Call me.

Reed — 8:41 AM
Much as I would like to fulfill such a polite and charming request, I cannot. For unknown reasons, cell phone use is not allowed at Bloomville Books. I'm currently getting a death stare from the guy behind the counter just for texting.

Marshall — 8:42 AM
If his nametag says Tim, that's one of the owners. He moved here recently from New York. He hates all electronic devices.

Have you seen this morning's paper?

Reed — 8:42 AM
Why yes, I'm looking at it now as I enjoy my Three Egg, Three Meat Combo Supreme.

Marshall — 8:42 AM
Have you seen IT?

Reed   8:42 AM

If you mean the listing you put in the paper for our childhood home, then yes, I have seen it. You apparently have a different sort of death wish than my fellow cell phone users, because the Judge is going to kill you when he sees it.

Marshall   8:43 AM

I'm not talking about that. I'm talking about the Letter to the Editor from your ex-girlfriend's mother.

Reed   8:44 AM

Why no, I missed that. I do not as a rule read Letters to the Editor, as I'm uninterested in local politics and government conspiracy theories.

Marshall   8:44 AM

She's calling on the citizens of Bloomville to boycott Shenanigans until they drop the charges against Mom and Dad.

Reed   8:45 AM

And this is a bad thing . . . why?

Marshall   8:45 AM

Carly and I are local business owners in this area. We can't be the cause—even indirectly—of a boycott against another business.

Reed   8:46 AM

Well, what am I supposed to do about it?

Marshall   8:46 AM

Obviously I want you to talk to her about it.

Reed   8:47 AM

You want me to talk to Becky Flowers's mother about her boycott against Shenanigans?

Marshall   8:47 AM

No, you idiot. Becky. Tell her she's got to get her mom to call it off.

Reed   8:48 AM

Goodbye, Marshall. I see now why Tim has his no cell phone rule.
I am going to continue enjoying my Three Egg, Three Meat Combo
Supreme in peace.

Marshall   8:48 AM

I'm serious, Reed. You've been gone a long time. You don't
understand how it is in this town anymore. The tire factory, the
limestone mill—they've all shut down, and left a lot of people out
of work. They feel bitter about it, and blame big corporations for
everything.

People are going to get all riled up over this thing, and you
know who's going to get hurt by it? We are. Not Shenanigans.
The Stewart family. And probably Becky, too. You've got to do
something.

Marshall   8:50 AM

Reed? Do not ignore me.

Marshall   8:51 AM

You're going to have to talk to her sometime, so it might as well
be over this.

Marshall   8:52 AM

Fine, don't answer me. But I know where you are. I'm coming
over there. You realize Bloomville Book's is literally around the
corner from our office, don't you?

Marshall   9:02 AM

Slick, Reed. Very slick. And sticking me with the bill? Classy.

I'll find you. This town isn't that big. There aren't that many places
you can hide.

BECKY FLOWERS	11:45AM	98%
TODAY	ALL	MISSED

Becky F — 11:26 AM
Mom, why did I just drive past the mall and see you standing outside with a sign that says Boycott Shenanigans with a big red slash through it?

Mom — 11:32 AM
Honey, I told you I was writing a letter to the editor. I just didn't think they'd print it so soon.

Becky F — 11:32 AM
That doesn't answer my question.

Mom — 11:32 AM
Well, I have to stand by my beliefs. Did you know that Grubb boy wouldn't take the $59 plus tip I tried to pay towards the Stewarts' bill?

Then again, he always was odd. Remember when he used to wear that black trench coat to school every day so he could look like the man from that movie about the matrix?

Becky F — 11:33 AM
Mom, I'm on my way to a meeting with the Stewarts RIGHT NOW. This is a total conflict of interest.

Mom — 11:35 AM
Well, I'm sorry, honey, but I have to do what I thought was right.

Becky F — 11:36 AM
Mom. Randy isn't a Girl Scout. It isn't your responsibility to set him straight.

Mom   11:36 AM
Actually, it is. It's my duty to leave this world a better place than I found it.

Becky F   11:36 AM
That's campsites, Mother. As a Girl Scout you're supposed to leave campsites cleaner than you found them.

Mom   11:36 AM
Yes, but Girl Scout Law also states I will do my best to make the WORLD a better place.

Becky F   11:37 AM
☹

Nicole F   11:40 AM
OMG I just saw a promo for the Channel 4 News at Noon with Jackie Monroe and MOM was on it protesting Shenanigans.

This is literally the best day of my life.

Becky F   11:40 AM
I'm already aware of what Mom is up to, Nicole. Do you have any idea what it's like to be driving to a client's house and see your own mother holding a protest sign on the side of the road?

Nicole F   11:40 AM
☺

Becky F   11:41 AM
I'm glad one of us is happy.

Nicole F   11:41 AM
Oh, come on. This is hilarious.

And it's good for Mom. She's been so down since Dad died.

Becky F   11:41 AM

I'm glad you can see the bright side of this, because I can't.

Nicole F   11:41 AM

Where are you, anyway? Not texting from a moving vehicle, I hope! Becky Flowers would NEVER break the law.

Becky F   11:42 AM

I'm parked down the street from their house.

Nicole F   11:42 AM

Of course you are. I know how you get. And that's with normal clients, not the parents of your ex. Are you psyching yourself up by listening to Beyoncé?

Becky F   11:42 AM

Maybe.

Nicole F   11:42 AM

Yes. You are.

Not to make things worse, but I saw on Antonelli's Facebook page that Reed Stewart bought four large pepperoni pizzas last night. It may be the most normal thing any boyfriend of yours has ever eaten. The lumbersexual always orders those weird pies with the figs and truffle honey and parma ham and blue cheese. Ugh. What is so wrong with pepperoni?

Becky F   11:43 AM

I swear to God Nicole, if you don't stop calling Graham a lumbersexual, I'm firing you.

Nicole F   11:43 AM

You can't fire me. I'm family. ☺

Becky F   11:44 AM

I can fire you, and I will.

Nicole F   11:45 AM

If you do, Mom will boycott. She'll start a protest outside of Moving Up!

Becky F   11:45 AM

You are not actually helping me feel less nervous right now.

Nicole F   11:45 AM

Yes, I am. Because now you're mad at me. Channel that energy!

Mom   11:46 AM

Honey, I feel badly for leaving work without checking to see if there was anything I could do to help you get ready for your big meeting. Is there anything I can do?

Becky F   11:47 AM

It isn't a big meeting, Mom. It's a normal meeting.

And no, there is nothing you can do to help me from outside Shenanigans, except call off the boycott.

Mom   11:48 AM

Well, you know I can't do that until Randy Grubb agrees to drop the charges. And who knows how long that will be.

Oh, honey, I can't chat anymore. That nice Rhonda Jenkins just showed up to protest with me! And she brought some of that delicious chicken of hers for lunch. Isn't that sweet?

Nicole F   11:48 AM

Hey, I might head over to the protest to help Mom for a little while.

Becky F   11:48 AM

No! Someone has to answer the landline!

Nicole F   11:48 AM

Just for a few minutes. I get a lunch break, you know, under OSHA.

Becky F   11:48 AM

There are no federal requirements for meal breaks in the state of Indiana. You just want some of Rhonda's chicken.

Nicole F   11:48 AM

Man, we chose the wrong state to be born in. At least you look hot in that outfit you wore today, Bex. Red is a good color on you.

Becky F   11:49 AM

Yes, looking hot for my ex's parents is of deep concern to me.

Okay, take your break. But please do not contact me while I'm with the Stewarts for any reason unless the office is burning down, Mom got arrested, or Doug in the garage has caught his finger in another sliding door, okay?

Nicole F   11:50 AM

Got it.

And Mom won't get arrested, they sent Henry to keep an eye on her, and he promised to get her out of there if there's trouble.

Anyway, send photos! Especially of the chandelier.

And if there are any squashed cats.

Becky F   11:50 AM

Nicole, that isn't funny. The Stewarts are distinguished members of the community. There aren't going to be any squashed cats, because they aren't hoarders.

Although I have to say, I can see quite a few cats in the yard from here. I'm not exactly sure what's going on with that.

But oh, well. Talk to you later, and save some chicken for me.

REED STEWART	11:45AM	38%
TODAY	ALL	MISSED

Carly — 11:22 AM
Hi, Reed, are we still on for our noon appointment?

Reed — 11:22 AM
Yes, but I'm curious to know where we're going. Your OB-GYN by any chance?

Carly — 11:25 AM
No, why would I ask you to come with me to the gynecologist? I told you, we're just doing boring legal stuff to do with your parents.

But first we should pick up lunch. I was going to get it from Shenanigans, but we can't with the boycott going on there.

So instead we're going to pick up a deli platter at Kroger. Sound OK?

Reed — 11:25 AM
Okay, except that I had a big breakfast. And who brings a deli platter to a lawyer's office?

Carly — 11:26 AM
Oh, it just seems like the polite thing to do. Some people don't get out much. What are you wearing?

Reed — 11:27 AM
Carly Stewart, are you sexting me? I'm shocked!

Carly — 11:27 AM
No, Reed, I am not "sexting" you. I just want you to look your best at this meeting.

Reed   11:28 AM

You business types are all the same. Actually I'm over at the range hitting balls, so I'm dressed down.

Carly   11:28 AM

Reed. There's still snow on the ground.

Reed   11:28 AM

The range is always open. I guess I could zip over to Target and buy a tie. Would that help me pass muster with the legal eagles?

Carly   11:29 AM

Yes, a tie would be good.

Reed   11:29 AM

OK. Then I'll meet you at your office after the tie has been secured.

Carly   11:29 AM

No, not the office. Marshall might be there.

Reed   11:29 AM

Oh, right. Are you avoiding Marshall, too?

Carly   11:30 AM

Well, let's just say it's better if Marshall doesn't know about this meeting. You know how he is.

Meet me in the Kroger parking lot after you've bought a tie. I'll have the deli platter, and then we can take my car to the meeting.

Reed   11:30 AM

This sounds like the weirdest meeting I've ever been to. But OK, the Kroger parking lot it is.

I kind of like all this sneaking around! It's fun.

Carly   11:30 AM

I really hope you still feel that way when you see where we're going.

Becky Flowers created chat "Reed Stewart"

Becky Flowers   12:17 PM
He's here.

Leeanne Matsumori   12:17 PM
What? Who is where? You woke me up. It's 1AM here.

Becky Flowers   12:17 PM
I'm sorry. I'm at his parents' house. The sister-in-law didn't tell me he was going to be here, but he's here.

Leeanne Matsumori   12:18 PM
OMG TELL ME EVERYTHING RIGHT NOW

Becky Flowers   12:18 PM
For some reason there's a deli platter.

Leeanne Matsumori   12:18 PM
Not that kind of stuff. About him. How does he look?

Becky Flowers   12:18 PM
Good. Too good. He's taller than I remember.

Leeanne Matsumori   12:18 PM
He grew.

Becky Flowers   12:19 PM
No.

Leeanne Matsumori   12:19 PM
Becky, yes. You were teenagers when you last saw one another. He's grown since then. You both have, in more ways than just physically, hopefully.

What else?

Becky Flowers   12:19 PM
He's wearing a tie. Oh, God, why did he have to be wearing a tie?

Leeanne Matsumori   12:19 PM
More, please. How did he react when he saw you?

Becky Flowers   12:20 PM
Startled. I don't think his sister-in-law told him I was going to be here.

Leeanne Matsumori   12:20 PM
Well, at least he didn't run again. MORE PLEASE.

Becky Flowers   12:20 PM
I can't tell you more. I'm in the bathroom. I excused myself because I was so freaked out. I needed a minute to collect myself.

Now I have to get back out there. His dad is telling me about his extensive hammer collection.

Leeanne Matsumori   12:20 PM
His what???

Becky Flowers   12:21 PM
Gavels. Sorry. They are judge's gavels. I think. I don't know. I'm so nervous. Why am I so nervous???

Leeanne Matsumori   12:21 PM
Because you haven't seen the guy in ten years and before that you two were the hottest couple in Bloomville history?

Becky Flowers   12:21 PM

Leeanne. The house, though. You don't even want to know.

Leeanne Matsumori   12:21 PM

Yes, I do. I really, really want to know.

Becky Flowers   12:21 PM

The word nightmare does not even begin to describe it.

The Stewarts are being so kind to me, though.

Leeanne Matsumori   12:21 PM

I don't care about them. I want to know about Reed!

Becky Flowers   12:22 PM

Polite but distant. He's eaten all the chicken salad from the deli platter.

Leeanne Matsumori   12:22 PM

Do not wake me up in the middle of the night to tell me about chicken salad.

I want to know about HIM HIM HIM.

Becky Flowers   12:22 PM

I don't know what else to say! He seems dazed. He's looking around the house like he doesn't recognize anything in it . . . which could be true, he's been gone a long time and his parents seem to have adopted some unusual habits in the past few years.

Leeanne Matsumori   12:22 PM

Drugs?

Becky Flowers   12:22 PM

Of course not. Collecting. A LOT. Look, I have to go back out there. They're going to think I have food poisoning from the deli platter.

Leeanne Matsumori   12:23 PM

Well, now I'm up, so text me and tell me every detail as it happens.

Becky Flowers   12:23 PM

That would be weird and unprofessional.

Leeanne Matsumori   12:24 PM

Oh, because Chat Apping me from the bathroom isn't.

Anyway, you can pretend like you're taking notes.

Becky Flowers   12:24 PM

No. Don't be silly. Go back to sleep. I'm sorry I woke you.

Leeanne Matsumori   12:24 PM

I can't believe this is happening without me. I'm coming home.

Becky Flowers   12:24 PM

What? Don't be crazy.

Leeanne Matsumori   12:24 PM

I'm looking into flights right now.

Becky Flowers   12:24 PM

You're insane. Goodbye, Leeanne.

From: Carly Stewart@StewartRealty.com
Date: March 15 12:30:39 PM EST
To: Marshall Stewart@StewartRealty.com
Subject: Your Parents

So remember how you made me swear on Blinky's life not to contact Becky Flowers? Well, don't be mad, but I had my fingers crossed.

Becky's here at your parents' house right now! And so is Reed!

But everything's going great. Better than great, anyway. Your parents are behaving like perfect angels. For the first time in ages, your dad isn't lecturing anyone about how the government should be spending our tax money to improve the infrastructure, and your mom hasn't mentioned her cats once.

Your parents could not be on better behavior. It's like no time at all has gone by since they last saw the two of them (and I'm not talking about the night Reed wrecked your dad's golf cart, either).

Becky's already told them that this house is much too big and drafty for them now that all the kids have moved out, and they've agreed.

She's like magic!

Well, okay, your mom did try to use the defense that "the grandkids still come over in the summertime to use the pool."

But Becky fenced with, "But that pool is much too expensive to maintain for a few visits a summer. Imagine if you had one in a smaller home that's somewhere warm year round. The kids could come for Christmas and Spring Break. Their visits would be so much more special."

Your mother seems to have fallen for it hook, line, and sinker.

I'm kind of sorry you're not here to watch.

And I KNOW you told me to stay out of it.

But I thought it would be a good idea to have a neutral third party here when I sprang your brother on your dad (and your dad on Reed).

I didn't think, given the amount of time that's passed since "the incident," that they'd snipe at one another in front of Becky.

And I was right (as I am about everything).

Because I arranged for us to arrive several minutes after Ms. Flowers (and carrying your dad's favorite food—well, second favorite, after Shenanigans—a cold cut and spring salad party platter from Kroger), all your dad could do when he saw Reed was say, "Hello, son," and give him a hug, which Reed returned (awkwardly).

It was heaven.

And unless I'm very, very wrong, there are some pretty heavy duty sparks flying between Becky and Reed. I've never seen any couple try to stay further apart than those two.

And you know what that means!

Anyway, I do think this was one of my better plans.

I'm not sure how you should reward me when I get home. I would say a full back massage to start with, and then of course, you're going to make dinner. Your Fettuccine Alfredo is probably in order. Because today I have solved all the problems in the world!!!

You're welcome.

XOXOXO

Carly

Carly R. Stewart | Accountant | Stewart Realty | 801 South Moore Pike, Bloomville, IN 47401 | phone (812) 555-8722 | Please visit StewartRealty.com for all your realty needs

From: Marshall Stewart@StewartRealty.com
Date: March 15 12:45:39 PM EST
To: Carly Stewart@StewartRealty.com
Subject: Re: Your Parents

If you think you've solved anything, you don't know my family at all. All you've done is create a giant mess that I'm going to have to clean up, and lit the fuse to a bomb that's going to blow in three . . . two . . . one . . .

From: Trimble Stewart-Antonelli@Stewart&Stewart.com
Date: March 15 12:56:29 PM EST
To: Carly Stewart@StewartRealty.com; Marshall Stewart@StewartRealty
.com; Reed Stewart@reedstewart.com
Subject: Mom and Dad

Why did Daddy just call me from his study and say that you clowns have hired one of Reed's exes to sell—or put into storage—all of Mommy's and Daddy's things?

This is NOT what we agreed on.

First, we don't need anyone snooping into Mom's and Dad's affairs. This is a private family matter. We do not need some kind of "moving consultant" or whatever this Becky Flowers person is, poking around in our business at a time when they've already been through a traumatic experience and we need to be keeping a LOW PROFILE.

And second, most of those things are MINE. I already told you that I get the chandelier, stemware, and dining room furniture.

But there are other things in there that I want. I need to get in there to see, but I don't have time at the moment. I'm extremely busy with the new restaurant and also a conflict Ty is having at school with a teacher.

Plus Tony is getting an award from the Kiwanis on Thursday night for all he's done for the community—which I notice none of you have congratulated him for, even though I posted about it on our Facebook page.

So could you please stop? NOTHING in that home is to be removed, or I will pursue legal action. And as executor of Mom and Dad's estate, I have every right to do so.

Trimble Stewart-Antonelli
Attorney at Law
Stewart & Stewart, LLC
1911 South Moore Pike
Bloomville, IN 47401
(812) 555-9721
www.stewart&stewart.com

From: Marshall Stewart@StewartRealty.com
Date: March 15 1:08:27 PM EST
To: Carly Stewart@StewartRealty.com
Subject: Re: Mom and Dad

Now do you see what I mean?

From: Carly Stewart@StewartRealty.com
Date: March 15 1:11:27 PM EST
To: Marshall Stewart@StewartRealty.com
Subject: Re: Mom and Dad

Oh, your sister can kiss my butt.

If she's such a great estate executor, why has she never been over here to take care of your parents when they've fallen or needed the trash taken out or given a holiday dinner? She lives down the street, for pity's sake, but hasn't noticed that your mother has about twenty feral cats, all of which are relieving themselves on her precious formal dining room furniture?

And by the way, since we got here, I've observed that a family of raccoons has built a nest in a hole in the living room ceiling.

When I mentioned it to your mother, she said, quite cheerfully, "Oh, yes. That's Ricky."

How did *you* fail to see any of this when you were over here dealing with the trash?

Carly R. Stewart | Accountant | Stewart Realty | 801 South Moore Pike, Bloomville, IN 47401 | phone (812) 555-8722 | Please visit StewartRealty.com for all your realty needs

From: Marshall Stewart@StewartRealty.com
Date: March 15 1:15:16 PM EST
To: Carly Stewart@StewartRealty.com
Subject: Re: Mom and Dad

I was in the basement, remember?

I'll deal with Trimble. Right after I call animal control.

Marshall   1:47 PM
I'm sorry, dude. I can't believe Carly did this to you.

Reed   1:47 PM
It's okay. I'm fine.

Marshall   1:47 PM
I know you're only saying that to save face. I'm on my way. I'm coming to get you.

Reed   1:48 PM
I wouldn't. Dad is more mad at you than he is at me, for a change.

Marshall   1:48 PM
What did *I* do?

Reed   1:48 PM
You listed his house for sale in today's paper. He's remarked on it several times already, and not in a positive manner.

Marshall   1:49 PM
Oh shoot I mean shot I mean, yeah, I forgot about that.

Well, I don't care. I'm still coming. Carly shouldn't have done this. She especially shouldn't have sprung Becky on you like this.

Reed   1:49 PM
It's okay. We're fine. It was awkward at first, but I'm an adult now. I've traveled the world. I can have a polite conversation with an ex-girlfriend from high school.

Marshall   1:50 PM

Dude, no, you can't. I've seen what that one looks like now, and no, you can't. I get why you creep on her. I'm coming to get you.

Reed   1:50 PM

I don't creep on her! And no, don't, it would be awkward. And she's making headway with Richard and Connie.

Marshall   1:50 PM

She's not. She's really not. Dad called Trimble from his study. He's mad as hello.

Reed   1:50 PM

Well, maybe he was, but right now Becky's got them eating out of her hand. They're talking about their future in Orlando.

Marshall   1:51 PM

What in the name of sweet Crisis are you talking about?

Reed   1:51 PM

I'm serious. She's actually really good at her job.

And your wife is not bad at the daughter-in-law thing, either. Between the two of them, they've got Richard and Connie admitting that Florida might not be a bad move. Good weather, good health care, lots of people their own age. I guess their friends, the Remacks, moved there last year, and love it?

Marshall   1:52 PM

Oh, yeah. I forgot about the Remacks.

But dude. Are you serious? Mom and Dad are excited about moving?

Reed   1:53 PM

Serious as the heart attack I'm pretty sure Richard will have if we don't get him the hell out of this place. It stinks like cat piss. And what is with all the newspapers?

Marshall   1:53 PM

Oh, yeah. Dad subscribes to four of them daily, and won't throw them out until he's read every article, which he never gets around to, because he's too busy looking at his stamps and writing disapproving letters to the President about the infrastructure. So they pile up.

Reed   1:53 PM

PILE UP?

Marshall, they're stacked up like high-rises all around the house. They're complete accidents waiting to happen. One of them could fall over at any time and wipe out Mom or one of the kids.

How could you not have noticed this?

Marshall   1:53 PM

They're not that bad. I mean, Dad's always done that.

Reed   1:53 PM

No, Marshall, the Judge hasn't "always" done that. This is a new thing he's started doing since I left.

Becky told him it's unhygienic. She found mouse droppings and pointed them out. Mom just about died.

I used the opportunity to chide them for firing Rhonda, and they both looked mortified.

None of this would be happening if they hadn't fired Rhonda.

Marshall   1:54 PM

Reed, this has nothing to do with Mom and Dad firing Rhonda. It has to do with you leaving. Dad started doing that after you left, as you would know if you'd ever once come to visit.

Dad wouldn't let Rhonda throw out the papers. That's why the papers have been sitting there for years.

Reed   1:54 PM

Oh.

Well, not anymore. They've agreed to let Becky's company come tomorrow to throw out the papers.

Marshall   1:54 PM

Are you shooting me?

Reed   1:55 PM

No, I am not shooting you. Why would I shoot you?

Marshall   1:55 PM

I've been trying to get Dad to throw out those papers for years.

Reed   1:55 PM

Well, you aren't Becky.

Marshall   1:55 PM

What is so great about Becky???

Reed   1:55 PM

Well, for one thing, Becky has a binder.

Marshall   1:55 PM

What the hello does that have to do with anything?

Reed   1:55 PM

She told me binders give people an air of authority.

Maybe you should try carrying a binder. You might sell more houses.

Marshall   1:55 PM

What about what Dad said, about only leaving Bloomville in a pine coffin?

Reed   1:55 PM

He told Becky that, too.

She told him that if he times it right, he could die here during a summer visit to you, and still get his wish.

Marshall   1:55 PM

What????

Reed   1:55 PM

Yeah. Right in your house.

That made Richard laugh, and Connie, too.

Marshall   1:56 PM

Well, I don't think that's funny.

And stop calling them Richard and Connie! Crest, I mean coast, I mean crust, I'm coming to get you. This whole thing was a honey trap for Mom and Dad, but YOU'RE the one falling for it. How can you not see that? And that girl is the honey!

Reed   1:56 PM

She's not a girl anymore. She's a woman. You should know better than to use sexist language like that.

Marshall   1:56 PM

Oh, Crust, where'd you hear that? Sexual harassment awareness training on the PGA circuit?

Reed   1:57 PM

Lifetime Channel. You should watch it sometime.

And I think Carly is right, Marshall. You need to see someone about your anger issues.

Marshall   1:57 PM

FUUUUUUUUUUUUUUUUUUUUUUDGE what is happening over there?????

BECKY FLOWERS	3:45PM	96%
TODAY	ALL	MISSED

Nicole F   2:26 PM
Where are you? Mom and I expected you to be back by now.

Becky F   2:26 PM
I know, sorry. It went a little longer than I expected. And I had to stop at the café for a caffeine fix. I'm feeling a little drained.

Nicole F   2:26 PM
That bad?

Becky F   2:26 AM
Oh, it's all right.

Nicole F   2:26 PM
How many PODS?

Becky F   2:27 PM
4 at least. I don't know how many Dumpsters. And possibly hazmat suits for the basement.

Nicole F   2:27 PM
4 PODS, you don't know how many Dumpsters, hazmat suits for the basement, and it's "all right"???

Becky, they're hoarders!!!! You assured me they were collectors! "Antiques, Nicole." That's what you said. "There's a Venetian glass chandelier in the dining room, Nicole." That's what you said!

And now we're talking about hazmat suits!

Becky F   2:27 PM

Well, I was wrong. The chandelier is still there. They've still got the other stuff, too.

But they've added to it. The Judge collects hammers. He must have a thousand of them.

And his wife's a cat lady. Live AND ceramic. One of the live ones leapt out at me from under a bed and tried to swipe at my ankles.

Thank God I wore boots today.

Nicole F   2:27 PM

I can't, Becky. Not cats. I draw the line at cats. Not after what happened at the Mayhews'.

Becky F   2:27 PM

I know.

But it's not as bad as the Mayhews, I swear. I think these mostly live outside. Mrs. Stewart said she only lets them in on special occasions.

Nicole F   2:28 PM

Oh, well, that makes it all right then. NOT.

You're not making this job sound very appealing, Bex.

Becky F   2:28 PM

We don't have a choice, Nicole. We have to help these people. It's not a healthy environment. They have the washer and dryer in the KITCHEN where the stove used to be. They've been eating fast food instead of cooking proper meals.

And there are stacks and stacks of the Judge's books and files and newspapers just piled up everywhere. It isn't a safe environment for anyone, let alone elderly people of questionable physical and possible mental health.

Some of the stacks were so unsteady even Reed looked scared to walk around them.

Nicole F	2:28 PM

Whoa. Back up. Reed?

REED STEWART WAS THERE?

Becky F	2:29 PM

Oh yes. Did I forget to tell you?

Nicole F	2:29 PM

Call me right now.

Becky F	2:29 PM

I can't. I told you, I'm at the café. You know how Tim is about cell phone conversations in the bookstore. Texting and emailing only.

Nicole F	2:29 PM

Fine. So WHAT DID HE LOOK LIKE? Did you kick him in the nads?

Becky F	2:30 PM

Yes, Nicole, I kicked the son of our potential clients in the groin. That is always the professional thing to do at an assessment.

Nicole F	2:30 PM

No, but really. What happened? Did he apologize for how he's ignored you for the past decade? Did he go down on bended knee and beg your forgiveness? Is that why you're considering a job that I know in your right mind, you would pass up?

Becky F	2:31 PM

Nicole, don't be ridiculous. Nothing happened. He looked great, just like he does when I see him on TV. He was very polite. He asked how I was, and how you were, and how Mom is. He said he was sorry Dad died.

Nicole F	2:31 PM

STALKER. He's a stalker.

Becky F   2:31 PM
Nicole.

Nicole F   2:32 PM
Well, if he knew Dad died, that means he's been stalking you
online.

Becky F   2:32 PM
Or one of his siblings could have told him.

In any case, he said he was sorry, and he really looked it, so that's
enough for me. I don't think his sister-in-law Carly told him that
I'd be there, though, any more than she told me that he'd be
there, so he looked shocked to see me.

But he pulled himself together enough to be very sincere in asking
after you and Mom, and saying he was sorry about Dad.

And that was it.

Nicole F   2:32 PM
That was it???? He didn't say anything about what happened
between you at Prom Night?

Becky F   2:33 PM
Well, we were never alone together. One of his parents or Carly
was always there. I was doing a walk-through his childhood home
to get an idea of how much we're going to charge to pack and
move all his parents' belongings from it. So it wasn't exactly an
intimate setting.

Nicole F   2:33 PM
Actually, it WAS. You know the saddest, most intimate thing about
him, that probably no one else on earth outside his immediate
family knows:

The parents of Reed Stewart, former #1 best professional golfer in
the world, are hoarders!

Becky F   2:33 PM
Yes, well, let's keep that to ourselves, all right, Nicole? Remember, we took an oath.

Nicole F   2:33 PM
How could I forget the oath we swore as members of the American Association of Senior Move Managers?

Becky F   2:34 PM
It's not a joke, Nicole. If we take this job, we're going to have to perform it to the best of our ability. The Stewart family needs our help.

Nicole F   2:34 PM
Oh, my God. Do you think maybe you're a little too personally involved even to be considering taking this job?

Becky F   2:34 PM
No.

Nicole F   2:34 PM
Are you sure?

Becky F   2:34 PM
Yes.

Now that Reed and I have gotten the initial awkwardness of meeting again out of the way, I think everything's going to be fine between us. We can be friends again.

Nicole F   2:35 PM
Everyone knows you can't be friends with an ex, Beck.

Becky F   2:35 PM
Of course you can. Millions of single parents do it every day.

Nicole F 2:35 PM
Oh, okay. That so applies to you and Reed. Because your kids are . . . his parents?

Becky F 2:35 PM
Well, right now, yes, I guess in a way.

Look, Reed and I were kids ourselves back when we dated. But we're adults now. We've both moved on. I have a boyfriend, and I'm sure he's seeing someone, too.

There's no reason we can't be friends. It's all good.

Nicole F 2:36 PM
Oh, you have a boyfriend, all right. He hasn't heard from you in forever.

Becky F 2:36 PM
What are you talking about?

Nicole F 2:36 PM
Nothing. Just that you might want to call Graham and let him know you're thinking about taking on a case involving your ex's parents. I bet he'd be pretty interested.

Becky F 2:36 PM
I haven't said we're taking the case.

Nicole F 2:36 PM
Sure.

Becky F 2:37 PM
We're probably not going to.

Nicole F 2:37 PM
I believe you.

Becky F	2:37 PM
It's too big a job and we have too many other things going on anyway.	

Nicole F	2:38 PM
Like the Blumenthals.	

Becky F	2:38 PM
Yes. Exactly.	

Nicole F	2:38 PM
So you aren't sitting there in the bookstore café writing out a relocation package proposal for the Stewarts, are you?	

Becky F	2:38 PM
Absolutely not.	

Nicole F	2:38 PM
Good. See you back here in the office soon, then.	

Becky F	2:38 PM
Yes. Absolutely.	

From: Becky Flowers Becky@MovingUp.com
Date: March 15 2:43:27 PM EST
To: Carly Stewart@StewartRealty.com
Subject: Pricing for Judge and Mrs. Stewart

Thank you for allowing Moving Up! Senior Move Management Consultants the opportunity to assist your husband's parents in downsizing to a smaller home.

I have some pricing ready for you derived from our meeting earlier today.

I believe that it will only require five days of preparation and packing to clear your parents' home. During these five visits my staff and I will help your in-laws sort their belongings and:

- **Pack** everything that is relocating with them immediately

- **Store** what they don't feel is necessary to bring right away

- **Donate** items in good condition they no longer care to keep

- **Sell** items of greater value they no longer care to keep

- **Dispose** of items of no value for which they no longer have any use

We are prepared to offer you our complete Relocation Preparation Package for a total price of: **$15,000.00.**

This price includes all packing, storage, and disposal materials, which we will deliver to your in-laws' home, and remove when the project is complete.

Also for your consideration:

We offer a "resettling package." When your husband's parents have chosen a new home, we will ship their items to the chosen destination, travel to that home, then unpack them and:

- **Set up** their furniture in their new home before their arrival

- **Make** all beds

- **Put away** kitchen items

- **Hang** all clothes

- **Organize** books and office materials

- **Remove** all packing materials, and

- **Have** their home move-in ready

The Resettling Package costs an average of $5,000.00 (depending on amount of items and distance shipped, and the cost of local overnight accommodations for the Moving Up! representative).

Since we have a number of other clients at the moment, it would be very much appreciated if you could get back to us as quickly as possible so we could place your husband's parents on our schedule. For your convenience, I've attached a contract for the Relocation Preparation Package for you to print out and sign should you choose to.

Please let us know if, in addition to our Relocation Preparation Package, you also wish to purchase our Resettling Package. It definitely changes the way we prepare and label items.

On a personal note, it would be a great honor to work with the Judge and Mrs. Stewart, as I've always sincerely admired them. I would do whatever I could to try to make this move as painless as possible for your entire family, as I understand what a difficult time this must be for you all.

Thank you for considering Moving Up! Senior Move Management Consultants.

Yours very sincerely,

Becky Flowers, CCSMM
Moving Up! Consulting LLC, President

From: Carly Stewart@StewartRealty.com
Date: March 15 3:15:19 PM EST
To: Marshall Stewart@StewartRealty.com; Reed Stewart@reedstewart.com
Subject: Re: Pricing for Judge and Mrs. Stewart

Hi. She's taking the job (don't ask me why). I'm forwarding the estimate. I think it's more than reasonable.

From: Becky Flowers Becky@MovingUp.com
Date: March 15 2:43:27 PM EST
To: Carly Stewart@StewartRealty.com
Subject: Pricing for Judge and Mrs. Stewart

Thank you for allowing Moving Up! Senior Move Management Consultants the opportunity to assist your husband's parents in downsizing to a smaller home.

I have some pricing ready for you derived from our meeting earlier today. . . .

Carly R. Stewart | Accountant | Stewart Realty | 801 South Moore Pike, Bloomville, IN 47401 | phone (812) 555-8722 | Please visit StewartRealty.com for all your realty needs

From: Marshall Stewart@StewartRealty.com
Date: March 15 3:17:12 PM EST
To: Carly Stewart@StewartRealty.com; Reed Stewart@reedstewart.com
Subject: Re: Pricing for Judge and Mrs. Stewart

You call $20,000 reasonable???

From: Reed Stewart@reedstewart.com
Date: March 15 3:20:02 PM EST
To: Marshall Stewart@StewartRealty.com; Carly Stewart@StewartRealty.com
Subject: Re: Pricing for Judge and Mrs. Stewart

You weren't there today, Marshall. You didn't see what I did in the basement.

From: Marshall Stewart@StewartRealty.com
Date: March 15 3:25:19 PM EST
To: Carly Stewart@StewartRealty.com; Reed Stewart@reedstewart.com
Subject: Re: Pricing for Judge and Mrs. Stewart

I've been in that basement plenty of times, Reed. "Don't touch any of it!
It's all worth millions!"—direct quote from Dad.

But fine, if you want to throw your money away, be my guest.

From: Reed Stewart@reedstewart.com
Date: March 15 3:28:07 PM EST
To: Marshall Stewart@StewartRealty.com; Carly Stewart@StewartRealty.com
Subject: Re: Pricing for Judge and Mrs. Stewart

What do you even care? It's my money to throw.

I'll write to Becky and tell her yes, Carly.

From: Carly Stewart@StewartRealty.com
Date: March 15 3:35:12 PM EST
To: Marshall Stewart@StewartRealty.com; Reed Stewart@reedstewart.com
Subject: Re: Pricing for Judge and Mrs. Stewart

You will? Well, thanks, Reed.

Carly R. Stewart | Accountant | Stewart Realty | 801 South Moore Pike, Bloomville, IN
47401 | phone (812) 555-8722 | Please visit StewartRealty.com for all your realty needs

From: Reed Stewart@reedstewart.com
Date: March 15 3:40:17 PM EST
To: Marshall Stewart@StewartRealty.com; Carly Stewart@StewartRealty.com
Subject: Re: Pricing for Judge and Mrs. Stewart

Of course! I said I was here to help.

And don't worry, you two. Uncle Reed will take the girls to dinner tonight, too. You two can have a romantic evening alone, to celebrate.

We have a senior moving consultant! Everything is going to be great!

From: Marshall Stewart@StewartRealty.com
Date: March 15 3:45:11 PM EST
To: Carly Stewart@StewartRealty.com
Subject: Re: Pricing for Judge and Mrs. Stewart

There's something deeply wrong with my brother, isn't there?

From: Carly Stewart@StewartRealty.com
Date: March 15 3:48:01 PM EST
To: Marshall Stewart@StewartRealty.com
Subject: Re: Pricing for Judge and Mrs. Stewart

No. He's in love, that's all.

Carly R. Stewart | Accountant | Stewart Realty | 801 South Moore Pike, Bloomville, IN 47401 | phone (812) 555-8722 | Please visit StewartRealty.com for all your realty needs

---

From: Marshall Stewart@StewartRealty.com
Date: March 15 3:55:17 PM EST
To: Carly Stewart@StewartRealty.com
Subject: Re: Pricing for Judge and Mrs. Stewart

Oh, God. This is going to be an even bigger disaster than I thought.

REED STEWART	5:45PM	51%
TODAY	ALL	MISSED

From: Reed Stewart@reedstewart.com
Date: March 15 5:06:10 PM EST
To: Becky@MovingUp.com
Subject: You

Dear Becky,

It seems inadequate to say "it's been a long time," but in this case, it's fitting.

Thanks so much for agreeing to help my parents. I'm attaching the signed contract, and yes, we would like the Resettling Package, as well.

We're still not exactly sure where my parents are going, or when, since for all we know, it could be prison, which I suppose will lower the bill for resettling considerably, as I suppose they won't need your bed-making skills in jail.

But they definitely need to get out of this town, as I know you're aware.

It's very generous of you, considering our past history, to agree to help facilitate this.

On that note, I'm sorry if I seemed awkward at my parents' house today. I'm sorry about a lot of things. I didn't know you were going to be there, and I had no idea what to say to you. Seeing you like that, in my parents' house, particularly in the state it was in . . . well, that wasn't the way I pictured the two of us meeting again after all these years.

And despite what you may think, I *have* pictured us meeting again. This is embarrassing to admit, but for years I've had this fantasy that when I came back to Bloomville, it would be as a rich man, like Captain Frederick Wentworth in *Persuasion* by Jane Austen. Do you remember him?

Captain Wentworth makes his fortune in the Navy, and returns not only to rescue the heroine Anne Elliot, but to show everyone in town, particularly her family, how wrong they'd been to misjudge him.

It was immature and pretentious of me, I know, since you were never the type of woman who needed rescuing. Even when we crashed into the pool, and you were in so much pain, you managed to get yourself out— though I swear to God I tried to rescue you then, too. I would have, if that security guard hadn't gotten to you first, and then, of course, the EMTs.

I never would have left your side if my father—and the cops—hadn't shown up, demanding explanations. But especially my father, who started shouting at me right then and there—in front of the police, the EMTs, and worst of all, you—about what a disappointment I was turning out to be to him, and that's when I just . . .

Well, I'm sure you remember the rest as well as I do.

I can't think of that night—the way I failed you—without breaking out into a cold sweat. I always swore when we met again, I'd show you how wrong my father was about me.

And now we finally do meet again, and what's happening? My dad is a shell of the man he once was, and it's partly my fault, because I've been off playing a stupid game. I can't even enjoy telling him how wrong he was about me, because that stupid game of mine is so off, I haven't had a win in years.

And you not only do not need rescuing, but are the only person for miles in a position to rescue *me*, from having to watch my parents destroy themselves.

Which makes me even more mortified about my past behavior, and the way I acted today at the house. When I saw you there, I was struck speechless, not only by your presence—which of course Carly didn't warn me about beforehand—but by what a beautiful and confident woman you've grown into.

Not that you weren't always gorgeous. And God knows you never had any problem speaking your mind.

But now there's something even more—I don't know what the right word is—about you.

I know how cheesy all of this must sound to you. I wouldn't blame you for hitting the delete button when you receive this.

But all I could think about when I saw you today was what a fool I was ten years ago, and have continued to be.

I know I don't have the right to ask anything of you, especially considering how generous you're being in agreeing to help us. But I had to get all this off my chest since it looks like you and I will be seeing quite a lot of one another in the next week or so.

So I was wondering if you'd consider being friends again. I know after the way I've treated you, I don't deserve your friendship, and I'm definitely not asking for anything more. I've heard about this guy you're with now, and I'm sure he must be great (you wouldn't settle for anything less). I would never want to do anything to disrupt that relationship (not that I could), or the nice life here in Bloomville you seem to have created for yourself. I'm genuinely happy for you!

But maybe I could take you out for coffee or a drink while I'm here, just for old times' sake? I promise I'll do all the driving! (Ha ha.)

Let me know.

Yours, always,
Reed

Becky Flowers created chat "Reed Stewart"

Becky Flowers   17:18 PM
Look what just landed in my inbox.

From: Reed Stewart@reedstewart.com
Date: March 15 5:06:10 PM EST
To: Becky@MovingUp.com
Subject: You

Dear Becky,

It seems inadequate to say "it's been a long time," but in this case, it's fitting.

Thanks so much for agreeing to help my parents. I'm attaching the signed contract, and yes, we would like the Resettling Package, as well. . . .

Leeanne Matsumori   17:20 PM
OMG. If anyone ever sent me a letter like that, I'd be so thirsty, I'd have to drink an entire bottle of vitamin water.

Becky Flowers   17:20 PM
I had to drink Lake Bloomville.

Leeanne Matsumori   17:20 PM
I would have had to drink Lake Michigan.

Becky Flowers   17:21 PM
I drank out of the flask Nicole keeps hidden in her desk and thinks I don't know about.

Leeanne Matsumori   17:21 PM
So what are you going to do about it?

Becky Flowers   17:22 PM
The flask? Or his letter? Both = nothing.

Leeanne Matsumori   17:22 PM
????!!!!!

Becky Flowers   17:22 PM
I can't get involved with the son of my clients. It would be unethical.

Leeanne Matsumori   17:23 PM
Oh, right.

Is this because of Graham?

Becky Flowers   17:23 PM
Yes. No. I don't know.

Leeanne Matsumori   17:23 PM
Oh, okay. So it's not because Reed said he only wants to be friends?

Becky Flowers   17:23 PM
No. Absolutely not.

Leeanne Matsumori   17:23 PM
Because you know that's only what he SAYS. He called you beautiful and confident. No one who wants to be friends says that. Has Graham ever called you that?

Becky Flowers   17:24 PM
No.

But Graham has other good qualities. Such as owning a business in the same town as me and not having a rescue complex or having abandoned me for ten years without a word.

Leeanne Matsumori 17:24 PM

OK, you read the letter, right? He explained all that. At least to my satisfaction. I'm not saying you should go running to him with open arms, but you could have a measly cup of coffee with the man.

And I like Graham, too, but wine and cheese are all he ever talks about. Maybe it's because I'm lactose intolerant and also can't process alcohol, but he seems a little dull. Does he even read Jane Austen?

Becky Flowers 17:24 PM

He reads *Bon Appetit* magazine. And he could find cheeses for you that are low in lactic acid that you could easily digest.

Leeanne Matsumori 17:25 PM

Believe me, I know. Every time I hang out with you guys, he tells me all about them.

And I will admit, he looks good in the photos on his timeline.

Like the one he posted on the Authentic Facebook page the other day, of him lying on that blanket with no shirt on and his baby niece next to him. He tagged it Baby Bliss.

Becky Flowers 17:25 PM

Oh, right, I saw that one. Graham likes babies.

Leeanne Matsumori 17:25 PM

Babies are nice. Babies are something I don't think golfers have a lot of time for, so that's another point in Graham's favor. You know, if you were doing a pro/con list of them both. Which I know you aren't.

Becky Flowers 17:26 PM

I'm definitely not. But you seem to be.

Leeanne Matsumori 17:26 PM

Well, I have a lot of time on my hands, since I'm sitting in the airport.

Becky Flowers   17:26 PM

What? Where are you going?

Leeanne Matsumori   17:26 PM

I told you before, I'm coming home. I'm not going to let you go through all this without me. I grabbed the cheapest flight I could. It's going to take me 24 hours, and I have to change planes in New York *and* Chicago before I get to Indianapolis, but I'll get home eventually.

Becky Flowers   17:26 PM

Oh, Lee! That's so sweet of you!

But you didn't have to. I'm fine.

Leeanne Matsumori   17:27 PM

I know you're fine. I read all about how you don't need rescuing. You got out of that pool at the country club by yourself with a dislocated shoulder.

But you haven't even seen that Reed's parents aren't the Dumbasses of the Week anymore.

Becky Flowers   17:27 PM

They aren't? How can there be a new Dumbass? The week isn't over yet.

Leeanne Matsumori   17:27 PM

I think there've been an extraordinarily high number of people acting like dumbasses lately.

Here look, here's the new one. I think it's someone Reed knows. I think we can add to the list of Reed's cons that he knows and/or is related to a lot of Dumbasses:

NEWYORKJOURNAL.COM

Where the World Goes For Its News, Celebrity Buzz, LOLs, and More

NEWS	CELEBRITY BUZZ	LOL	FAIL	WTF

DUMBASS OF THE WEEK

It's sad when a good man goes bad.

But that's exactly what appears to have happened to Number 1 ranked professional golfer Cobb Cutler.

After posting a sweet message of goodbye to his wife, Russian model Ava Kuznetsov, upon signing their divorce papers, Cutler then posted the unthinkable:

The death of my marriage to you, Ava, is more painful than the death of my own father, and even the death of my old dog, Blue.

Who can forget the tragic death of Cutler's beloved Golden Retriever, Blue, who, while accompanying Cutler on a fishing trip off the coast of Southern California, was attacked by a freakishly aggressive dolphin that leapt from the sea and delivered a fatal blow to the head of the eleven-year-old canine?

A grieving Cutler met Kuznetsov online just a few months later. The two wed within the year, though friends whispered that the pair had nothing in common.

The marriage was notoriously troubled from the start, with Kuznetsov preferring her fast-paced Manhattan lifestyle, and Cutler his more laid-back ways out West.

"It's very painful to see him dismissing Blue's memory in this way," said Joyce Kilpatrick, president of the Golden Retriever Club of America. "But dog lovers all over the world are quickly realizing that Cobb Cutler's not the man we once thought he was."

When you publicly call your divorce from a woman with whom you barely lived more painful than the death of your own father AND your canine best friend, that makes you:

NY JOURNAL'S DUMBASS OF THE WEEK!!

Your reaction?

LOL	Fail	WTF
35	510,972	317,459

Becky Flowers   17:28 PM
Wow. That is depressing.

Leeanne Matsumori   17:28 PM
I know, right? Men.

Becky Flowers   17:28 PM
Men? What about dolphins?

Leeanne Matsumori   17:28 PM
Seriously. Who knew? Assassins of the sea. And dolphins were my spirit
animal!

Becky Flowers   17:28 PM
You should consider rethinking that.

Leeanne Matsumori   17:28 PM
I will.

But you might want to consider the fact that Reed isn't Cobb Cutler.

Becky Flowers   17:28 PM
I have considered that.

Leeanne Matsumori   17:29 PM
Ha! I knew it! So you ARE thinking about taking him up on his offer for a
drink!

Becky Flowers   17:29 PM
No. Like I said, that would be a conflict of interest.

But I'm not ready for kids yet, either, and Graham seems to have them
on the brain.

Leeanne Matsumori   17:29 PM
Who needs babies when you're a beautiful and confident business owner?

Becky Flowers   17:29 PM
Who also happens to have cellulite. I'm never going to be mistaken for a model, that's for sure.

Leeanne Matsumori   17:29 PM
See, this is why I'm coming. Guarding your heart is one thing.

But it's like you think your heart is one of your client's vases, or something. You've put so much bubble wrap around it that you can't even enjoy it anymore.

Becky Flowers   17:30 PM
Well, I don't want to risk giving my heart to someone who's going to abuse it. Again.

Leeanne Matsumori   17:30 PM
I know. I get it. But sometimes people learn from their mistakes. And by people I mean men. And by men I mean Reed. I don't think it's a coincidence that of all the senior move managers in this state, he hired you. I think he did it on purpose because he wants you back.

Becky Flowers   17:30 PM
Leeanne, I'm the only senior move manager in the tri-county area.

Leeanne Matsumori   17:30 PM
Oh. Well, what does your sister say to do?

Becky Flowers   17:30 PM
If I showed that letter to Nicole, she'd grab Henry's taser and go shoot Reed with it.

Leeanne Matsumori	17:30 PM

Oh. OK, so maybe don't show it to Nicole.

Becky Flowers	17:30 PM

Look, thanks for the chat. I know what I need to do.

Leeanne Matsumori	17:30 PM

You do? What? Tell me!

Becky Flowers	17:31 PM

What any sensible Austen heroine would do.

Leeanne Matsumori	17:31 PM

Go to the milliner's for a new hat?

Becky Flowers	17:31 PM

I'll talk to you later, Lee. Have a safe flight.

PHONE SCREEN OF REED STEWART

From: Becky@MovingUp.com
Date: March 15 6:12:10 PM EST
To: Reed Stewart@reedstewart.com
Subject: You

Dear Reed,

Thank you so much for your note and the signed contract. I'm so glad your family has agreed to hire Moving Up! Senior Move Management Consultants. We'll certainly do our best to make your parents' transition as stress free as possible.

Like you, I'm glad we can finally move forward as two adults who've learned to put our past mistakes behind us. I'm sorry it has to be under these circumstances, since your parents really do seem to have fallen into difficult times—through no fault of their own, or the rest of your family's.

I've actually seen this happen before. I can assure you it's more common than you think, especially someone like your father, who has such a strong personality and is too prideful to accept outside help.

I would be very happy to sit down with you or any other of your family members any time you'd like to go over my strategy for dealing with your parents' situation in more detail.

But as I've now received a signed contract from you employing Moving Up! as your parents' senior moving consultants, you are technically a client, and I make it a policy never to interact socially with clients. So I'm afraid having coffee or a drink as friends won't be possible.

I do hope you understand. It simply wouldn't be appropriate, and might make it difficult for me to supply the best care I can for your parents.

Tomorrow some of my employees and I will be delivering several Dumpsters and portable on demand storage units to your parents' home. I think it would probably be best if you were not there, as I think feelings might be running high, and your presence could exacerbate the situation. (With your parents, of course. Not with me.)

When your parents are more used to the idea of downsizing, I'm sure your company will be more welcome! I hope you understand.

Fondly,

Becky Flowers, CSMM
Moving Up! Consulting LLC, President

P.S. I don't know if you got my texts, letters, and messages from ten years ago, but I want to take this opportunity to thank you, once again, for what you did in taking the blame for your father's golf cart ending up in the pool. I know it caused a great rift between you and the Judge, and I've always been so, so sorry about that.

I do hope you know how grateful I am for what you did.

Becky

> **Reed Stewart**   10:01 PM EST
> Alvarez, I need your help, bud. I need it more than I've ever needed it before in my life.

Enrique Alvarez   10:05 PM EST
What is it now? I already spent three hours today looking at condos for you. If I have to hear about "space for entertaining" one more time, I'm going to kill myself.

> **Reed Stewart**   10:05 PM EST
> I saw her today.

Enrique Alvarez   10:05 PM EST
Who? Valerie? She stalked you to your hometown? Man, I told you that one was trouble. But do you ever listen to me? No. Like at the 16th hole at Augusta.

Reed Stewart   10:05 PM EST

Not Valery. My ex. She was at my parents' house. My sister-in-law hired her to help my parents' move. She owns a moving company.

Enrique Alvarez   10:05 PM EST

Your ex owns a moving company? Now that is a good business to invest in.

Because everyone has to move at least a few times in their life, and you can't always count on friends to help you. So hiring a moving company always makes it a lot easier, if you can find one to do it at a fair price. How are her prices?

Reed Stewart   10:06 PM EST

As usual, Alvarez, YOU ARE MISSING THE POINT.

It is HER. It is BECKY.

Enrique Alvarez   10:06 PM EST

Oh, BECKY. I didn't know Becky is the one with the moving company. Wait, that is who your sister-in-law hired to move your parents to this condo I'm picking out for you in Orlando?

HA! Boudro! You are screwed.

Reed Stewart   10:07 PM EST

Thank you, Alvarez. Thank you so much. I realized that when I asked her out and she shot me down because I'm now technically a client, and she makes it a policy never to interact socially with clients.

Enrique Alvarez   10:07 PM EST

HA HA HA! I wish I had been there to see that.

Reed Stewart   10:07 PM EST

Thank you for the sympathy. So what do I do about it? You're always telling me which club I should use. You must know something about relationships.

Enrique Alvarez   10:07 PM EST

Well, I know you always screw up yours. Almost as much as you've screwed up your swing lately.

Reed Stewart   10:08 PM EST

I am aware of that. That's why I'm asking for your advice. How should I proceed? Because I already screwed up this relationship once, and this time—if she'll give me a second chance—I'd like not to.

Enrique Alvarez   10:08 PM EST

She already told you "no," man. What part of "no" do you not understand?

Reed Stewart   10:08 PM EST

I get that. But surely there must be some way around the client thing.

Enrique Alvarez   10:08 PM EST

First I'm your caddy, then I'm your realtor, now I'm supposed to give you love advice?

I'm the one who said "Call her" when you first told me about her five years ago. You didn't listen to me then, just like you didn't listen at Doral when I told you to go for the wedge on the 17th hole.

Why is this woman so important to you, anyway? There are plenty of other ladies you could have who aren't working for you.

Reed Stewart   10:08 PM EST

Maybe because I've seen things today—horrible, horrible things— that have helped me realize what's truly important in life, Alvarez.

I don't want to die surrounded by THINGS and not people who love me. Least of all the woman I've always loved.

Enrique Alvarez   10:09 PM EST

Boudro, that is profound, man! What happened? Did you finally watch the tape of Augusta, like I asked you?

Reed Stewart   10:09 PM EST

No. I went to my parents' house.

Enrique Alvarez   10:09 PM EST

Oh. Well, then, the only advice I have for you when it comes to this young lady is: Big Bertha.

Reed Stewart   10:10 PM EST

I don't even know what that means.

Enrique Alvarez   10:10 PM EST

Of course you know what that means. Don't embarrass me, man.

Reed Stewart   10:10 PM EST

I understand Big Bertha is the heaviest club in the bag, Alvarez, and it's the one you wanted me to use at Augusta and I didn't, and you think that's why I lost.

I don't understand what it means in the context of my ex.

Enrique Alvarez   10:11 PM EST

Did you know they named that club after the German Big Bertha howitzer? That's an artillery cannon they used in World War I to smash down forts.

Reed Stewart   10:12 PM EST

Becky isn't a fort, Alvarez. She's a woman.

Enrique Alvarez   10:12 PM EST

She's got her walls up against you, doesn't she?

Reed Stewart   10:12 PM EST

Still, I'm not going to hit her with a stainless steel driver.

Enrique Alvarez 10:12 PM EST

It's a metaphor, you idiot.

When you've got a big problem, you have to hit it with the biggest weapon in your arsenal.

You wouldn't know this, of course, because you've never had to try very hard before, either on the course or with women.

But now, with age, you might actually have to take out the heavy artillery, which on the greens are the big sticks, and with women is your charm—if you have any, which I'm starting to doubt.

Reed Stewart 10:13 PM EST

Thanks, boudro. You always know the right thing to say.

Enrique Alvarez 10:13 PM EST

Yes, because I'm a caddy. Now Cutler's caddy and I are off to Epcot Brazil to enjoy dinner on both of your expense accounts.

Check out the photos I emailed, there's a place on there I think will work for your parents. It's near the Golden Palm golf resort, in case you ever decide to come back to work.

Reed Stewart 10:14 PM EST

Funny. No, really, very amusing.

But thanks for the advice.

Enrique Alvarez 10:14 PM EST

I hope it works, for both our sakes. I could use the extra cash if you start winning again.

Blessings Journal

of

BECKY FLOWERS

Today I feel blessed because:

I do not feel blessed!!!

Oh, God, I don't know what's happening to me. What am I even doing with my life?

Why did I send him that email? Why didn't I tell him the truth? That I'd love, love, LOVE to meet him for coffee, drinks, ANYTHING?

But I can't. What would be the point? He's right, I *have* built a successful life and business here. I can't allow a boy—well, a man, now—from my past to blow back into it and destroy everything I've worked so hard for. Especially my peace of mind. I'm happy. *I'm finally happy now.* I'm not going to let him ruin that.

But oh! He looked so good. Especially in that tie, with that dark hair of his, and those eyes, those eyes! How could I have forgotten how bright and shiny and blue they are? Well, I guess because on television, he's usually wearing sunglasses out on the course.

And what if Leeanne is right? What if I *am* overprotecting myself, keeping my heart in too much bubble wrap?

But why shouldn't I? I didn't before, and got hurt.

Things are different now. I'm a confident business owner. With a kind, handsome boyfriend (who's left four texts I haven't answered. I really need to get back to Graham soon, or he's going to start suspecting something is up).

Okay, breathe. I have everything under control. I'm going to ACE this Stewart job (I've already shoved the Blumenthals off on Nicole, so that's taken care of).

All I need to do is get a good night's sleep, go to the Stewarts' bright and early tomorrow morning, and get them to start sorting. Everything is going to be fine. As long as I can keep Reed away, it should run smooth as silk. Smooth as a St. Andre French triple cream.

God! I have to stop thinking about cheese.

And men.

Especially one man. And I will!

I truly *am* blessed. It's all going to go great.

I just need to bring enough packing materials.

Especially bubble wrap.

Not-So-Crazy Cat Lady

Reviewer ranking: #2,350
93% helpful
votes received on reviews

Reviewed
Welcome Cat Figurine
$39.00 + Shipping

As pictured
March 15

This funny little critter is simply impossible to resist.

So how could I not snap up this tiny treasure, especially after the hard day I had dealing with my own little kiddies (pun intended).

Of course, they don't seem to be so pleased with me and their father anymore—so much so that they're making us feel a bit unwelcome— in our own home, no less!

Not that I blame them. I know we've embarrassed them very much over the years.

But I didn't know that we'd displeased them so much that they'd listed our home for sale and hired a stranger (well, a relative stranger) to force us to pack up our belongings and move away from the town we've known and loved for so many years.

But I suppose this happens to all of us—we outgrow our usefulness, or do one silly thing—and it's "Bye-bye. You aren't welcome anymore."

Oh, of course my daughter-in-law has said things over the past few months about our house getting to be "too big" and the way we spend our money being "not right."

But don't we have the right to live in whatever size house we choose to, and spend our money how we see fit?

For instance, I prefer to spend my money on adorable kitties like this, instead of on something boring, like the water bill. Water should be free! It comes from the sky, doesn't it?

Oh, well, here I am going on about my problems when really I meant to tell you about this cute figurine. It is lovely, so exquisitely crafted and perfect. You couldn't add a finer one to your collection.

So do so at once, before someone comes along and tries to take all your beloved things away!

10 out of 10 people found this review helpful.

The Bloomville Herald

The Tri-County Area's Only
Daily Newspaper
• Thursday, March 16 • Vol. 142 •
Still Only 50 Cents!

BLOOMVILLE RESTAURANT
FACES BOYCOTT

BY CHRISTINA MARTINEZ Herald Staff

Bloomville, Ind.—A restaurant in Bloomville's Old Towne Mall is facing a massive backlash following reports that a retired judge and his wife were arrested there after an alleged misunderstanding concerning a postage stamp.

Resident Beverly Flowers, 64, called for a boycott of the casual family eatery Shenanigans for prosecuting locally beloved Judge Richard Stewart and his wife, Constance, for attempting to pay for a $59 meal with an antique postage stamp worth only $4.

What began as a suggestion in a letter to the editor in yesterday's edition of the *Herald* soon spread like wildfire across social media as others joined Flowers's campaign.

A small handful of protesters outside the restaurant had grown to as many as two dozen by press time yesterday. Although the protesters were peaceful, two Bloomville police officers were dispatched to the area in order to assure the smooth flow of traffic along Old Towne Mall Road.

When contacted for comment, Flowers said she

was not surprised that so many people felt the same way she did.

"I'm doing this because what they did to Judge Stewart isn't right," said Mrs. Flowers, the office manager of Moving Up! Senior Move Management Consultants, who spent several hours outside of Shenanigans Neighborhood Bar and Grill yesterday persuading would-be customers to dine elsewhere.

Another protester, Ward Hicks, 59, agreed.

"Judge Stewart saved my boy's life. Instead of throwing him in jail, like he could have, Judge Stewart gave him another chance, and put him in a job program. Now my boy is a trained electrician, and drug free."

Shenanigans' day manager, Heather MacIntosh, 37, admits that "Judge Stewart is one of the most admired men ever to have lived in Bloomville. That's why they named the courthouse after him. This situation has put some of us in a very difficult position. There are definitely those of us who work here who sympathize with the protesters."

Not all Bloomville residents feel the same way.

"This is where I always come for a salad and smoothie after yoga," said Bloomville resident Summer Hayes, 32. "Now I can't get in without being accosted by dirty hipsters. This seems very unsafe, especially for the children."

Shenanigans' night manager, Randy Grubb, 35, agrees.

"It's gotten out of hand. People need to remember that postage stamps are not currency. The Stewarts should not have been trying to use one to pay for anything, regardless of what they thought it was worth."

"If postage stamps are not currency," one

commenter wrote on the restaurant's Facebook page after Grubb expressed a similar sentiment there, "then why is there a monetary value written on them? Grubb needs to get over himself."

"I've got a good home and savings for my four grandkids because Judge Stewart gave me a second chance after I made some poor choices," said Rhonda Jenkins, housekeeper, 62. "Why can't we give Judge Stewart a second chance?"

Shenanigans Corporate Headquarters addressed the growing firestorm in a post to its Facebook page yesterday afternoon.

"As always, we appreciate feedback from our customers," the company wrote. "We will do everything possible to try to support the concerns of our patrons. But we also support decisions made at the local level of our franchises, and agree with Mr. Grubb's actions in this case."

Their statement only seemed to further enrage some critics.

"My boyfriend and I moved to Bloomville because we were tired of the city and loved the small-town feel of the place," wrote commenter Tim Grabowksi, co-owner of Bloomville Books. "We try to patronize only businesses owned by locals, and this Shenanigans incident is a good example of why: Big corporations just don't care."

Mrs. Flowers said more protests are planned all week, which on Friday could disrupt the restaurant's St. Patrick's Day business, which has traditionally been brisk.

Judge Stewart and his wife were released on $1,600 bond early Monday morning, but could face federal charges.

From: Judge Richard Stewart@Stewart&Stewart.com
Date: March 16 8:06:27 AM EST
To: Trimble Stewart-Antonelli@Stewart&Stewart.com; Marshall
Stewart@StewartRealty.com; Reed Stewart@reedstewart.com
Cc: Tony Antonelli@AntonelliPizza.com; Carly Stewart@StewartRealty.com
Subject: Attempt to Sabotage

Dear Children,

It has come to the attention of your mother and I that the three of you—
and apparently your spouses—think that your parents are too mentally
and physically unfit to continue living in the home we've owned for 35
years.

I do not know what could have occurred recently to cause you to think
this.

Yes, there was a minor mix-up at a local dining establishment where
your mother and I attempted to gift a young local girl with an incredible
financial opportunity.

But that was only because I was swindled by a philatelist in Andersonville
against whom I will be seeking legal compensation, as this is not the first
time he's bamboozled me.

And yes, your mother and I both had accidents in and around the house
this past year. And yes, perhaps a few critters have crept in.

But this winter has been exceedingly harsh, and though we pay exorbitant
fees to the Bloomville Country Club community board, somehow they
always seem to plow our driveway last.

And you know your mother has a tender heart when it comes to
animals, and will always offer them a warm hearth and bowls of food
and water.

Some of you have accused our housekeeping habits of slipping. The plain
fact of the matter is, we had to let Rhonda go, because your mother was
tired of Rhonda's complaining about having to dust her cat figurines, and
I did not like having my paperwork moved. You know how important my
reading is to me. How can I do my reading if I can't find it?

I understand that there is some concern about the way we've chosen to spend our money. How is that the business of you children? It is up to us to decide how and when we'll spend our fortune.

I suppose some of you are concerned that, with our "profligate spending," there won't be any inheritance left for the grandchildren.

Well, never you worry. The grandchildren will receive their fair share of the family fortune. Maybe it will be in the form of some unique vintage heirlooms. Hopefully they will be more appreciative of our taste than their parents are!

Now I ask each of you to think about how you would feel if a "de-cluttering, moving expert" were brought into your home uninvited, and allowed to look through all your rooms.

Though Miss Flowers is a perfectly charming girl, and we in no way blame her for any of this, we never asked for her help. We can only assume, since Reed is involved, that this is in some way his fault. It appears to be his primary goal in life to bedevil poor Miss Flowers, and dash her hopes and dreams.

As for Reed, I no longer harbor any animosity towards you. It was, in fact, good to see you. Although you did not choose to live your life the way I would have chosen for you to live it, you have obviously chosen well for yourself, and become what I suppose some young people today might consider a success.

But what is going to happen, I wonder, if the ball continues to no longer fly as straight or as long as it once did? Have you given any sort of thought to that, my boy?

This letter is not to condemn the three of you, or your chosen life mates. We know you did what you did out of some sort of misdirected love and concern for us.

This is merely to remind you that it is we, not you, who are the parents, and you who are the children, and that you do not know what is best for us, any more than we, apparently, know what is best for you.

"Treat your parents with loving care for you will only know their value when you see their empty chair."

I hope you all know who said that!

I also hope you all know that as of today, none of you (except the grandchildren, who are innocent of any wrongdoing, and of course Miss Flowers, who clearly knew nothing of your machinations) will ever again be admitted into this house. Consider yourselves "persona non grata"!

The Honorable Richard Stewart

From: Trimble Stewart-Antonelli@Stewart&Stewart.com
Date: March 16 8:16:20 AM EST
To: Carly Stewart@StewartRealty.com; Marshall Stewart@StewartRealty.com; Reed Stewart@reedstewart.com
Subject: Re: Attempt to Sabotage

Nice going, idiots.

Trimble Stewart-Antonelli
Attorney at Law
Stewart & Stewart, LLC
1911 South Moore Pike
Bloomville, IN 47401
(812) 555-9721
www.stewart&stewart.com

From: Reed Stewart@reedstewart.com
Date: March 16 8:20:39 AM EST
To: Carly Stewart@StewartRealty.com; Marshall Stewart@StewartRealty.com
Subject: Re: Attempt to Sabotage

I'm the one who made poor choices?

At least I'm not about to be foreclosed on for failing to pay my mortgage, and thrown in jail by the IRS for not paying taxes, and Shenanigans for trying to pay for dinner with a 2 cent stamp!

And I never meant to bedevil Becky Flowers, much less dash her hopes and dreams! I was trying to do right by her!

What is the old man even talking about?

From: Carly Stewart@StewartRealty.com
Date: March 16 8:22:09 AM EST
To: Reed Stewart@reedstewart.com; Marshall Stewart@StewartRealty.com
Subject: Re: Attempt to Sabotage

See, this is proof of exactly what I've been telling you: your father's lost his mind.

I'm forwarding this letter to Jimmy Abrams. He can definitely use it as evidence to get your parents declared *non compos mentis*.

Carly R. Stewart | Accountant | Stewart Realty | 801 South Moore Pike, Bloomville, IN 47401 | phone (812) 555-8722 | Please visit StewartRealty.com for all your realty needs

From: Marshall Stewart@StewartRealty.com
Date: March 16 8:29:29 AM EST
To: Reed Stewart@reedstewart.com; Carly Stewart@StewartRealty.com
Subject: Re: Attempt to Sabotage

There's no way you're going to be able to use Dad's email as evidence of him being mentally incompetent, Carly. The man is perfectly lucid, and knows exactly what he wants.

If you're going to forward it to anyone, forward it to Becky Flowers. She's got a right to know Reed *has* dashed her hopes and dreams . . . at least of getting $20,000 out of us.

From: Reed Stewart@reedstewart.com
Date: March 16 8:30:36 AM EST
To: Marshall Stewart@StewartRealty.com; Carly Stewart@StewartRealty.com
Subject: Re: Attempt to Sabotage

Wait, no! We don't have to tell Becky about this! I'm sure she's trained to handle this kind of thing.

And Dad said they'll let her in!

From: Carly Stewart@StewartRealty.com
Date: March 16 8:32:17 AM EST
To: Reed Stewart@reedstewart.com; Marshall Stewart@StewartRealty.com
Subject: Re: Attempt to Sabotage

Seriously, Marshall, you can't STILL be in denial about your parents' mental health. After the cats?

After the *raccoons*?

Carly R. Stewart | Accountant | Stewart Realty | 801 South Moore Pike, Bloomville, IN 47401 | phone (812) 555-8722 | Please visit StewartRealty.com for all your realty needs

---

From: Marshall Stewart@StewartRealty.com
Date: March 16 8:35:12 AM EST
To: Reed Stewart@reedstewart.com; Carly Stewart@StewartRealty.com
Subject: Re: Attempt to Sabotage

This is America. A man has a right to allow raccoons to nest in his ceiling if he wants to.

From: Carly Stewart@StewartRealty.com
Date: March 16 8:37:35 AM EST
To: Reed Stewart@reedstewart.com; Marshall Stewart@StewartRealty.com
Subject: Re: Attempt to Sabotage

Yes, and I have the right never to allow my children to visit their grandparents in their home again, thanks to the potentially rabid animals there.

Carly R. Stewart | Accountant | Stewart Realty | 801 South Moore Pike, Bloomville, IN 47401 | phone (812) 555-8722 | Please visit StewartRealty.com for all your realty needs

---

From: Reed Stewart@reedstewart.com
Date: March 16 8:40:29 AM EST
To: Marshall Stewart@StewartRealty.com; Carly Stewart@StewartRealty.com
Subject: Re: Attempt to Sabotage

Can't we all just get along????

From: Carly Stewart@StewartRealty.com
Date: March 16 8:42:39 AM EST
To: Reed Stewart@reedstewart.com; Marshall Stewart@StewartRealty.com
Subject: Re: Attempt to Sabotage

It's too late, Reed, I'm sorry. I already forwarded your father's email to her. I think it's important a *professional* see it.

Carly R. Stewart | Accountant | Stewart Realty | 801 South Moore Pike, Bloomville, IN 47401 | phone (812) 555-8722 | Please visit StewartRealty.com for all your realty needs

---

From: Reed Stewart@reedstewart.com
Date: March 16 8:43:01 AM EST
To: Marshall Stewart@StewartRealty.com; Carly Stewart@StewartRealty.com
Subject: Re: Attempt to Sabotage

NOOOOOOOOOOOOOOOOOOO!

What is wrong with you people? Are you trying to dash all of *my* hopes and dreams?

From: Marshall Stewart@StewartRealty.com
Date: March 16 8:45:29 AM EST
To: Reed Stewart@reedstewart.com; Carly Stewart@StewartRealty.com
Subject: Re: Attempt to Sabotage

You forwarded her that email to spite me, didn't you, Carly?

And as for you, Reed, I never saw anybody more anxious to throw 20 grand away on an ex.

And what exactly happened during that dinner you had last night with the girls? For the first time in months, Bailey didn't want to wear her Chief Massasoit costume to school this morning. She insisted on wearing a new costume that she said her uncle Reed got her at the Walmart in Dearborn:

Ant-Man.

From: Reed Stewart@reedstewart.com
Date: March 16 8:46:19 AM EST
To: Marshall Stewart@StewartRealty.com; Carly Stewart@StewartRealty.com
Subject: Re: Attempt to Sabotage

She did? That's fantastic!

From: Marshall Stewart@StewartRealty.com
Date: March 16 8:48:27 AM EST
To: Reed Stewart@reedstewart.com; Carly Stewart@StewartRealty.com
Subject: Re: Attempt to Sabotage

No, it is not fantastic, Reed. We are trying to convince our child to dress as *herself* for school, not as the historic leader of a Native American tribe or a fictional superhero, who, by the way, is male. Bailey, in case you hadn't noticed, is a girl.

From: Reed Stewart@reedstewart.com
Date: March 16 8:49:03 AM EST
To: Marshall Stewart@StewartRealty.com; Carly Stewart@StewartRealty.com
Subject: Re: Attempt to Sabotage

Marshall, biological sex and gender are social constructs and your child has the right to wear whatever makes her feel most comfortable.

From: Marshall Stewart@StewartRealty.com
Date: March 16 8:50:17 AM EST
To: Reed Stewart@reedstewart.com; Carly Stewart@StewartRealty.com
Subject: Re: Attempt to Sabotage

Where are you right now? Because I'll be happy to drive over there and strangle you with my bare hands.

From: Carly Stewart@StewartRealty.com
Date: March 16 8:51:11 AM EST
To: Reed Stewart@reedstewart.com; Marshall Stewart@StewartRealty.com
Subject: Re: Attempt to Sabotage

Will you two cut it out? I for one am happy that Bailey has found a different costume that she likes. It's given me a chance to put old Chief Massasoit in the wash.

And Marshall, I did not send Becky Flowers your dad's email just to spite you. I sent it because it's unhealthy for seniors to live with feral cats and raccoons, and that is not the kind of home I care to have my children visiting during the holidays.

I was sure a normal, rational person like Becky would agree with me, and I was right, since she's already replied. Here's what she says:

To: Carly Stewart@StewartRealty.com
Sent: March 16 8:45:11 AM EST
From: Becky@MovingUp.com
Subject: Marshall's Parents

Dear Carly,

This kind of response from Judge Stewart is perfectly normal. I see it all the time.

Often after the first flush of excitement over a move, clients get cold feet. They're nervous at the idea of relocating, especially to somewhere they've never been before.

In the case of your husband's parents, it's even more unsettling, because they've resided in this community for so long and don't know where they're going, and this has all happened very, very quickly!

It would be great if you had photos of where they might be headed, so we can use them—please excuse the cliché—as the carrot at the end of the stick to get them excited about their future.

I'm a great fan of the Judge's, and ordinarily I would say if he wanted to age in place, he should.

But considering what I saw yesterday, I feel that it's in the best interest of your husband's parents to downsize to a smaller, safer home, preferably in a warmer environment than Bloomville.

Since they're open to my presence, I'll go over there again today with photos, a positive attitude, and some comfort food—and of course some Dumpsters so we can begin purging the more dangerous materials from the home, as there really are some health hazards that need to be addressed immediately.

Let me know, however, if you feel differently, and we can discuss at any time.

Becky Flowers, Certified Senior Move Manager
Moving Up! Consulting LLC, President

Carly R. Stewart | Accountant | Stewart Realty | 801 South Moore Pike, Bloomville, IN 47401 | phone (812) 555-8722 | Please visit StewartRealty.com for all your realty needs

---

From: Marshall Stewart@StewartRealty.com
Date: March 16 8:52:36 AM EST
To: Reed Stewart@reedstewart.com; Carly Stewart@StewartRealty.com
Subject: Re: Attempt to Sabotage

You just love being right, don't you, Carly?

Becky Flowers should work for the UN. She's a real diplomat.

"In your husband's parents best interest to downsize."

What she really meant was "in their best interest not to die under piles of old newspapers and dead cats," am I right?

She should have just come out and said it.

From: Carly Stewart@StewartRealty.com
Date: March 16 8:55:44 AM EST
To: Reed Stewart@reedstewart.com; Marshall Stewart@StewartRealty.com
Subject: Re: Attempt to Sabotage

So are you finally coming out and admitting, Marshall, that your parents need professional help? Because that would be a step in the right direction.

Also a miracle.

And yes, for your information, I do love being right.

Carly R. Stewart | Accountant | Stewart Realty | 801 South Moore Pike, Bloomville, IN 47401 | phone (812) 555-8722 | Please visit StewartRealty.com for all your realty needs

From: Marshall Stewart@StewartRealty.com
Date: March 16 8:59:06 AM EST
To: Reed Stewart@reedstewart.com; Carly Stewart@StewartRealty.com
Subject: Re: Attempt to Sabotage

I admit nothing.

Where exactly does she suggest we get these photos of where they're going, though? We have no idea where they're going. I mean, except to jail for fraud and tax evasion.

From: Reed Stewart@reedstewart.com
Date: March 16 9:00:01 AM EST
To: Carly Stewart@StewartRealty.com; Marshall Stewart@StewartRealty.com
Subject: Re: Attempt to Sabotage

C'mon you two, don't fight. I've got this!

From: Marshall Stewart@StewartRealty.com
Date: March 16 9:02:09 AM EST
To: Reed Stewart@reedstewart.com; Carly Stewart@StewartRealty.com
Subject: Re: Attempt to Sabotage

Got what? Since when have you had anything except an amazing ability to annoy me?

From: Reed Stewart@reedstewart.com
Date: March 16 9:05:12 AM EST
To: Carly Stewart@StewartRealty.com; Marshall Stewart@StewartRealty.com
Subject: Re: Attempt to Sabotage

I've had someone condo hunting for Mom and Dad in Orlando. I told you I'd handle that one. I've got photos. I'll go over there and tell her. I mean, show them to Richard and Connie.

From: Marshall Stewart@StewartRealty.com
Date: March 16 9:12:29 AM EST
To: Reed Stewart@reedstewart.com; Carly Stewart@StewartRealty.com
Subject: Re: Attempt to Sabotage

Dad specifically said he didn't want you at the house.

From: Reed Stewart@reedstewart.com
Date: March 16 9:15:03 AM EST
To: Carly Stewart@StewartRealty.com, Marshall Stewart@StewartRealty.com
Subject: Re: Attempt to Sabotage

I know. But I need to Big Bertha it.

From: Carly Stewart@StewartRealty.com
Date: March 16 9:16:11 AM EST
To: Reed Stewart@reedstewart.com; Marshall Stewart@StewartRealty.com
Subject: Re: Attempt to Sabotage

Who is Bertha?

Carly R. Stewart | Accountant | Stewart Realty | 801 South Moore Pike, Bloomville, IN
47401 | phone (812) 555-8722 | Please visit StewartRealty.com for all your realty needs

---

From: Marshall Stewart@StewartRealty.com
Date: March 16 9:19:27 AM EST
To: Carly Stewart@StewartRealty.com
Subject: Re: Attempt to Sabotage

Just ignore him.

Maybe we should start looking at condos in Florida for ourselves. Because
I have the feeling you and I might need to enter the witness protection
program before this is all over. Dad's going to be on the warpath.

From: Carly Stewart@StewartRealty.com
Date: March 16 9:21:18 AM EST
To: Marshall Stewart@StewartRealty.com
Subject: Re: Attempt to Sabotage

Marshall, the phrase "on the warpath" is culturally insensitive to
indigenous peoples.

Carly R. Stewart | Accountant | Stewart Realty | 801 South Moore Pike, Bloomville, IN
47401 | phone (812) 555-8722 | Please visit StewartRealty.com for all your realty needs

From: Marshall Stewart@StewartRealty.com
Date: March 16 9:25:52 AM EST
To: Carly Stewart@StewartRealty.com
Subject: Re: Attempt to Sabotage

Damn it!

PHONE SCREEN OF BECKY FLOWERS

Becky F — 11:28 AM
Where are you?

Nicole F — 11:28 AM
I'm still in line at the café counter at Bloomville Books, waiting to order those sandwiches you wanted.

Becky F — 11:28 AM
There's a line? There's never a line at the bookstore.

Nicole F — 11:28 AM
Well, where else are people going to go grab a quick lunch? We're supposed to be boycotting Shenanigans, and the sushi from Matsumori's is a little difficult to eat at your desk or on the run.

Becky F — 11:29 AM
Oh, God, I forgot about the boycott. Mom better not be there.

Nicole F — 11:29 AM
Don't worry, she's back at her desk. Rhonda Jenkins has taken over the boycott. I guess she used to be the Stewarts' housekeeper. She's hopping mad at Randy.

Becky F — 11:29 AM
Good. We need all hands on deck for this. The Dumpsters were just delivered. The PODS are on their way.

Nicole F — 11:29 AM
How are they taking it?

Becky F   11:29 AM

The Stewarts? Well, Mrs. Stewart flipped out and yelled dramatically, "If this is what our children think of us, fine, they can have everything," and threw her wedding dress into Dumpster #1.

Nicole F   11:29 AM

DAMMIT! I miss all the good stuff!

Becky F   11:29 AM

You really do.

Nicole F   11:30 AM

What's she doing now?

Becky F   11:30 AM

Sobbing on the back porch.

But I didn't notice any actual tears, and she's eating Lucky Charms straight out of the box, while petting the orange tabby cat. It's her favorite.

I think we may have a case of Hanger.

Nicole F   11:30 AM

Angry hunger? Oh no! There's nothing worse.

Becky F   11:30 AM

The sooner she and her husband get some real food into their bellies, the better. Part of their problem is there's nothing but ice cream in their refrigerator, ceramic cats in the cabinets, and they got rid of the stove. I can't even fix them a cup of soup.

Nicole F   11:30 AM

Seniors are weird. Have you given them their instructions?

Becky F   11:30 AM

Ditch, Donate, Save? Oh, yes, they know. That's why she threw the wedding gown in the Dumpster. I fished it out later, of course, when she wasn't looking.

Now I'm having the two of them sticker so Doug will know what goes and what stays.

Of course Judge Stewart has put a Save sticker on every pile of newspapers in the house.

Nicole F   11:31 AM

Oh no. What are you going to do?

Becky F   11:31 AM

The usual. I'll have the sister-in-law come over after school with the grandkids to lure them both out of the house. Then we'll do a quick load-and-dash to the recycling center.

It's possible, considering how out of it he is, that by the time they get back, the Judge won't even notice the newspapers are gone.

Nicole F   11:31 AM

Do you know why I love you, besides the fact that you're my big sister?

Because you're such an optimist.

Becky F   11:31 AM

I've explained that all of the articles from the papers are available on the Internet, and that the silverfish, mice, and raccoon droppings constitute a health hazard.

But the Judge doesn't believe me. He asked if I was accusing him of having a slovenly home.

Nicole F   11:31 AM
Do you want me to drop some wine off along with the sandwiches on my way to the Blumenthals? Because I think you're going to need it.

Becky F   11:31 AM
Oh, no. I'll be all right. I like the Judge. I think he's—oh God.

Nicole F   11:32 AM
What?

Becky F   11:32 AM
He's here.

Nicole F   11:32 AM
Who's where?

Becky F   11:32 AM
Reed. He just walked in. When I told him specifically not to come!

Nicole F   11:33 AM
That despicable rake! Want me to call Henry? He could come over and tase him.

Becky F   11:33 AM
He says he wants to help.

Nicole F   11:33 AM
With the stickering?

Becky F   11:33 AM
With everything.

Nicole F   11:34 AM
Someone's still got a crush!

Becky F   11:34 AM
I most certainly do not.

Nicole F   11:34 AM
I meant him, not you. I don't think he'd be there if you weren't.

Becky F   11:34 AM
He sent me a letter. Can you pick up an extra sandwich for him?

Nicole F   11:34 AM
Wait. What?

Becky F   11:34 AM
Chicken. He likes chicken.

Nicole F   11:35 AM
I meant what letter, not what kind of sandwich.

Becky F   11:35 AM
Email. It was an email. Oh, no, his dad just saw him.

Nicole F   11:35 AM
WHAT DID THE LETTER SAY????

Becky F   11:35 AM
His dad is letting him have it.

Nicole F   11:35 AM
That's fine. Don't tell me anything about the letter.

So what kind of chicken? They've got chicken salad, roast chicken breast, fried chicken, chicken and pesto, chicken parm.

Becky F   11:35 AM
It was an apology letter, for the way he behaved that night. You know. And after. And then he asked me out. But only as friends.

Nicole F — 11:36 AM
As friends! Right. I knew it.

I knew this was going to happen!

I hope you said no.

Becky F — 11:36 AM
Of course I did.

Chicken salad.

Nicole F — 11:36 AM
WHAT?

Becky F — 11:36 AM
He likes chicken salad. At least he used to.

His dad is really laying into him. I guess I should intervene.

Nicole F — 11:36 AM
No, don't. Reed deserves it.

Chicken salad it is. He's not getting chips though. When you don't call my sister for ten years, you don't get chips, even if you do write an apology email.

Becky F — 11:36 AM
OK, gotta go. His mom's getting into it now. She's just thrown one of the family photo albums into Dumpster #2 and says she wishes they were all dead.

Nicole F — 11:37 AM
God, Reed Stewart's family is so amazing. Who wouldn't want to marry him, if you could have in-laws like that?

Becky F   11:37 AM

Don't make fun of the Stewarts. They're in crisis.

Wait . . . he's got photos.

Nicole F   11:37 AM

I thought the photos were in the Dumpster.

Becky F   11:37 AM

No. He's got photos of condos in Orlando.

Nicole F   11:38 AM

Wait, he actually did something useful for a change? I might die of shock.

Becky F   11:38 AM

The photos are of The Town.

Nicole F   11:38 AM

The fastest growing retirement community in America, where the residents can drive golf carts instead of cars?

The Judge should love that.

Becky F   11:39 AM

He does. He's actually stopped yelling.

So has Mrs. Stewart. They're looking at the photos on Reed's phone.

Nicole F   11:39 AM

Wow. The prodigal son returneth, and doeth something good.

Maybe I'll get him chips after all.

REED STEWART	3:45PM	42%
TODAY	ALL	MISSED

From: Reed Stewart@reedstewart.com
Date: March 16 2:12:13 PM EST
To: Carly Stewart@StewartRealty.com; Marshall Stewart@StewartRealty.com
Subject: Hi from Mom and Dad's House

Yes, Dad is right. It's all worth millions!

From: Carly Stewart@StewartRealty.com
Date: March 16 2:16:11 PM EST
To: Reed Stewart@reedstewart.com; Marshall Stewart@StewartRealty.com
Subject: Re: Hi from Mom and Dad's House

I'm crying with laughter. Did you find the Maxi Pads from 1982?

Carly R. Stewart | Accountant | Stewart Realty | 801 South Moore Pike, Bloomville, IN
47401 | phone (812) 555-8722 | Please visit StewartRealty.com for all your realty needs

From: Marshall Stewart@StewartRealty.com
Date: March 16 2:14:11 AM EST
To: Reed Stewart@reedstewart.com; Carly Stewart@StewartRealty.com
Subject: Re: Hi from Mom and Dad's House

You two aren't funny.

Any why are you even there, Reed? I thought the whole reason we hired
your ex-girlfriend was so that she could do this.

From: Reed Stewart@reedstewart.com
Date: March 16 2:17:33 PM EST
To: Carly Stewart@StewartRealty.com; Marshall Stewart@StewartRealty.com
Subject: Hi from Mom and Dad's House

I'm just trying to show Becky what a warm and caring person I am by
helping out.

From: Marshall Stewart@StewartRealty.com
Date: March 16 2:19:27 AM EST
To: Carly Stewart@StewartRealty.com
Subject: Re: Hi from Mom and Dad's House

Carly, you should warn that poor girl. My brother is a degenerate who will
dash her hopes and dreams.

From: Carly Stewart@StewartRealty.com
Date: March 16 2:22:07 PM EST
To: Marshall Stewart@StewartRealty.com
Subject: Re: Hi from Mom and Dad's House

I think this is romantic. They're getting to know one another again.

Carly R. Stewart | Accountant | Stewart Realty | 801 South Moore Pike, Bloomville, IN
47401 | phone (812) 555-8722 | Please visit StewartRealty.com for all your realty needs

From: Marshall Stewart@StewartRealty.com
Date: March 16 2:25:39 AM EST
To: Carly Stewart@StewartRealty.com
Subject: Re: Hi from Mom and Dad's House

Romantic? They're rooting through my parents' garbage. Why can't he take her to a restaurant, like a normal person?

From: Reed Stewart@reedstewart.com
Date: March 16 2:30:33 PM EST
To: Carly Stewart@StewartRealty.com; Marshall Stewart@StewartRealty.com
Subject: Hi from Mom and Dad's House

I guess this is one of the cushions from that dining room set Trimble really wants. Did I just do a bad thing?

From: Carly Stewart@StewartRealty.com
Date: March 16 2:35:46 PM EST
To: Reed Stewart@reedstewart.com; Marshall Stewart@StewartRealty.com
Subject: Re: Hi from Mom and Dad's House

So sad.

Carly R. Stewart | Accountant | Stewart Realty | 801 South Moore Pike, Bloomville, IN
47401 | phone (812) 555-8722 | Please visit StewartRealty.com for all your realty needs

---

From: Reed Stewart@reedstewart.com
Date: March 16 2:45:53 PM EST
To: Carly Stewart@StewartRealty.com; Marshall Stewart@StewartRealty.com
Subject: Hi from Mom and Dad's House

Oh, no, too late! I hope Trimble won't be mad.

From: Carly Stewart@StewartRealty.com
Date: March 16 2:50:41 AM EST
To: Reed Stewart@reedstewart.com; Marshall Stewart@StewartRealty.com
Subject: Hi from Mom and Dad's House

Maybe Too Bad Tony can jump in there and find the cushions for her.

How is this even happening? Your parents would never let us TOUCH their stuff.

Carly R. Stewart | Accountant | Stewart Realty | 801 South Moore Pike, Bloomville, IN 47401 | phone (812) 555-8722 | Please visit StewartRealty.com for all your realty needs

---

From: Reed Stewart@reedstewart.com
Date: March 16 2:55:53 PM EST
To: Carly Stewart@StewartRealty.com; Marshall Stewart@StewartRealty.com
Subject: Hi from Mom and Dad's House

It's called Becky Flowers. She is magical.

From: Carly Stewart@StewartRealty.com
Date: March 16 3:05:17 PM EST
To: Reed Stewart@reedstewart.com; Marshall Stewart@StewartRealty.com
Subject: Hi from Mom and Dad's House

Worth every penny!

Carly R. Stewart | Accountant | Stewart Realty | 801 South Moore Pike, Bloomville, IN 47401 | phone (812) 555-8722 | Please visit StewartRealty.com for all your realty needs

---

From: Marshall Stewart@StewartRealty.com
Date: March 16 3:17:55 AM EST
To: Reed Stewart@reedstewart.com; Carly Stewart@StewartRealty.com
Subject: Hi from Mom and Dad's House

Would you two please stop it? Some of us are trying to work at our actual jobs.

And between the two of you, Mom and Dad, Trimble, the fact that one of my kids won't stop dressing in costume, and my only listing being an asbestos-laden school, I'm starting to get an ulcer.

From: Reed Stewart@reedstewart.com
Date: March 16 3:15:43 PM EST
To: Carly Stewart@StewartRealty.com; Marshall Stewart@StewartRealty.com
Subject: Hi from Mom and Dad's House

You know what you should try in order to reduce the stress in your life, Marshall?

Golf.

Reed Stewart   4:12 PM
So, I don't know how you're doing this, but it's impressive.

Becky Flowers   4:12 PM
Thanks. But it's my job.

I can't believe you're texting me from across your parents' living room.

Reed Stewart   4:12 PM
I didn't want to tell you in front of my dad how impressed I am that you got him to part with all seventy of his copies of the Encyclopaedia Britannica from 1982.

Becky Flowers   4:12 PM
Well, most of the information in them is a little outdated.

Reed Stewart   4:13 PM
I think it was pointing out to him that Argentine forces no longer occupy the Falkland Islands that did the job.

Becky Flowers   4:13 PM
Thank you, yes, I felt that was a stroke of brilliance myself.

You didn't do so bad, either, with the photos from The Town.

Reed Stewart   4:13 PM
Thanks. I have a man on the inside.

Becky Flowers   4:13 PM
I told you that once they had a sense of where they're going, they'd be more excited about it.

Your mother looks as if she's beginning to flag, however.

Reed Stewart   4:13 PM
Yes. The battle over the fondue pots took a lot out of her.

Becky Flowers   4:13 PM
Why would anyone insist on keeping seven fondue pots?

Reed Stewart   4:13 PM
Why would anyone want ONE?

Becky Flowers   4:13 PM
Reed! I am shocked. I thought you of all people would have an appreciation for the culinary art of fondue.

Reed Stewart   4:13 PM
Why me of all people?

Becky Flowers   4:14 PM
Well, sticks, holes.

Reed Stewart   4:14 PM
Becky Flowers! Are you flirting with me?

Becky Flowers   4:14 PM
No, I'm sorry. That was unprofessional. I apologize.

Reed Stewart   4:14 PM
Are you kidding? I'm sitting here sorting through four boxes of monogrammed highball glasses. I could use a little flirting.

Becky Flowers   4:14 PM
Monogrammed highball glasses are the height of stylish entertaining, Reed.

Reed Stewart   4:15 PM

Maybe in 1987, if you were Magnum PI.

But 1997 is the last time I remember my parents having had a party, and neither of them is a suave mustachioed private investigator who drives a Ferrari.

Becky Flowers   4:15 PM

But tell them that they'll definitely use those highball glasses when they move to Orlando. It will cheer them up.

Reed Stewart   4:15 PM

But not 200 of them.

Uh-oh, look out. Here comes Richard.

Reed Stewart   4:22 PM

Brilliantly done.

I enjoyed how you parried that there probably wasn't going to be a wall large enough in the new condo to display all 800 of his gavels, but that if he put them in storage until the market for them got any hotter, he might miss Peak Gavel Sales entirely.

Becky Flowers   4:22 PM

Thank you. Like I said, it's my job.

But you shouldn't make fun of him. Your dad is a good man.

Reed Stewart   4:22 PM

A good man who squandered all his retirement savings on gavels and worthless stamps.

Becky Flowers   4:22 PM

The gavels actually didn't cost that much. Your dad told me how much he paid for each one as he gave me the official tour.

Reed Stewart   4:22 PM

He gave you a tour of his gavel collection?

Becky Flowers   4:23 PM
He's proud of them. They symbolize something to him.

Reed Stewart   4:23 PM
Now I'm officially the most mortified I've ever been in my life. I thought the cats were the worst.

Becky Flowers   4:23 PM
Don't be embarrassed.

And I actually think the cats belong to other homeowners in the area. They just hang around because your mother is feeding them. Did you see how the orange tabby has a collar with a tag? Its name is Gelato.

Reed Stewart   4:24 PM
My God. The horror. The horror.

Becky Flowers   4:24 PM
Stop being so silly and ask your mom which set of those glasses she wants to keep. The rest she should donate. Or we can sell them at the consignment store.

Reed Stewart   4:24 PM
Consignment. They need the money.

Though I don't know who's going to buy 180 highball glasses monogrammed with the letters RDS.

Becky Flowers   4:25 PM
You could, actually. Those are your initials.

Wait, are your parents really broke?

Reed Stewart   4:25 PM
You remember my middle name? No one remembers my middle name.

Becky Flowers   4:25 PM

A name like Reed Duncan Stewart is hard to forget.

How can your parents be broke?

Reed Stewart   4:25 PM

Rebecca Catherine Flowers is hard to forget, too.

Becky Flowers   4:25 PM

And yet you managed to do so for ten years.

Reed Stewart   4:25 PM

I never forgot you, Flowers. It took me ten years to feel *worthy* of you.

Not that I do now.

Becky Flowers   4:25 PM

Nice save.

Okay, so what's all this about your parents allegedly being broke?

Reed Stewart   4:25 PM

Fine. Between the gavels, his stamp collection, and Mom's cat figurines, my parents haven't got a dime. Why do you think we're selling the place? I mean, besides the obvious—they're going to have to flee to Canada to escape the long arm of the law if Shenanigans doesn't drop the charges.

Becky Flowers   4:26 PM

Reed, I've been doing this for a long time, and I haven't seen anything in this house so far that is expensive enough to account for your parents having lost *all* their savings.

Reed Stewart   4:26 PM

Connie apparently loves her scratch-offs.

Becky Flowers   4:27 PM

Is she also frequenting the riverboat casinos?

Reed Stewart   4:27 PM

Jesus, I hope so. I would pay money to see Connie hitting the blackjack table.

Becky Flowers   4:27 PM

So would I.

But if it really is the case that your parents are broke, I'd look into the possibility of some kind of fraud or elder abuse. It happens more often than you think, and many of my clients have been able to get their parents' money back.

Reed Stewart   4:28 PM

Bex, are you serious?

Becky Flowers   4:28 PM

Of course. Your dad has always been such a prominent and beloved figure in the community, but he has made a few enemies. There are definitely people out there who don't agree with some of the decisions he made, and swore they'd get back at him if they could.

Reed Stewart   4:28 PM

You realize you're talking about me. I'm one of those people.

Becky Flowers   4:29 PM

Reed, don't be ridiculous. Of course I'm not talking about you. Why would you swindle your own father out of his savings?

Reed Stewart   4:29 PM

Because I resent him for . . . a lot of things.

Becky Flowers   4:29 PM

Now you're just talking nonsense. Even if you had reason to resent your dad, you wouldn't take his money. What would you need it for? You have plenty of your own.

Reed Stewart   4:29 PM

Sure, but if I really resented him, I'd steal his money anyway, and donate it to the orphans in Bolivia, or something.

Becky Flowers   4:29 PM

Are there orphans in Bolivia?

Reed Stewart   4:29 PM

I don't know. I was just using that as an example of how devious I could be, if I were someone who wanted to get back at my dad.

You shouldn't rule me out as a suspect.

Becky Flowers   4:29 PM

Now you're simply being obtuse.

If you really want to help, why don't you go down into the basement and help your dad sort through all those boxes?

Reed Stewart   4:29 PM

Uh, no thank you. First of all, Miss, Flowers, everything down there is worth millions. MILLIONS, understand? You're never going to get what that stuff is really worth selling it in a consignment shop. It needs to go on *Antiques Road Show*, where there are experts who can value its true worth.

And secondly, I found our old high school yearbook. Do you know what you wrote in mine?

Becky Flowers   4:30 PM

I don't remember writing anything in it.

> **Reed Stewart**   4:30 PM
>
> Exactly! Because my dad kicked me out of the house before graduation. My copy of our yearbook was shipped here, so I never saw it until now. It's empty.

Becky Flowers   4:30 PM

Don't you have more important things to worry about right now than the fact that I didn't sign your yearbook?

> **Reed Stewart**   4:30 PM
>
> You mean how many *World's Greatest Grandma* mugs my mother should take with her to the new condo? Twenty? Is twenty too many? I'm thinking it probably is.

Becky Flowers   4:30 PM

You're an idiot.

Listen, I know you're not taking this seriously, but there are people around here who might take advantage of the fact that since your parents' health has declined, they haven't been quite on top of things as they used to be. Financial elder abuse is an avenue you and the rest of your family might want to explore.

> **Reed Stewart**   4:31 PM
>
> Are you text lecturing at me?

Becky Flowers   4:31 PM

Yes. I'm sorry, but yes. Your mother is in here, and I don't want her to know what we're discussing.

I find your statement that your parents have no money curious when, so far, except for the famous stamp over which your father says he was swindled, I've seen no expensive items in this home.

And if he did get "swindled" over that stamp, that's something to look into, as well.

Reed Stewart   4:31 PM

The Judge wasn't swindled over the stamp. I saw the receipt in that huge pile of junk on his desk in the study. It was wedged in between two letters, one to the President of the United States discussing our relations with China, and one to Tiger Woods, advising him on how to improve his golf swing.

Becky Flowers   4:31 PM

Well, that's one question answered.

Reed Stewart   4:32 PM

What?

Becky Flowers   4:32 PM

One of the ways the state assesses whether an older person is mentally fit enough to handle their own affairs is by whether or not they can name the date, their own address, and the President of the United States.

Both of your parents pass that test with flying colors.

Reed Stewart   4:32 PM

That's the problem, right? It's the other ones—physical and financial functions—in which they're failing.

But because they pass the first one, we can't get—what is it called? My sister mentioned it, I think.

Becky Flowers   4:32 PM

Power of attorney. Right. Not without your parents' consent, unless you can prove they're mentally incapacitated.

From what I know about your father, it seems unlikely he's going to give it willingly.

But it's usually good for older members of the family to give someone they trust access to their bank accounts to deposit or withdraw funds, pay bills, or check their credit card accounts . . . especially in the event that the older person is in some way incapacitated.

I've had older clients suffering from dementia take the family car and drive off, and the only way the family was able to find them was through the charges on the missing elderly person's credit cards, which the family was only able to access because they'd been given POA.

The police couldn't access the charges because there was no evidence the person was in danger, or hadn't left of his own volition.

Reed Stewart   4:32 PM

Jesus.

Becky Flowers   4:32 PM

Sorry. I don't mean to scare you. I'm just letting you know.

Reed Stewart   4:32 PM

It's OK. This all might turn out to have a silver lining.

Becky Flowers   4:32 PM

How?

Reed Stewart   4:33 PM

Well, you think this fraud/elder abuse/power of attorney thing is something my siblings and I should explore more fully?

Becky Flowers   4:33 PM
Oh, yes, definitely.

You know a lot of people didn't agree with your dad over the Dumbbell Killer. Some people thought he should never have instructed that jury to consider a lesser charge than murder, let alone manslaughter. Someone could be trying to get back at him for that. It could be someone who works at the bank!

Or anyone. I'm just saying.

Reed Stewart   4:33 PM
I see. Would helping us look into this—or that power of attorney thing—fall under your job description?

Becky Flowers   4:33 PM
Well, no, not really.

But I'd be happy to refer you to people who could help.

Reed Stewart   4:33 PM
Maybe you and I should meet to discuss this further face-to-face, somewhere my parents can't overhear, so you don't have to keep sending me such long texts about it.

Becky Flowers   4:33 PM
I'm having your sister-in-law Carly pick up your parents to take them to dinner with your nieces at six o'clock. We can talk then, either here or, if you prefer, at my office.

Reed Stewart   4:34 PM
Great.

Or, since today I witnessed my mother throw her wedding dress in a Dumpster, maybe you could join me in drinking myself blind at Bud's Stick and Stein over on the turnpike.

That was my plan for later, anyway.

Becky Flowers   4:34 PM
You did not actually see your mother do that.

Reed Stewart   4:34 PM
You described it to me. And also how you climbed into the Dumpster to retrieve it. That was just as traumatic as witnessing it myself.

Becky Flowers   4:34 PM
I'm sorry I had to tell you about it, but as you are my employer, I was obligated to.

But don't take your mother's actions personally. She was highly stressed. I'm sure she'll feel better in a few days when she sees how much better the house looks without all this clutter. I'm going to have the floors professionally cleaned, so the cat smell should be gone by then, as well.

And really, you shouldn't drink at Bud's. It's gotten very dicey over the past few years. There was a fight there not too long ago. One trucker broke a pool cue over the head of another after a disagreement stemming from the ownership of a Blake Shelton CD.

Reed Stewart   4:35 PM
Come with me to that new place on the square, then, Authentic. I highly doubt anyone's ever been in a fight there over a country music CD.

Becky Flowers   4:36 PM
Thank you, but no. My boyfriend owns that place.

Reed Stewart   4:36 PM
Why would that be a problem? You said we have to keep this strictly professional, so wouldn't he know that's what this is?

Becky Flowers   4:36 PM
I think you need to stop slacking off and work harder.

Reed Stewart   4:36 PM

I beg your pardon. I've done a lot already. Have you seen the boxes I sorted from the dining room alone? By size and color, ready for removal by "your guys" to the POD.

I give you exhibit A.

Becky Flowers   4:37 PM

That is really not very impressive considering how much more of the house we have left.

Reed Stewart   4:38 PM

Look. Look, Becky. Gelato has come in and is sitting on my lap. Gelato likes me. Why don't you?

Becky Flowers   4:38 PM

Well . . . I will admit, Gelato is quite discriminating. So if Gelato likes you, I suppose I could have one drink. At Matsumori's. At 7.

But only as friends to discuss this problem with your family's finances. Nothing more.

Reed Stewart   4:38 PM
"Friendship is certainly the finest balm for the pangs of disappointed love."

Becky Flowers   4:38 PM
Emma?

Reed Stewart   4:38 PM
Forsooth, Flowers, that's from *Northanger Abbey*. You're slipping.

Becky Flowers   4:38 PM
Isn't that your dad I hear calling from the basement? I think he wants to show you something. I hope it's another box of gavels! Too bad there's no cell service down there.

Reed Stewart   4:38 PM
Wow. And I used to think the women in LA were the cattiest in the world.

Becky Flowers   4:38 PM
See you at 7 ☺

Timeline | About | Photos | Reviews | More

Authentic Wine and Cheese Boutique

added an event

13 hrs

St. Patrick's Day Wine and Cheese Tasting
Tomorrow between 6pm and 10pm!
Sample some of our prize-winning
Irish Cheddars, Beara Blues, Clover Reds,
and Concannon Crimsons!
10% discount for any members of law enforcement
or the Armed Forces!

Henry de Santos, Tony Antonelli, Summer Hayes, Nicole Flowers, and 179 others like this.

TOP COMMENTS

Henry De Santos—Really cool of you to honor the Men and Women in Blue, bro!
Today at 2:16 PM

Graham Tucker—It's my pleasure! Thanks for all that you do!
Today at 2:37

Nicole Flowers—Save me some of those ice wines.
Today at 2:45

Graham Tucker—You know I will! Is your sister coming?
Today at 3:12 PM

Nicole Flowers—I'm not my sister's keeper, but I'm pretty sure she'll be there.
Today at 3:15

Graham Tucker—Well, that's good. It's just that I haven't heard from her much lately.
Today at 3:30

Nicole Flowers—Well, she got some new clients, so she's been kind of busy.
Today at 3:45

Graham Tucker—Oh, I see! Well, let her know I'm thinking of her.
Today at 3:47

Nicole Flowers—I sure will!
Today at 4:05

Tony Antonelli—I'll be there!
Today at 4:45 PM

Graham Tucker—Great, see you then.
Today at 4:50 PM

Trimble Stewart-Antonelli—Actually Tony and I won't be able to attend. We have that award ceremony tomorrow night, don't we, Tony?
Today at 6:15 PM

Tony Antonelli—Whoops! Sorry, I forgot.
Today at 6:20 PM

Graham Tucker—It's all good. Next time!
Today at 6:40 PM

Going (228)
Recent Guests (20+ new)
Maybe (350)
Invited (1059)

Sweetie Ty

Reviewer ranking: #1,162,357
13% helpful
votes received on reviews

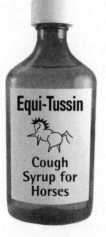

Reviewed:
Equi-Tussin Cough Syrup for Horses, 1 qt.
An effective decongestant and expectorant for horses, formulated for
the treatment of the equine cold, flu, allergies and stable cough.

As pictured
March 16

My idea of a fun party is *not* to have a bunch of people come over to
my house and drink punch with horse syrup in it.

No, that would be my idiot brother Tony Jr.'s idea.

But he busted me with Mom's credit card (whatever. I was going to
buy this totally hot Marc Jacobs beach cover-up for Spring Break and
he walked in just as I was about to hit *Order Now*).

Tony Jr. said he'd rat me out unless I help him whip up a batch of
lean, which—for all my classy readers out there who don't know—is a

mixed drink that immature high school kids who think they're OG and can't get proper party beverages consume.

So now I have to buy this disgusting horse cough syrup.

It hasn't arrived yet, so I can't tell you how it is.

I won't list all the other ingredients of lean here because this is an upscale site. The fact that one of them is cough syrup should give you a clue.

But it isn't supposed to be HORSE COUGH SYRUP.

I tried to argue with him, but Tony Jr. is Tony Jr. He still wears his baseball caps backwards. Enough said.

Anyway I have no choice but to attend this horrible soirée (which means party. I have straight As in French) because it's tomorrow night on St. Patrick's Day when our parents will be at the Kiwanis Club because they are giving our dad some kind of medal (which, lol, whatever) and I don't trust Tony Jr.'s idiot friends unsupervised in our home.

I own over six pairs of Christian Louboutins and three Pradas and a signed Harry Styles poster. I'm not about to let some Tussed-up tweaker barf horse cough syrup and green Jolly Ranchers all over my perfect Harry.

And I still haven't seen my uncle Reed, even though my friend Sundae texted that she saw him just now at Matsumori's Tiki Palace with a lady.

Sundae says she couldn't get a good look at the lady because she and my uncle Reed were at the bar, and you aren't allowed at the bar at Matsumori's unless you're 21 or over, and Sundae couldn't use her fake ID because she was there with her parents.

But she said the lady def wasn't Ava Kuznetsov.

Ugh, my life SUX. I wish I had been born in London, England, instead of boring Bloomville, Indiana. There is nothing to do here at all, even if you aren't grounded, which is why people like my brother make drinks like lean, which by the way caused L'il Wayne to be hospitalized. Allegedly.

And he didn't even use horse cough syrup.

1 out of 10 people found this review helpful.

REED STEWART	11:45PM	2%
TODAY	ALL	MISSED

From: Dolly Vargas l.Vargas@VTM.com
Date: March 16 8:42:10 PM EST
To: Reed Stewart@reedstewart.com
Subject: Lyrexica Offer

Are your ears ringing? Because I've been talking about you all day, darling. Lyrexica has upped their offer again:

Seven figures!

That's right. One million dollars for your beautiful, shaggy head.

I know. I can hardly believe it myself. I'd like to think it has something to do with my amazing negotiating skills.

But I think it probably has more to do with the fact that your old buddy Cobb Cutler has made a complete jackass of himself on social media. Who is stupid enough to post that his divorce from a woman he barely lived with is more painful than the loss of his own father, let alone the death of his beloved dog? That's simply un-American.

A guy with parents who tried to hoodwink a waitress with a phony stamp looks pretty good in comparison!

Be sure to get back to me soon, though. You can only ignore these big pharma phonies for so long.

Oh, and I finally figured out where I'd heard of Bloomville: A former colleague of mine, Tim Grabowski, left a successful job in IT to open up an antique shop or a bookstore or something ridiculously quaint like that. So be sure to tell him hi from me when you see him!

Anyway, did I ever tell you that you're my favorite client? You and that brilliantly shiny head of hair of yours.

XOXOX

Dolly
Dolly Vargas
Vargas Talent Management
Los Angeles, CA

From: Reed Stewart@reedstewart.com
Date: March 16 11:27:21 PM EST
To: Lyle Stewart@FountainHill.org
Subject: Her

Dear Uncle Lyle,

I tried what you said in your last email about going back and reexamining decisions made when one was in one's youth, then changing one's behavior.

It didn't work.

In fact, it was a huge disaster.

I saw Becky again today, and I actually convinced her to spend time with me alone—well, not alone, exactly. We went to Matsumori's for drinks, and somehow drinks turned into appetizers, and then appetizers turned into dinner, and before we knew it—well, before *she* knew it, anyway, because *I* was hoping for it all along—we'd spent the whole night together.

Not like that. Get your mind out of the gutter. Ha, kidding, I know you're not like that. Well, of course you ARE like that, but you keep it to yourself like a gentleman. We spent the *evening* together, but it was only dinner.

It was exactly like it used to be, only better, because neither of us had a curfew and we didn't have to worry about finishing our homework (not like I ever worried so much about that).

It was like no time had gone by at all since we'd last been together—she's exactly the same, only sadder, I guess, because of her dad dying, and her having had to take over the family business. Did you know she's only ever been out of the state a couple of times? And never out of the country. She never had the money or the time. She wanted to know all about my trips to Scotland and China.

It made me feel good, thinking about taking her overseas. I could see us traveling together, showing her things she's never seen before, being with her when she tries haggis and dim sum for the first time. Well, maybe not haggis, but you get what I'm saying.

Is it weird that I feel this way? Is it weird that I've traveled the whole world and met women from nearly every country, and the one I still have the most fun with and am most excited by is the one from my hometown, whom I've known since kindergarten?

Is it wrong that I want to take her away from her terrible job cleaning up other people's messes and show her what she's been missing? There's an incredible world out there that she's never experienced.

She's never seen Paris. She's never seen your orchids. She's never seen the month of March without snow!

But somehow I think I managed to fall for the one woman who is more into books and binders than she is into private jets and beaches.

Still, after we left the restaurant tonight (which didn't happen until closing time—they started putting the chairs on the tables, so they could sweep beneath them, which goes to show how deep into our own conversation we were: we didn't even notice we were the only two customers left in the place), and started walking towards our cars, something came over me.

Maybe it was because the moon was shining and the air was so crisp and sharp in that way it never gets in LA because it so rarely dips below freezing. Someone somewhere in Bloomville had a fire going in their fireplace, and I could smell that good clean scent of burning pine.

Anyway, even though I know now that it was the worst idea in the world, I did something terrible:

I went in for a good-night kiss.

(Look, you've told me what went on in the Seventies on Fire Island. You can bear with me for this, which is tame in comparison.)

I was just feeling so happy and free and hopeful about the future . . . and, okay, maybe a little drunk from the sake and the smell of the burning pine.

And she looked so beautiful in the moonlight, and she was smiling, and I didn't think it would be a bad thing.

So I reached out and took her hand and pulled her over to me, and she didn't stop smiling, or anything. She just looked up, kind of inquisitively, like, "Yes?"

I couldn't help myself. I cupped her face in my hands and I kissed her, the way I'd kissed her a thousand times before, back when we used to go out.

Only this time there was something different about it.

This time it wasn't sweet and pleasant and fun, like I remember it being, the way I'd *wanted* it to be.

This time it was deep and dark and *serious*.

She didn't turn it that way. *I* did. The minute I touched her, this . . . *longing* just about kicked me in the solar plexus. I don't know any other way to describe it. All I knew was that this time, I wasn't letting her go, and that this was a kiss for keeps, because even though it wasn't like old times, it *was*. All the old memories of those nights in the boathouse and her bedroom and my bedroom came flooding back . . .

. . . only this was no trip down memory lane. It was a *rocket ride*.

I don't think I ever would have let her go, either, if she hadn't suddenly pushed me away—recoiled, maybe, is a better word for it. She *recoiled* from me—and gasped.

When she'd staggered what she must have decided was a safe distance (about ten feet away, which is nice to know. She feels like she needs to keep a ten foot parameter between us), she cried, her eyes blazing in the moonlight, "I've got a boyfriend, remember?"

Can you believe it? She boyfriended me!

I nearly lost it. Boyfriend? What boyfriend? We spent the whole evening drinking sake and eating spicy tuna rolls, while her best friend's mother brought out special after special, such as miso-marinated black cod and hamachi kama, telling us how glad she was to see us, especially since

"Leeanne" was on her way home and was going to be so glad to see us, too.

The implication was "see us back *together*," as in "a couple," and Becky never batted an eye.

Then, after we have the most explosive kiss in the history of time, the boyfriend suddenly matters?

And this boyfriend, let me tell you, I checked him out. You bet I did! He owns just about the lamest wine and cheese place you've ever seen. If it were in Palm Springs, you and all your friends would drive right past it since it would be filled with trophy wives in their yoga pants drinking pinot noir because their neurologists told them it won't give them migraines.

Plus, he's got a *beard*, and wears slim fit crewnecks to show off his biceps.

But she likes him anyway!

"Besides," she goes on. "I thought we agreed to keep this professional."

This was the best kiss of the century, and she wants to keep it professional!

What could I say? What could I do?

I know I'm the one who messed it all up.

But how could I have stayed ten years ago? I couldn't. You know I couldn't.

And deep down, she knows it, too. Just like she knows I couldn't have asked her to come with me. Unlike me, she was college material. She got that great scholarship. She had to go.

That's the real reason I couldn't answer any of her phone calls or letters. What was I going to say? Ask her to wait for me? I had no idea how long it was going to take me to make something out of myself. That wouldn't have been fair to her. It was better to make a clean break of it.

Enrique—you know Enrique—thinks I should have called her years ago, and that I don't have a snowball's chance of getting her back now.

He's probably right. I'm sure he and the other caddies are taking bets on how badly I'm going to lose at the Palm because of all this. There's no way I'm ever going to get my swing back or my head on straight in time for the tournament after this.

I don't know what I was thinking. I told her I wasn't here to rescue her. So what was I doing? It's obvious she loves her life here. The way she talked about it tonight . . . she was interested in the places I've been, but more the way someone is interested in the plot of a movie they'd like to see someday, but aren't feeling deprived for having missed, because they've seen plenty of other good movies.

God, why am I telling you all this? You didn't even ask. You wanted to know how Mom and Dad are doing.

Well, the answer is bad. You should see the basement. It's like a black pit of despair. How does anyone let anything get that way? I never want to end up living like that.

But Becky is going to save them. Because that's what she does. She thinks someone might even be defrauding them. She doesn't understand how they could have so little money and yet so little to show for it. She wants us kids to look into it. Because that's another thing she does—rights injustices, or tries to, when she sees them.

I should have known it was going to turn out like this. I should have followed my first instinct, gone straight to Orlando, and just sent a check to help out Mom and Dad. I don't know what I was thinking.

Okay, I've stayed up too late, writing this. Tomorrow I have to get up early to go to the house to finish packing. Also because the girls get up at the crack of dawn, which is apparently what small children do. They like to burst into my room screaming, "Wake up, Uncle Reed! Wake up!"

This is not as delightful as it might sound.

I don't expect a reply to this. I'm aware that you're busy with the Expo, and also that I sound like a lunatic. I *feel* like one. I feel like I'm going slowly insane. I got a huge endorsement deal today (for a pharmaceutical product. You would not approve), and I can't even be happy about it, because what is the point of having a lot of money if the woman you love (or man, sorry to be gender-specific) doesn't love you back?

I'll be glad when this is all over, and I can head off to Florida and play and get this woman (person) out of my system for good.

Although actually it won't be for good, because I doubt I'll ever get her out of my system.

Anyway, sorry to burden you with all this. I'm going to bed. Good luck with the Expo. I hope your *Phalaenopsis amabilis* wins.

Love,
Your Favorite Nephew (although possibly not after you've read this),
Reed

Blessings Journal

of

BECKY FLOWERS

Today I feel blessed because:

_____

I can't. I just can't. I don't even—

How am I going to look at him tomorrow?

This is all a complete disaster.

How could I have let it happen? I've never been one of those people who could do the friends with benefits thing. I tried to do that with Reed, and look what happened.

I have to break up with Graham, that's all. I have to make it clear once and for all that we're not compatible and we never were and it's over. It's over.

Dear Graham,

I'm so sorry, but

No, that sounds terrible. I have nothing to be sorry for.

Dear Graham,

I'm sure by now you've realized that

God, what is wrong with me?

Dear Graham,

Due to unforeseen circumstances, I am no longer going to be able to see you socially, at least not for the next few weeks while I—

get my ex-boyfriend out of my head because all I can think about is jumping his bones.

Oh, my God. I am in so much trouble.

I wish I were a dolphin.

The Bloomville Herald

The Tri-County Area's Only
Daily Newspaper
• Friday, March 17 • Vol. 143 •
Still Only 50 Cents!

RESTAURANT DROPS CHARGES

BY CHRISTINA MARTINEZ Herald Staff

Bloomville, Ind.—All charges against Judge Richard Stewart and his wife, Constance, for attempting to pay for a meal at Shenanigans Neighborhood Bar and Grill with a postage stamp will be dropped, according to a corporate spokesperson for Shenanigans.

A night manager at a local franchise of the restaurant in Bloomville's Old Towne Mall will also be transferred, says Felicia Forchette, director of communications at Shenanigans International, Inc.

"Mr. Grubb's decision was technically the correct one," said Ms. Forchette when reached by phone late yesterday evening. "However, we expect our managers to be flexible and work with the local community, so we feel Mr. Grubb's talents could be best utilized elsewhere."

Forchette denied that the transfer of Randy Grubb, the night manager who insisted on the elderly couple's prosecution, was punitive, or had anything to do with the arrest or the subsequent boycott of the restaurant launched by Beverly Flowers, 64.

The boycott, which included a protest outside the restaurant that at times grew to number as many as two dozen people, has now been called off. Forchette had no comment when asked if the timing of the chain's decision had anything to do with St. Patrick's Day, a traditionally profitable holiday for the corporation.

When contacted for comment on the restaurant's decision, Flowers said she was "overwhelmed."

"I'm so pleased, I could cry. I might just have to run over to Shenanigans for a great big Blarney Burger!"

Judge Stewart's reaction to the news was typically stoic for the well-known man of law:

"Well, that's good to hear. Real good."

Matsumori's
Tiki Palace

HAPPY HOUR SPECIAL

Half Off Drinks and Appetizers
4PM-6:30PM

Complimentary Parking With Dinner

ANTONELLI'S PIZZA

WE LOVE OUR CUSTOMERS!

Every Pizza on Our Menu $10
when you are seated by 6PM

ANTONELLI'S PIZZA

Your Pizza is Free
on your birthday
with customer photo ID

Come home to

Shenanigans!
We miss YOU!

Blarney Burgers with Shamrock Fries
ALL DAY only $5.99
Beer on tap only $2
with this coupon limit one per customer

BLOOMVILLE UNITED COMMUNITY CHURCH

partnering with the City of Bloomville Police Department welcomes you to

THE
SAVE THE STEWARTS
FUNDRAISER

Friday, March 17

5PM-7PM

at the Bloomville High School Gym

Did you know—
Beloved local Judge Stewart isn't doing as well
financially as people might think? That's why his house
is for sale. But YOU can help by attending our

Save the Stewarts

St. Patrick's Day Fundraiser!

A Donation of just $10 ($5 for kids) will get you:

All-You-Can-Eat Baked Chicken, Baked Beans, Potato
Salad, Green Salad, Rolls and Pies! Ice Cream! Bounce
House! Face Painting! Petting Zoo! Hula Hoop Contest
And Much Much More Family Fun!

FREE PERFORMANCE BY
HARRISON AND THE FORDS!!!!

Plenty of Parking Available!

**Help Judge and Mrs. Stewart battle their legal fees,
pay off debts, relocate to a warmer climate!**

Judge Stewart gave YOU a 2nd Chance!
Now it's your turn to give one to HIM!

Call Rhonda for more information: 812-555-0663

————————————Today————————————

Summer Hayes   8:15 AM

Hi, Carly! So, I saw the ad in today's paper for the benefit tonight, and now I just feel so wretched about what I wrote to you earlier this week, I could scream. I had no idea your in-laws were going through all that!

It's no wonder your little Bailey has been acting out the way she has. I'm surprised, really, that you all have been holding up as well as you have.

My Britney has been collecting canned goods all month to take up to the Mission Ministries in Indy for Easter Sunday, but when I told her how her friend Courtney's grandparents are in need, she said she'd much rather give her canned goods to them.

Isn't that sweet? What time would be good for me to drop them by? Or would it be better for me to bring them directly to the benefit?

You hang in there!

☺ Summer ☺
Britney's Super Mom!

From: Carly Stewart@StewartRealty.com
Date: March 17 9:05:17 AM EST
To: Reed Stewart@reedstewart.com; Marshall Stewart@StewartRealty.com
Subject: Your Parents

Look at today's Bloomville Herald. Page 7. LOOK AT IT RIGHT NOW.

Carly R. Stewart | Accountant | Stewart Realty | 801 South Moore Pike, Bloomville, IN 47401 | phone (812) 555-8722 | Please visit StewartRealty.com for all your realty needs

From: Marshall Stewart@StewartRealty.com
Date: March 17 9:06:05 AM EST
To: Reed Stewart@reedstewart.com; Carly Stewart@StewartRealty.com
Subject: Re: Your Parents

FUUUUUUUUUUUUUUUDDDDDGGGGGGEE

From: Marshall Stewart@StewartRealty.com
Date: March 17 9:07:42 AM EST
To: Reed Stewart@reedstewart.com; Carly Stewart@StewartRealty.com
Subject: Re: Your Parents

Reed, why did you tell Rhonda that our parents are broke?

From: Reed Stewart@reedstewart.com
Date: March 17 9:10:12 AM EST
To: Carly Stewart@StewartRealty.com; Marshall Stewart@StewartRealty.com
Subject: Re: Your Parents

I didn't. I swear to God I haven't spoken to Rhonda since I got here. I have no idea how she could have found out. I'm so, so sorry about this, guys.

But it is kind of awesome, in a way.

From: Carly Stewart@StewartRealty.com
Date: March 17 9:14:53 AM EST
To: Reed Stewart@reedstewart.com; Marshall Stewart@StewartRealty.com
Subject: Re: Your Parents

HOW IS IT AWESOME? How is Summer Hayes wanting to drop canned goods off at my in-laws anything but embarrassing and horrible?

Carly R. Stewart | Accountant | Stewart Realty | 801 South Moore Pike, Bloomville, IN 47401 | phone (812) 555-8722 | Please visit StewartRealty.com for all your realty needs

From: Marshall Stewart@StewartRealty.com
Date: March 17 9:18:17 PM EST
To: Reed Stewart@reedstewart.com; Carly Stewart@StewartRealty.com
Subject: Re: Your Parents

He means it's awesome for him. It's free press that I'm sure his "people" will be eating up. Didn't you see the piece on *SportsCenter* last night about our parents, and how "eccentric" they are? Everyone was making a big deal about how great it is that Reed's flown here to help them instead of concentrating on improving his swing for the Golden Palm next week.

From: Carly Stewart@StewartRealty.com
Date: March 17 9:21:25 AM EST
To: Reed Stewart@reedstewart.com; Marshall Stewart@StewartRealty.com
Subject: Re: Your Parents

Uh, no, I did not see that, Marshall. I was too busy making dinner, helping Courtney with her homework, drying the feathers on Bailey's Chief Massasoit costume—which she insists she's going to wear tomorrow, by the way—getting Taylor to stop braiding the dog's hair, and trying not to strangle YOUR FATHER as he told me his latest scheme for how he's going to strike it rich selling his gavel collection online.

How did YOU have so much time to watch it?

Carly R. Stewart | Accountant | Stewart Realty | 801 South Moore Pike, Bloomville, IN 47401 | phone (812) 555-8722 | Please visit StewartRealty.com for all your realty needs

---

From: Marshall Stewart@StewartRealty.com
Date: March 17 9:23:17 PM EST
To: Reed Stewart@reedstewart.com; Carly Stewart@StewartRealty.com
Subject: Re: Your Parents

Uh, never mind. That's not important right now.

The important thing is, Reed is RICHER THAN EVER.

From: Reed Stewart@reedstewart.com
Date: March 17 9:25:43 AM EST
To: Carly Stewart@StewartRealty.com; Marshall Stewart@StewartRealty.com
Subject: Re: Your Parents

Look, you guys, can we not fight?

I'll talk to Rhonda and get her to call it off. I'm sure it's nothing but a little misunderstanding.

From: Marshall Stewart@StewartRealty.com
Date: March 17 9:27:04 AM EST
To: Reed Stewart@reedstewart.com; Carly Stewart@StewartRealty.com
Subject: Re: Your Parents

Rhonda can't call it off, Reed. It's in the paper! Everyone is going to show up at the high school tonight expecting to see Harrison and the Fords play, get their faces painted, donate money to Mom and Dad, and have some pie. It's Friday night—St. Patrick's Day—in a small town, not L.A., where people don't have a lot of different options for their entertainment dollars.

From: Reed Stewart@reedstewart.com
Date: March 17 9:30:13 AM EST
To: Carly Stewart@StewartRealty.com; Marshall Stewart@StewartRealty.com
Subject: Re: Your Parents

OK, fine.

But Rhonda doesn't have to give the proceeds to Richard and Connie. We can get the Judge to go and give a speech about how much he appreciates everyone's help on his behalf, but that the charges have been dropped— which they obviously didn't know when they paid for this ad and organized the benefit—so they need to give the money to someone else. Someone who really needs it.

From: Carly Stewart@StewartRealty.com
Date: March 17 9:35:14 AM EST
To: Reed Stewart@reedstewart.com; Marshall Stewart@StewartRealty.com
Subject: Re: Your Parents

That's actually not a bad suggestion. I think your brother may have come up with a pretty reasonable solution to the problem, Marshall.

Carly R. Stewart | Accountant | Stewart Realty | 801 South Moore Pike, Bloomville, IN 47401 | phone (812) 555-8722 | Please visit StewartRealty.com for all your realty needs

---

From: Reed Stewart@reedstewart.com
Date: March 17 9:37:48 AM EST
To: Carly Stewart@StewartRealty.com; Marshall Stewart@StewartRealty.com
Subject: Re: Your Parents

See? No harm, no foul.

From: Trimble Stewart-Antonelli@Stewart&Stewart.com
Date: March 17 9:40:26 AM EST
To: Carly Stewart@StewartRealty.com; Marshall Stewart@StewartRealty
.com; Reed Stewart@reedstewart.com
Cc: Tony Antonelli@AntonelliPizza.com
Subject: Our Parents

Could someone please explain to me why our former housekeeper is holding a fundraiser to save my parents from financial ruin? And on the same day that the Kiwanis are giving my husband an award for his generous civic contributions to this town?

I thought you people said you were going to handle this problem. I thought you people said you'd TAKE CARE OF IT.

From where I'm sitting, absolutely NOTHING is getting taken care of.

Trimble Stewart-Antonelli
Attorney at Law
Stewart & Stewart, LLC
1911 South Moore Pike
Bloomville, IN 47401
(812) 555-9721
www.stewart&stewart.com

From: Marshall Stewart@StewartRealty.com
Date: March 17 9:42:15 AM EST
To: Reed Stewart@reedstewart.com; Carly Stewart@StewartRealty.com
Subject: Re: Your Parents

Correction, dude: Both harm and foul. As usual, Reed, you spoke too soon.

From: Reed Stewart@reedstewart.com
Date: March 17 9:47:03 AM EST
To: Trimble Stewart-Antonelli@Stewart&Stewart.com; Carly Stewart@ StewartRealty.com; Marshall Stewart@StewartRealty.com
Subject: Re: Our Parents

Take it easy, Trimble. I'm handling this.

From: Trimble Stewart-Antonelli@Stewart&Stewart.com
Date: March 17 9:52:26 AM EST
To: Carly Stewart@StewartRealty.com; Marshall Stewart@StewartRealty .com; Reed Stewart@reedstewart.com
Cc: Tony Antonelli@AntonelliPizza.com
Subject: Our Parents

"Take it easy, Trimble"? You're seriously telling me to *take it easy*?

How dare you come back to this town after years of doing nothing but causing pain for Mommy and Daddy, then tell ME to take it easy?

You'd better be "handling" this. Because you're the one who caused it.

Trimble Stewart-Antonelli
Attorney at Law
Stewart & Stewart, LLC

1911 South Moore Pike
Bloomville, IN 47401
(812) 555-9721
www.stewart&stewart.com

From: Reed Stewart@reedstewart.com
Date: March 17 9:58:53 AM EST
To: Carly Stewart@StewartRealty.com; Marshall Stewart@StewartRealty
.com; Trimble Stewart-Antonelli@Stewart&Stewart.com
Subject: Re: Our Parents

I didn't, actually.

But like I said, I'll handle it.

From: Trimble Stewart-Antonelli@Stewart&Stewart.com
Date: March 17 10:06:21 AM EST
To: Carly Stewart@StewartRealty.com; Marshall Stewart@StewartRealty
.com; Reed Stewart@reedstewart.com
Cc: Tony Antonelli@AntonelliPizza.com
Subject: Re: Our Parents

Oh, really? You didn't cause this by hiring that ex-girlfriend of yours,
whatever her name is, to paw through Mommy's and Daddy's things?
She's probably been lying to everyone in town that Daddy is broke.

Trimble Stewart-Antonelli
Attorney at Law
Stewart & Stewart, LLC
1911 South Moore Pike
Bloomville, IN 47401
(812) 555-9721
www.stewart&stewart.com

From: Reed Stewart@reedstewart.com
Date: March 17 10:10:08 AM EST
To: Trimble Stewart-Antonelli@Stewart&Stewart.com; Carly Stewart@
StewartRealty.com; Marshall Stewart@StewartRealty.com
Subject: Re: Our parents

First of all, her name is Becky, as you know perfectly well.

Second of all, she would never do that. She has the strongest sense of professional ethics of anyone I've ever met. Trust me, I know.

And third, it isn't a lie. The Judge *is* broke.

From: Trimble Stewart-Antonelli@Stewart&Stewart.com
Date: March 17 10:17:28 AM EST
To: Carly Stewart@StewartRealty.com; Marshall Stewart@StewartRealty
.com; Reed Stewart@reedstewart.com
Subject: Re: Our Parents

Mommy and Daddy may be having cash flow problems at the moment, but in this economy, who isn't?

And don't you think it's a little coincidental that Rhonda is the one throwing this fundraiser, and Rhonda is also the one who was named in the paper as having attended the boycott against Shenanigans that was organized by Becky's mother?

She obviously heard some things there from Mrs. Flowers, who could only have heard them from Becky. Mrs. Flowers works at Moving Up!

And Becky's sister, Nicki, or whatever her name is, dates a cop. The fundraiser is being co-sponsored by the Bloomville PD.

How stupid can you people be?

Trimble Stewart-Antonelli
Attorney at Law
Stewart & Stewart, LLC
1911 South Moore Pike
Bloomville, IN 47401
(812) 555-9721
www.stewart&stewart.com

From: Marshall Stewart@StewartRealty.com
Date: March 17 10:20:08 AM EST
To: Carly Stewart@StewartRealty.com; Reed Stewart@reedstewart.com
Subject: Re: Our Parents

Sorry, Reed. Trimble's right. This isn't looking very good for your girl.

From: Reed Stewart@reedstewart.com
Date: March 17 10:22:52 AM EST
To: Trimble Stewart-Antonelli@Stewart&Stewart.com; Carly Stewart@StewartRealty.com; Marshall Stewart@StewartRealty.com
Subject: Re: Our parents

Sorry to burst your bubble, guys, but it's not possible. I didn't mention anything to Becky about Richard and Connie being broke until yesterday, so she couldn't have told her mom before that.

Rhonda had to have started organizing this fundraiser at least the day before yesterday, even if only to buy the ad space in the newspaper.

From: Carly Stewart@StewartRealty.com
Date: March 17 10:25:17 AM EST
To: Trimble Stewart-Antonelli@Stewart&Stewart.com; Marshall Stewart@StewartRealty.com; Reed Stewart@reedstewart.com
Subject: Re: Our Parents

Reed's right. Marshall, you know we have to reserve ad space in the *Herald* 48 hours in advance.

And for Rhonda to have reserved the gym at the high school for her event? She had to have done that Tuesday, at the earliest.

And Becky hadn't even agreed to work for us at that point.

Carly R. Stewart | Accountant | Stewart Realty | 801 South Moore Pike, Bloomville, IN 47401 | phone (812) 555-8722 | Please visit StewartRealty.com for all your realty needs

From: Trimble Stewart-Antonelli@Stewart&Stewart.com
Date: March 17 10:31:22 AM EST
To: Carly Stewart@StewartRealty.com; Marshall Stewart@StewartRealty
.com; Reed Stewart@reedstewart.com
Subject: Re: Our Parents

Well, it had to have come from someone. Who was it?

Trimble Stewart-Antonelli
Attorney at Law
Stewart & Stewart, LLC
1911 South Moore Pike
Bloomville, IN 47401
(812) 555-9721
www.stewart&stewart.com

From: Reed Stewart@reedstewart.com
Date: March 17 10:36:52 AM EST
To: Trimble Stewart-Antonelli@Stewart&Stewart.com; Carly Stewart@
StewartRealty.com; Marshall Stewart@StewartRealty.com
Subject: Re: Our parents

Well, I guess we'll find out tonight when we see Rhonda at the benefit,
won't we? We can just ask her.

From: Trimble Stewart-Antonelli@Stewart&Stewart.com
Date: March 17 10:42:27 AM EST
To: Carly Stewart@StewartRealty.com; Marshall Stewart@StewartRealty
.com; Reed Stewart@reedstewart.com
Subject: Re: Our Parents

Are you joking? I'm not going to that thing.

Trimble Stewart-Antonelli
Attorney at Law
Stewart & Stewart, LLC
1911 South Moore Pike
Bloomville, IN 47401
(812) 555-9721
www.stewart&stewart.com

From: Carly Stewart@StewartRealty.com
Date: March 17 10:45:27 AM EST
To: Trimble Stewart-Antonelli@Stewart&Stewart.com; Marshall
Stewart@StewartRealty.com; Reed Stewart@reedstewart.com
Subject: Re: Our Parents

Trimble, you have to. It's very kind of Rhonda and the Bloomville Police Department to be doing this. You and Tony and your kids really should go, just for a little while, out of politeness. Marshall and I are going, with Reed and our kids. And of course we're going to bring your mom and dad.

Carly R. Stewart | Accountant | Stewart Realty | 801 South Moore Pike, Bloomville, IN 47401 | phone (812) 555-8722 | Please visit StewartRealty.com for all your realty needs

---

From: Trimble Stewart-Antonelli@Stewart&Stewart.com
Date: March 17 10:49:16 AM EST
To: Carly Stewart@StewartRealty.com; Marshall Stewart@StewartRealty
.com; Reed Stewart@reedstewart.com
Subject: Re: Our Parents

I told you, we have a previous engagement. Tony is being honored tonight at an award dinner by the Kiwanis.

And I'm really surprised you would subject Mommy and Daddy to something so tawdry. They've been under enough stress this week, don't you think? Mom just called me, weeping, because of all the things that horrible Flowers girl is making her throw out. I had to console her over the phone.

You really ought to be ashamed of yourselves.

Trimble Stewart-Antonelli
Attorney at Law
Stewart & Stewart, LLC
1911 South Moore Pike
Bloomville, IN 47401
(812) 555-9721
www.stewart&stewart.com

From: Marshall Stewart@StewartRealty.com
Date: March 17 10:55:08 AM EST
**To: Trimble Stewart-Antonelli@Stewart&Stewart.com; Carly Stewart@
StewartRealty.com; Reed Stewart@reedstewart.com**
Subject: Re: Our Parents

You can go to both, Trimble. You can go to the fundraiser, and then go to
the dinner.

Try to remember that as a business owner in this town, you have an image
to maintain.

From: Reed Stewart@reedstewart.com
Date: March 17 11:01:52 AM EST
**To: Trimble Stewart-Antonelli@Stewart&Stewart.com; Carly Stewart@
StewartRealty.com; Marshall Stewart@StewartRealty.com**
Subject: Re: Our parents

And that's interesting about the weepy call you just got from Connie,
Trimble, considering the fact that I'm sitting with her right now, and she's
calmly sorting through her cat figurines, deciding which ones are her
favorites. She's allowed to take twenty to the new condo I'm buying her.
The rest she's selling in the new Etsy store that Becky's sister, Nicole, is
setting up for her.

What time, exactly, was this alleged call you had with Connie?

From: Trimble Stewart-Antonelli@Stewart&Stewart.com
Date: March 17 11:04:28 AM EST
**To: Carly Stewart@StewartRealty.com; Marshall Stewart@StewartRealty
.com; Reed Stewart@reedstewart.com**
Subject: Re: Our Parents

Technically the call came last night after Carly brought Mom and Dad
home from dinner, and Daddy discovered that someone had removed all
of his newspapers.

Daddy was livid!

He's been saving those newspapers for years, and that ex-girlfriend of
yours had the nerve to throw them away like they were trash.

Trimble Stewart-Antonelli
Attorney at Law
Stewart & Stewart, LLC
1911 South Moore Pike
Bloomville, IN 47401
(812) 555-9721
www.stewart&stewart.com

From: Carly Stewart@StewartRealty.com
Date: March 17 10:45:27 AM EST
To: Trimble Stewart-Antonelli@Stewart&Stewart.com; Marshall
Stewart@StewartRealty.com; Reed Stewart@reedstewart.com
Subject: Re: Our Parents

Newspapers *are* trash, Trimble. Well, they're recycling, anyway, especially after they
become a few weeks old. Your dad should have let go of them a long time ago.

Did you point out to him that he has that iPad Marshall and I got him for
Christmas and he could have looked up any one of those newspapers on it,
and read all of the articles there? He has online subscriptions to all of them.

Carly R. Stewart | Accountant | Stewart Realty | 801 South Moore Pike, Bloomville, IN
47401 | phone (812) 555-8722 | Please visit StewartRealty.com for all your realty needs

---

From: Trimble Stewart-Antonelli@Stewart&Stewart.com
Date: March 17 11:04:28 AM EST
To: Carly Stewart@StewartRealty.com; Marshall Stewart@StewartRealty
.com; Reed Stewart@reedstewart.com
Subject: Re: Our Parents

No, I did not. I agreed with Mom that his rights had been violated. I was
too furious on his behalf.

Trimble Stewart-Antonelli
Attorney at Law
Stewart & Stewart, LLC
1911 South Moore Pike
Bloomville, IN 47401
(812) 555-9721
www.stewart&stewart.com

From: Reed Stewart@reedstewart.com
Date: March 17 11:07:12 AM EST
To: Trimble Stewart-Antonelli@Stewart&Stewart.com; Carly Stewart@ StewartRealty.com; Marshall Stewart@StewartRealty.com
Subject: Re: Our parents

I can tell. Is that why you came over here last night and pawed through all my carefully sorted boxes?

From: Trimble Stewart-Antonelli@Stewart&Stewart.com
Date: March 17 11:12:08 AM EST
To: Carly Stewart@StewartRealty.com; Marshall Stewart@StewartRealty .com; Reed Stewart@reedstewart.com
Subject: Re: Our Parents

Some of those things are mine! Mom and Dad promised them to me after they die. You have no right to sell them or donate them or whatever it is you think you're doing. I'm executor of their will, you know, not you.

Trimble Stewart-Antonelli
Attorney at Law
Stewart & Stewart, LLC
1911 South Moore Pike
Bloomville, IN 47401
(812) 555-9721
www.stewart&stewart.com

From: Reed Stewart@reedstewart.com
Date: March 17 11:16:33 AM EST
To: Trimble Stewart-Antonelli@Stewart&Stewart.com; Carly Stewart@ StewartRealty.com; Marshall Stewart@StewartRealty.com
Subject: Re: Our parents

Trimble, as a lawyer you of all people should know that people who are appointed estate executors are only supposed to handle the affairs of the deceased. Mom and Dad are broke, not dead.

We're getting rid of those things so we can pay off some of their debt and provide them with income and a new, safer place to live.

What we need to do now is get them to let us give one of us power of attorney. That way we can find out what happened to all their money.

Why is this so difficult for you to understand?

___

From: Trimble Stewart-Antonelli@Stewart&Stewart.com
Date: March 17 11:18:28 AM EST
To: Carly Stewart@StewartRealty.com; Marshall Stewart@StewartRealty
.com; Reed Stewart@reedstewart.com
Subject: Re: Our Parents

Wow, aren't you hoity-toity today? Who have you been speaking to about estate law? Your ex-girlfriend, I suppose.

Well, you don't need to worry about it, because like I said, Mom and Dad aren't broke. That's just that girl putting ideas into your head.

Trimble Stewart-Antonelli
Attorney at Law
Stewart & Stewart, LLC
1911 South Moore Pike
Bloomville, IN 47401
(812) 555-9721
www.stewart&stewart.com

___

From: Marshall Stewart@StewartRealty.com
Date: March 17 11:20:12 AM EST
To: Trimble Stewart-Antonelli@Stewart&Stewart.com; Reed Stewart@
reedstewart.com; Carly Stewart@StewartRealty.com;
Subject: Re: Our parents

No, Trimble, that was you. You're the one who found all their past due notices and told us, remember?

___

From: Reed Stewart@reedstewart.com
Date: March 17 11:22:11 AM EST
To: Trimble Stewart-Antonelli@Stewart&Stewart.com; Marshall
Stewart@StewartRealty.com; Carly Stewart@StewartRealty.com
Subject: Re: Our parents

Which I notice are missing from Dad's study this morning. Did you take them when you were here last night because you and Tony have decided you want to help out with Richard and Connie after all, Trimble?

From: Carly Stewart@StewartRealty.com
Date: March 17 11:25:07 AM EST
To: Marshall Stewart@StewartRealty.com; Reed Stewart@reedstewart.com
Subject: Re: Our Parents

Ha! Good one, Reed!

Carly R. Stewart | Accountant | Stewart Realty | 801 South Moore Pike, Bloomville, IN
47401 | phone (812) 555-8722 | Please visit StewartRealty.com for all your realty needs

---

From: Trimble Stewart-Antonelli@Stewart&Stewart.com
Date: March 17 11:28:28 AM EST
To: Carly Stewart@StewartRealty.com; Marshall Stewart@StewartRealty
.com; Reed Stewart@reedstewart.com
Subject: Re: Our Parents

Yes. After we got Mom's phone call, Tony said we had to do something. He
said it would be the right thing to do. So we took those bills to pitch in to help.

Trimble Stewart-Antonelli
Attorney at Law
Stewart & Stewart, LLC
1911 South Moore Pike
Bloomville, IN 47401
(812) 555-9721
www.stewart&stewart.com

From: Carly Stewart@StewartRealty.com
Date: March 17 11:31:12 AM EST
To: Marshall Stewart@StewartRealty.com; Reed Stewart@reedstewart.com
Subject: Re: Our Parents

Wait. What is happening??? Is Trimble turning over a new leaf?

Carly R. Stewart | Accountant | Stewart Realty | 801 South Moore Pike, Bloomville, IN
47401 | phone (812) 555-8722 | Please visit StewartRealty.com for all your realty needs

From: Marshall Stewart@StewartRealty.com
Date: March 17 11:35:27 AM EST
To: Trimble Stewart-Antonelli@Stewart&Stewart.com; Carly Stewart@
StewartRealty.com; Reed Stewart@reedstewart.com
Subject: Re: Our Parents

Wow. Thank you, Trimble. That's really kind of you and Tony.

From: Carly Stewart@StewartRealty.com
Date: March 17 11:37:24 AM EST
To: Marshall Stewart@StewartRealty.com; Reed Stewart@reedstewart.com
Subject: Re: Our Parents

What? No. Don'T THANK her. She's faking it!

Carly R. Stewart | Accountant | Stewart Realty | 801 South Moore Pike, Bloomville, IN
47401 | phone (812) 555-8722 | Please visit StewartRealty.com for all your realty needs

---

From: Trimble Stewart-Antonelli@Stewart&Stewart.com
Date: March 17 11:42:02 AM EST
To: Carly Stewart@StewartRealty.com; Marshall Stewart@StewartRealty
.com; Reed Stewart@reedstewart.com
Subject: Re: Our Parents

You're welcome. We all need to work together at a time like this.

Well, keep me posted on what you find out about who is spreading these
nasty rumors about Mommy and Daddy being broke. I'll talk to you later,
I guess.

Trimble Stewart-Antonelli
Attorney at Law
Stewart & Stewart, LLC
1911 South Moore Pike
Bloomville, IN 47401
(812) 555-9721
www.stewart&stewart.com

From: Carly Stewart@StewartRealty.com
Date: March 17 11:45:25 AM EST
To: Marshall Stewart@StewartRealty.com; Reed Stewart@reedstewart.com
Subject: Re: Our Parents

That did NOT just happen.

Carly R. Stewart | Accountant | Stewart Realty | 801 South Moore Pike, Bloomville, IN
47401 | phone (812) 555-8722 | Please visit StewartRealty.com for all your realty needs

From: Marshall Stewart@StewartRealty.com
Date: March 17 11:47:48 AM EST
To: Carly Stewart@StewartRealty.com; Reed Stewart@reedstewart.com
Subject: Re: Our Parents

Carly, my sister can be kind sometimes. She's not a witch out of a Disney
cartoon, however much you might like to pretend she is.

From: Carly Stewart@StewartRealty.com
Date: March 17 11:49:00 AM EST
To: Marshall Stewart@StewartRealty.com; Reed Stewart@reedstewart.com
Subject: Re: Our Parents

Oh, no! She's fine! She's great. Have I ever mentioned how much I love
your sister? She is just so charming and sweet and in no need of therapy.

Carly R. Stewart | Accountant | Stewart Realty | 801 South Moore Pike, Bloomville, IN
47401 | phone (812) 555-8722 | Please visit StewartRealty.com for all your realty needs

From: Reed Stewart@reedstewart.com
Date: March 17 11:52:11 AM EST
To: Carly Stewart@StewartRealty.com; Marshall Stewart@StewartRealty.com
Subject: Re: Our Parents

I have to go.

From: Carly Stewart@StewartRealty.com
Date: March 17 11:54:01 AM EST
To: Marshall Stewart@StewartRealty.com; Reed Stewart@reedstewart.com
Subject: Re: Our Parents

To therapy? Don't we all.

Carly R. Stewart | Accountant | Stewart Realty | 801 South Moore Pike, Bloomville, IN
47401 | phone (812) 555-8722 | Please visit StewartRealty.com for all your realty needs

---

From: Reed Stewart@reedstewart.com
Date: March 17 11:57:16 AM EST
To: Carly Stewart@StewartRealty.com; Marshall Stewart@StewartRealty.com
Subject: Re: Our Parents

No, I have to go. I just saw Becky's car pull up. Although for some reason
she hasn't gotten out of it.

She was here earlier, Connie said, then left when I got here—said she had
some kind of errand to run. Now she's back, but she's just sitting in her car.

We had a date last night, and it didn't go well. Maybe she's afraid to come
inside. Should I go out there?

From: Marshall Stewart@StewartRealty.com
Date: March 17 12:00:22 AM EST
To: Carly Stewart@StewartRealty.com; Reed Stewart@reedstewart.com
Subject: Re: Our Parents

Yes, Reed, a really good idea would be for you to go out there holding a
boom box over your head blaring Peter Gabriel and stare at her longingly.

From: Carly Stewart@StewartRealty.com
Date: March 17 12:00:27 PM EST
To: Marshall Stewart@StewartRealty.com; Reed Stewart@reedstewart.com
Subject: Re: Our Parents

Marshall, don't be so mean.

Reed, don't listen to him. I'm sure she's on her phone, or going over her
notes or something.

Tell me about your date. Why didn't it go well? What happened?

From: Reed Stewart@reedstewart.com
Date: March 17 12:02:26 PM EST
To: Carly Stewart@StewartRealty.com; Marshall Stewart@StewartRealty.com
Subject: Re: Our Parents

Nothing happened on our date. Nothing that I'm going to tell *you* guys about, anyway.

I think she's sitting there listening to music. I think it's . . . Beyoncé.

From: Marshall Stewart@StewartRealty.com
Date: March 17 12:03:22 PM EST
To: Carly Stewart@StewartRealty.com; Reed Stewart@reedstewart.com
Subject: Re: Our Parents

Oh, bro. You are so screwed.

From: Carly Stewart@StewartRealty.com
Date: March 17 12:05:54 PM EST
To: Marshall Stewart@StewartRealty.com; Reed Stewart@reedstewart.com
Subject: Re: Our Parents

Marshall, stop it!

Reed, I'm sure whatever happened last night isn't as awful as you think it is. Just talk to her.

From: Reed Stewart@reedstewart.com
Date: March 17 12:07:46 PM EST
To: Carly Stewart@StewartRealty.com; Marshall Stewart@StewartRealty.com
Subject: Re: Our Parents

Fine. I guess I can try.

Reed   12:25 PM
Hi.

Becky   12:25 PM
Hello.

Reed   12:25 PM
So, sorry about last night.

Becky   12:25 PM
You have nothing to apologize for. It was my fault.

Reed   12:25 PM
How was it your fault? You said you wanted to keep things professional and I got carried away. Although I think the moonlight had a little something to do with it.

Becky   12:26 PM
Funny, I was thinking it was the sake.

Reed   12:26 PM
There was a lot of that, too. In any case, it won't happen again. Unless of course you want it to.

Becky   12:26 PM
I think we can easily avoid it by staying away from moonlight and sake. This setting, for instance, does not lend itself to romance. What do you think happened in here? It was completely organized when I left last night.

Reed   12:26 PM

Oh, yeah, sorry about that. It was my sister, also known as Hurricane Trimble. Apparently Richard wasn't too happy at finding his newspapers gone when he got back from dinner, so he called her to complain.

She came over and decided to take what she thought she was owed by birthright, which it looks like included several of the fondue pots, an assortment of the monogrammed highball glasses, and quite a bit of the dining room furniture.

Becky   12:26 PM

How nice. She raided the storage units, too, I see.

Reed   12:26 PM

Apparently. And the Dumpsters. My sister is nothing if not thorough. I imagine she'll be coming by later for the chandelier.

Becky   12:26 PM

It's good to have things to look forward to. Your sister was always a very independent thinker.

Reed   12:26 PM

That's one way of putting it.

Becky   12:27 PM

So I hear congratulations are in order.

Reed   12:27 PM

Oh, you heard about the Lyrexica deal?

Becky   12:27 PM

I don't know what Lyrexica is. I meant about Shenanigans dropping the charges against your parents.

Reed   12:27 PM

Oh, right. Yes, that's good. We owe all that to your mother, I think.

Becky 12:27 PM

Oh, I don't know about that. But yes, when she gets fired up about a cause, she's always been very good at getting other people to champion it, and then organizing a solution.

Reed 12:27 PM

Like mother, like daughter.

Becky 12:27 PM

Stop it, you're making me blush.

I thought we agreed to be professional.

Reed 12:27 PM

Sorry. But it's true.

Becky 12:28 PM

My mom got something out of her little boycott, too. She sold about a million Blessie Sticks to the other protesters.

Reed 12:28 PM

What's a Blessie Stick?

Becky 12:28 PM

It's—never mind.

Are you going to the fundraiser tonight? She'll be selling them there, too.

Reed 12:28 PM

How could I miss the fundraiser to benefit my own parents? Marshall says we have to go, or our image in this town will be forever tarnished.

Becky 12:28 PM

I can see that you're smiling, and your parents think it's funny, too—but how do you really feel about it?

I know you. You must be mortified.

Reed   12:28 PM

It's going to get even more mortifying when the press gets hold of the story, and it's all over *PTI*.

Becky   12:28 PM

What's *PTI*?

Reed   12:29 PM

Pardon the Interruption. It's a sport show on—now YOU never mind.

You know what, it's fine. It's kind, what the people of this town are doing for my parents. I don't remember them being this kind when I lived here.

Becky   12:29 PM

Well, Bloomville may be a tiny town in the middle of nowhere, but it has its bright spots. One of them is the people who live here.

Reed   12:29 PM

I would definitely agree with that.

Becky   12:29 PM

If you're ever in a jam, they will be there to help you out.

Reed   12:29 PM

This is so true, it's making me wonder why I ever left.

Becky   12:29 PM

You mean besides the fact that your father kicked you out?

Reed   12:29 PM

Yes. But I'm starting to think I should have had more of a backbone about it, and fought harder to stay. I should have fought harder for a lot of things.

Becky   12:30 PM
I don't know about that. If you hadn't left, you wouldn't be who you are today.

Reed   12:30 PM
I'm not sure that would be such a bad thing.

Becky   12:30 PM
Fishing for compliments, are we?

Reed   12:30 PM
You caught me.

OK, let me put it another way: If I hadn't left, maybe YOU wouldn't have turned out to be who you are today—which is pretty great!

Becky   12:30 PM
That's more like it. Speaking of which, I thought today I'd use my greatness to tackle the master bedroom. There are going to be things in there I don't think you're going to want to see. So I suggest you stick with the office.

Reed   12:30 PM
What kind of things?

Becky   12:30 PM
What kind of things do YOU keep in YOUR bedroom?

Reed   12:30 PM
My parents do NOT have porn in their bedroom. And neither do I. You're only implying that to keep me away from you because you're hot for me and you know you can't resist my manly form.

Becky   12:30 PM
Actually, I can easily resist your manly form, and I did not mean porn at all. I meant things like adult diapers. A lot of seniors wear them. It's nothing to be ashamed of, but it often makes their children embarrassed when they find out. . . .

Reed   12:31 PM
Jesus Christ! I'll stay in the office with Dad.

Becky   12:31 PM
Aw, you wrote Dad.

Reed   12:31 PM
What?

Becky   12:31 PM
It's the first time you've called him Dad and not Richard or the Judge. Perhaps you're beginning to warm up to him again.

Reed   12:31 PM
I'm warming up to someone, but it isn't my dad.

Becky   12:31 PM
Inappropriate. You are banished. Good luck sorting through all that paperwork. It looks like Hurricane Trimble struck in the office, too.

Reed   12:32 PM
You don't deserve to have this now because you're being so unkind, but here, my niece Courtney made this for you.

Becky   12:32 PM
What are you talking about?

Reed   12:32 PM
I'm sending it as an attachment. Courtney was very impressed upon meeting you yesterday when Carly brought the girls over to pick up Grandma and Grandpa to take them for dinner—not knowing, of course, that it was all part of an elaborate scheme to deprive Grandpa of one of his great joys in life, his newspaper collection.

Anyway, when Courtney got home, she was apparently inspired to include you in an essay about her family that she was assigned to write. Carly was so amused by it that she scanned it so you could have a copy. I think it's A+ work, but you can decide for yourself. Enjoy.

My Family

By

Courtney Stewart

My family is made up of my mom, my dad, me, my sister Bailey, my youngest sister Taylor, and our dog, Blinky.

We all live in Bloomville, Indiana, USA, planet Earth, in a house on Rock Cliff Road, only there is no cliff there.

My sister Bailey is seven years old and likes to dress as Ant-Man or an Indian chief. My mom says Bailey just needs to get this out of her system and to ignore it.

My sister Taylor is 4 and likes princesses. My moms says she has to get this out of her system, too.

My aunt Trimble and Uncle Tony live in the same town only on a different street with my two cousins, Tony Jr. and Ty. Tony Jr. and Ty are teenagers and they go to a different school. They do not have any pets. My mom says Aunt Trimble says pets are dirty and have germs.

Mom says our dog Blinky is not dirty which I know is true because we give him a bath once a month.

My grandpa and grandma also live in my town except now they are moving to Florida because grandpa keeps falling down in the snow. My mom says one of these days he is going to break a hip.

My uncle Reed is visiting right now from California to help Grandma and Grandpa move. He is sleeping in my bed. He sings us funny songs about a big mouthed frog and also one about a cowboy named Joe. He showed us a movie about an alien until Mom came home and said it was too scary and to turn it off.

Uncle Reed hired a lady named Miss Flowers to help Grandma and Grandpa move. She brought a lot of big storage things to their house. Also Dumpsters. Mom said "Do not get in the Dumpsters" but Uncle Reed said it was OK and so Bailey got in one and found a shoe and Uncle Reed said she could keep it, so she did.

Uncle Reed says Miss Flowers helps people when they have too much stuff. My grandma and grandpa have so much stuff you can't even move around in their house and it makes my dad sad and sometimes mad, so he yells. Mom says he just needs to get this out of his system.

I'm glad Miss Flowers is now in our family. Uncle Reed says when she's done with her job, I'll be able to visit my grandma and grandpa in Florida and go swimming and see DISNEY WORLD. I can't WAIT!

Note from Uncle Reed: Uncle Reed talks about Miss Flowers a lot. That's because he can't get her out of his system.

online

Becky Flowers created chat "Reed Stewart"

Leeanne Matsumori   12:44
(No reply)

Leeanne Matsumori   12:44
(No reply)

Leeanne Matsumori   12:44
(No reply)

Becky Flowers   12:45
Ugh, you're not there! I know it's because you're somewhere over the Pacific right now, flying home, and won't get this for hours, if ever.

But I have to tell someone:

I love him.

I still love him, now more than ever.

And it's killing me!

He is killing me. Every time he says my name, or looks my way, every time he laughs, even if he's only telling one of his stupid jokes about his parents idiotic World's Greatest Grandparents mugs, he is taking my heart, pulling it from my chest, crumpling it into a little ball, and stuffing it into his pocket, as casually as if it were a napkin he'd used to wipe his mouth.

And it's killing me! He doesn't even know it.

But it's true.

And there's not a blessed thing I can do about it.

And when he leaves—because of course he's going to leave. Why would he stay here, of all places? Especially *now* when I told him there could never be anything between us—he'll take my heart away with him, exactly like he did before.

And just like before, I'll be left with nothing, *nothing*, no heart, no will to live, not even a pulse. I'll be like the Tin Man from *The Wizard of Oz*, with an empty metal shell where my heart was supposed to be that echoes emptily when anyone taps on it.

And I don't even care. I can't do anything about it. I can't stop it, or quit this job and walk away to protect myself, like I should, because I don't want to. That would mean being away from him, and I can't stand being away from him. That's how weak I am.

When he walks into the room, I lose my breath. When he asks, "What are we having for lunch?" all I can think is "You, you, *you*."

I try. I did try. I left this morning for an hour—I pretended to go to Home Depot for more packing tape, but really I just drove around, thinking, *What am I doing? Don't go back.*

But I went back, and sat in the car for five minutes listening to Beyoncé for strength before he came out of the house to ask me something, I don't even remember now what it was. When I saw his dark hair gleaming in the sunlight—why does his hair have to be so thick and dark and messy?—all I could think was, *I'm lost. I'm lost to him forever.*

What is wrong with me? I wasn't this bad before, and that was high school. We haven't even slept together this time, all we did was kiss, and when his hand accidentally brushed mine while we were stuffing packing paper into a box a few minutes ago, I thought every single one of my nerve endings was going to explode.

AND I HAVE A BOYFRIEND. WHO ISN'T HIM.

I've lost my soul to Reed Stewart, after I swore to myself that I wouldn't. Not again.

What am I going to do?

I even let him pick up Blarney Burgers from Shenanigans for his parents for lunch. For all of us. It's what the Judge and Connie wanted, and even though I'm fairly certain it's the worst thing for a man with a history of heart disease to eat, one glance into those pale blue eyes as he shrugged, as if to say, "Oh, well, sorry, they're my parents and they're old, what are you going to do?" and I caved.

That's how far I've sunk. I'm letting him kill his own parents with high sodium and saturated fats.

I'm doomed, Leeanne. Please come home soon and save me.

REED STEWART	2:20PM	72%
TODAY	ALL	MISSED

From: Lyle Stewart@FountainHill.org
Date: March 17 1:08:22 PM EST
To: Reed Stewart@reedstewart.com
Subject: Re: Her

My dearest boy, I must make this short as my *Phalaenopsis amabilis*
is currently being judged (and if I do say so myself is most likely to win
in multiple categories. This is not bragging, but simple truth. I don't
know what is wrong with today's gardeners. They seem to have lost any
common sense).

But I found your recent email most amusing. Not that I don't sympathize
with your plight—it is never pleasant to have one's romantic overtures
struck down.

The answer to your problem, however, is obvious. And yet you can't seem
to see it . . . or aren't yet ready.

Look over your past emails to me. You yourself wrote down the answer.

Perhaps when we are young, we are too blind to see what our own heart
most desires, even when it is directly in front of us. I sometimes wonder
why that is the case. Is it misplaced pride, or a desire to lead a more
exciting life than our ancestors before us?

In your case, I believe a part of you fears to take the road that fate has
laid out for you, perhaps because you feel it's only going to take you to a
dark and gloomy place—one you've visited many times before, and have
disliked since you were a child.

What you don't seem to realize, however, is that everyone's road is their
own, with its own individual twists and turns, that takes them to their own
destination. Your road isn't necessarily going to take you to that same dark
and gloomy place, even if, on the surface, it appears to. Your road could
lead you somewhere completely different . . . somewhere better than you
ever imagined.

Until you realize this, Reed, you will always be unhappy, and never achieve your ultimate goal.

That's all I can tell you.

They're calling us now to hand out the awards. I have faith you'll make the right decision. Eventually, you always seem to, though I must say you take your damned time about. Good luck.

Yours truly,
Uncle Lyle

From: Reed Stewart@reedstewart.com
Date: March 17 1:25:15 PM EST
To: Lyle Stewart@FountainHill.org
Subject: Re: Her

Dear Uncle Lyle,

Thanks for the email. I really appreciate it.

But if you thought it was at all helpful, or supposed to make sense to me, well, it wasn't, and it didn't. I have no idea what you're talking about. What road? What gloomy place?

Was that supposed to be some kind of weird Jedi stuff? Or Buddhist, or something?

Again, thanks for trying, though.

I do hope your flower wins.

Love,
Your Favorite Nephew,
Reed

BECKY FLOWERS	2:45PM	94%
TODAY	ALL	MISSED

From: Graham Tucker@AuthenticWineCheeseBoutique.com
Date: March 17 2:24:11 AM EST
To: Becky@MovingUp.com
Subject: You

Dear Becky,

Hi, just checking that everything is okay! I haven't heard from you at all in a couple of days. I know you have that new job (your sister told me) so you've been busy.

But I was wondering if I'm going to see you tonight? We're having a pretty exciting tasting at the boutique. We've got some Irish cheddars that will blow you away. I know how much my girl loves her cheeses.

I'm just hoping she still loves me?

XOXO
Graham

Visit Authentic for the most AUTHENTIC taste sensation
you've ever experienced!
Authentic—Bloomville Courthouse Square—Bloomville, Indiana

From: Becky@MovingUp.com
Date: March 17 2:35:19 AM EST
To: Graham Tucker@AuthenticWineCheeseBoutique.com
Subject: You

Hi, Graham. I'm sorry I've been so distant lately. Like Nicole said, this new job really has got me burning the candle at both ends.

I don't think I'm going to make it to Authentic tonight. I really should attend the fundraiser for the Stewarts over at the high school.

I'd ask you come with me, but I know you have your own celebration to throw.

And truthfully, Graham, I've been doing a lot of thinking lately, and I'm not sure right now is the best time for me to be seeing anyone romantically. I seem to be going through some kind of quarter-century crisis. I think I need to spend some time with myself before I can commit to a romantic partner.

I'm sorry to tell you this in an email, but I thought it was better that you heard it now than wait until I could tell you in person, since I know you think it was something you did, and it absolutely was not.

Everyone jokes about the "It's not you, it's me" thing, but in this case, it *absolutely* has nothing to do with you. I really do need to take some time off to get to know me better, and I wouldn't dream of asking you to wait, since I know you want to start a family, and that's not a plan you should put on hold.

I hope you understand and that we can still be friends. I wish you the best.

Becky
Becky Flowers, CSMM
Moving Up! Consulting LLC, President

Sent from my handheld device, please excuse typos

From: Graham Tucker@AuthenticWineCheeseBoutique.com
Date: March 17 2:45:23 AM EST
To: Becky@MovingUp.com
Subject: You

Dear Becky,

Of course I understand. I'm sad to hear it, because I thought we got along and would have made a great team.

But I absolutely wish you the best as well, and am glad you were so honest with me (I wouldn't have expected anything less, since your integrity is one of the qualities that attracted me to you in the first place).

I'm actually quite relieved to receive this because I'd been hearing rumors (it's a small town, as you know) that an ex-boyfriend of yours was back, and that you were working for his parents, and I'd begun to worry that

that was why I hadn't heard from you in so long—that the two of you had gotten back together, or something.

I should have known that that wasn't the case. You're not that kind of girl!

Glad we can still be friends, at least. There'll always be an ergonomically designed stool for you at Authentic ;-)

Graham

Visit Authentic for the most AUTHENTIC taste sensation
you've ever experienced!
Authentic—Bloomville Courthouse Square—Bloomville, Indiana

Becky Flowers created chat "Reed Stewart"

Leeanne Matsumori	15:04
(No reply)	

Leeanne Matsumori	15:04
(No reply)	

Leeanne Matsumori	15:05
(No reply)	

Leeanne Matsumori	15:06
(No reply)	

Becky Flowers   15:06
Just kill me. Please. I'm begging you.

Becky Flowers   15:07
Okay, not really.

But if a small earthquake occurred right now and knocked the weather vane off the top of the courthouse and it landed on my head and knocked me unconscious for the next twenty-four hours, I would not mind, so long as there was no permanent damage.

To my head, not the weather vane.

REED STEWART	3:45PM	63%
TODAY	ALL	MISSED

Enrique Alvarez   3:12 PM EST
Just checking in to see if you got those photos I sent. What do you think?

Reed Stewart   3:12 PM EST
It's perfect. Richard and Connie love it.

Enrique Alvarez   3:12 PM EST
Who the hell are Richard and Connie?

Reed Stewart   3:12 PM EST
My parents, genius.

Enrique Alvarez   3:12 PM EST
You call your parents by their first names? What kind of disrespect is that?

Reed Stewart   3:12 PM EST
The kind my dad deserves. Hey, your advice about women sucks, by the way. SHE Big Bertha'd ME.

Enrique Alvarez   3:12 PM EST
Why, what did you do to her?

Reed Stewart   3:12 PM EST
Nothing. Showed her an amazingly romantic evening and then kissed her good night in the moonlight.

Enrique Alvarez   3:13 PM EST
What is your problem, man? That is the direct opposite of what I told you to do.

Reed Stewart   3:13 PM EST

How is that the opposite of what you told me to do? You told me to Big Bertha the problem.

Enrique Alvarez   3:13 PM EST

When I said to Big Bertha her, I meant show her the man you've become as opposed to the boy you were when she last saw you, boudro.

A man who cares about the things she cares about.

A man of sophistication and worldly charm.

I didn't mean a man who goes around taking advantage of vulnerable small town businesswomen by chowing down on them the way a monkey chows down on bananas.

Reed Stewart   3:13 PM EST

Thanks, Alvarez. You really know how to make a guy's day.

How the hell am I going to get back together with her if she won't go out with me?

Enrique Alvarez   3:13 PM EST

What do you mean get back together with her? I thought you meant sleep with her.

Reed Stewart   3:13 PM EST

Sure, yes, of course that's what I mean.

Enrique Alvarez   3:13 PM EST

Oh good cuz for a second there I thought you meant have an actual real relationship with a woman that lasts longer than 3 months.

Reed Stewart   3:13 PM EST

Well, I mean, I feel like with Becky it could be something more. I don't know.

Enrique Alvarez   3:13 PM EST
You don't know.

Is one of the things you don't know how a relationship with her is supposed to work if she lives in Indiana and you live in LA?

Reed Stewart   3:14 PM EST
I don't know. Maybe.

Enrique Alvarez   3:14 PM EST
Maybe that's one of the things she doesn't know either. Maybe that's why she Big Bertha'd you.

Reed Stewart   3:14 PM EST
Yeah, but we could work out the long-distance thing.

Enrique Alvarez   3:14 PM EST
How? With her business and you on the circuit?

Reed Stewart   3:14 PM EST
People do it.

Enrique Alvarez   3:15 PM EST
What people? Are you talking about Cutler? Have you seen the news about Cutler lately?

Reed Stewart   3:15 PM EST
Yeah, well, I'm not Cutler.

Enrique Alvarez   3:15 PM EST
Yes, I am aware of that. If you were, I'd be making more money.

Reed Stewart   3:15 PM EST
Ow. Really, Alvarez? Kick a man when he's down, why don't you.

Enrique Alvarez   3:15 PM EST
I think I see now why the young lady objects to you.

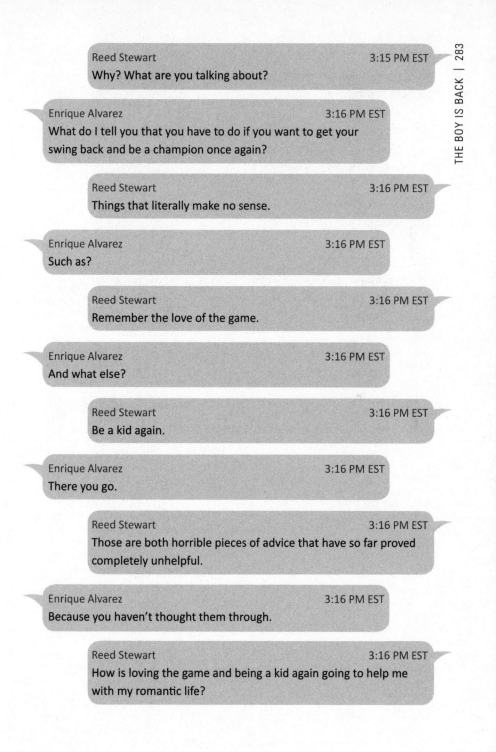

Reed Stewart — 3:15 PM EST
Why? What are you talking about?

Enrique Alvarez — 3:16 PM EST
What do I tell you that you have to do if you want to get your swing back and be a champion once again?

Reed Stewart — 3:16 PM EST
Things that literally make no sense.

Enrique Alvarez — 3:16 PM EST
Such as?

Reed Stewart — 3:16 PM EST
Remember the love of the game.

Enrique Alvarez — 3:16 PM EST
And what else?

Reed Stewart — 3:16 PM EST
Be a kid again.

Enrique Alvarez — 3:16 PM EST
There you go.

Reed Stewart — 3:16 PM EST
Those are both horrible pieces of advice that have so far proved completely unhelpful.

Enrique Alvarez — 3:16 PM EST
Because you haven't thought them through.

Reed Stewart — 3:16 PM EST
How is loving the game and being a kid again going to help me with my romantic life?

Enrique Alvarez   3:16 PM EST

You'll figure it out. Or you won't. And you'll keep losing at both love and sports.

Reed Stewart   3:16 PM EST

Alvarez, are you drunk? Oh my God, you are. You're drunk with Cutler's caddy, aren't you?

Enrique Alvarez   3:16 PM EST

Erin go Bragh.

Reed Stewart   3:16 PM EST

I forgot. It's St. Patrick's Day. You guys are at the United Kingdom Pavilion at Epcot drinking green beer. Hilarious, Alvarez. Just hilarious.

Reed Stewart   3:16 PM EST

Alvarez?

Reed Stewart   3:17 PM EST

You better not be using the expense account.

BECKY FLOWERS	3:45PM	98%
TODAY	ALL	MISSED

Nicole F — 3:28 PM
Holy crap, did you just break up with the lumbersexual?

Becky F — 3:28 PM
How . . . ?????

Nicole F — 3:28 PM
Henry just ran into the lumbersexual at Kroger and he told him.

Becky F — 3:28 PM
Why is Henry at Kroger in the middle of a workday?

Nicole F — 3:28 PM
He got a call there. It's St Patrick's Day. Two drunk idiots are fighting over a pound of bacon.

Tell me what is going on with you and the lumbersexual.

Becky F — 3:28 PM
Nothing is going on. I'm just not ready to be in a committed relationship right now.

Nicole F — 3:29 PM
OMG. Then it's true? You're really broken up?

And you say it's because YOU are not ready to be in a committed relationship anymore?

Do you realize this is like the pope quitting his job because he's decided he's an atheist?

Becky F — 3:29 PM
Nicole, could you please stop? How is Mrs. Stewart's Etsy store going?

Nicole F   3:29 PM

Great. I've got an auctioneer lined up to come next week to take a look at the Judge's gavels, too. Ha, I wrote "the Judge's gavels." But whatever.

Did you break up with the lumbersexual because of Reed? Tell me the truth.

Becky F   3:29 PM

I don't have time for this, Nicole. Animal control is coming over in a few minutes to trap the raccoon and I need to emotionally prepare Mrs. Stewart. She's grown very close to Ricky.

Nicole F   3:29 PM

She's not the only one who's grown very close to someone in that house. You and Reed were spotted together last night, you know.

Becky F   3:29 PM

So? I don't deny that we were together last night. We had dinner at Matsumori's. We spent the whole time talking about his parents. I used the gold AmEx because I intend to write it off as a business expense.

Nicole F   3:29 PM

No, you didn't, because I checked the file as soon as I heard and there's no receipt in there. He paid, didn't he? So you DIDN'T only talk about business, which is why you felt too guilty to charge it to the business AmEx, AND why you let him pay. I know you.

And then you let him kiss you.

Becky F   3:30 PM

I did not.

Nicole F   3:30 PM

Yes, you did, because Henry's sister's boyfriend's cousin plays pool at Stick and Stein every night with one of the waiters at Matsumori's, and he said the waiter said he saw you kissing Reed Stewart in the parking lot after his shift last night.

Becky F   3:30 PM

God, this town is WAY too small.

Anyway, whatever. It was a good-night kiss before we got into our cars.

Nicole F   3:30 PM

Right. Because we kiss all our clients' good-looking pro golfer sons goodnight before we leave for the day. And then the next day, we break up with our longtime boyfriends.

Becky F   3:31 PM

I'm not texting with you about this. I'll talk to you about it later, when we get home. Maybe.

Nicole F   3:31 PM

You bet you will. And I want details. Like where the wedding is going to be. And am I going to be maid-of-honor, or Leeanne?

I think I should be, because Leeanne doesn't even live here anymore.

Becky F   3:32 PM

It's not like that, Nic. Reed Stewart and I are not back together. And please don't tell people that we are.

Nicole F   3:32 PM

Sure, I won't. I get the basement apartment when you move out.

Becky F   3:32 PM

I'm not going anywhere, Nicole. I can assure you.

Nicole F   3:32 PM

I think you'll like it in LA. I mean, I hear it's smoggy, but they probably need senior moving consultants there, too. I genuinely think they force people to move away from there as soon as they hit 50.

Maybe even thirty.

Becky F   3:33 PM

You're not funny. Or right about any of this. It's sad how wrong you are, as a matter of fact.

Nicole F   3:33 PM

I was right about the lumbersexual being all wrong for you. I'm right about this, too.

Oh, Mom wants to know: What time are you meeting her to go to the Stewart fundraiser?

Becky F   3:34 PM

I'll meet her there at 5:15. And tell her no, I won't take any Blessie Sticks in my car.

Nicole F   3:34 PM

Good luck with that.

Goodbye, Mrs. Reed Stewart.

Becky F   3:34 PM

You're not funny.

Reed — 5:15 PM

Hey, it's me. I'm here. Where are you? I don't see you guys.

Marshall — 5:15 PM

We're by the bouncy castle, Reed. Where else? I have small daughters. My whole life is about bouncy castles and will be for the next foreseeable decade.

Reed — 5:15 PM

Well, excuse me. It could easily have been the face painting or ice cream.

Marshall — 5:15 PM

Bouncy castle, Reed. I see bouncy castles when I close my eyes to sleep at night.

Reed — 5:15 PM

I will join you momentarily. I have spied a distraction.

Marshall — 5:15 PM

You spent ALL DAY WITH HER. Give the poor girl time to miss you.

Reed — 5:15 PM

I meant Rhonda's baked chicken. Oh, and Rhonda. I'm going over to say hi.

And also ask her how she found out about Richard and Connie losing all their scratch.

Marshall   5:15 PM

Stop talking about them as if they were characters out of the movie *Barfly*.

And Carly is insisting we be seen eating together as a family. Do not fill up on chicken without us.

Reed   5:15 PM

Do you not remember how much of Rhonda's chicken I can consume?

Marshall   5:15 PM

Oh, right. Please save some for the rest of us.

And don't abandon me to the bouncy castle!

BECKY FLOWERS	5:45PM	85%
TODAY	ALL	MISSED

Becky F   5:28 PM
Where are you?

Nicole F   5:28 PM
I'm getting my face painted. What should I be, Ninja Warrior Fairy Princess or Unicorn Dragon Lady?

Becky F   5:28 PM
Neither. You should come help me at Mom's Blessie Stick booth. We're under siege.

Nicole F   5:28 PM
I thought you said you weren't going to let her put any sticks in your car.

Becky F   5:28 PM
I didn't. I got here and the booth is right as you walk in and she was being flooded by customers. How could you not have seen it?

Nicole F   5:28 PM
Maybe I did and ran to the face-painting booth to acquire my disguise.

Becky F   5:28 PM
It's not that bad. All the proceeds are going to the Stewarts.

Nicole F   5:29 PM
It's still pretty embarrassing.

Becky F   5:29 PM

That your mother, a widow, is making a small fortune off something she invented, handcrafts, and promotes herself? Now who's embarrassing?

Stop being such a little baby and get over here. I haven't had anything to eat since lunch.

Nicole F   5:29 PM

Fine, you're right. I'm coming.

But take my advice and don't go near the baked chicken.

Becky F   5:30 PM

Why, what's wrong with it?

Nicole F   5:30 PM

Nothing, it's amazing.

I just wouldn't go near the table where it's being served right now if you want to avoid a certain ex-boyfriend of yours.

Becky F   5:30 PM

Graham is here? That's so weird, I thought he'd be at the boutique all night.

Nicole F   5:31 PM

No, your OTHER ex-boyfriend.

Wow, your life sure has gotten complicated lately.

But funny how it's the lumbersexual your mind jumped to first when I typed "avoid."

I think I just figured out why you dumped him. That kiss last night in the parking lot was more than a friendly good-night peck after all, wasn't it????

Becky F 5:31 PM
You should have gotten your face painted like a jackass because that's what you are.

Nicole F 5:31 PM
Oh ha ha, burn. Whatevs.

At least my ex-boyfriend from high school isn't walking towards me RIGHT NOW holding a plate of cherry pie.

You know, you two look good together.

So why are you blushing so much?

Reed 5:33 PM
Hi.

Becky 5:33 PM
Hi.

Reed 5:33 PM
It's really loud in here.

Becky 5:33 PM
Yes. Harrison and the Fords make up for their lack of talent with their enthusiasm.

Reed 5:33 PM
I don't think my dad approves.

Becky 5:33 PM
No. He's frowning. But your mom looks happy.

Reed 5:33 PM
She looks like she's waiting for my dad to ask her to dance. Which she probably is. I think they met in this gymnasium forty-something years ago. Or so the story goes.

Becky   5:33 PM

I think that's sweet.

Reed   5:33 PM

I guess. We look like idiots, standing here texting. Well, not you. You look amazing, as always.

Becky   5:34 PM

Thanks. I actually came over here for some chicken.

Reed   5:34 PM

Me, too. And to talk to Rhonda about how she knows my parents are broke. But she seems swamped. The closest I could get is some pie. Would you like some?

Becky   5:34 PM

Are you asking if I'd like to share your pie, Reed Stewart?

Reed   5:34 PM

Are you flirting with me, Becky Flowers?

Becky   5:34 PM

Absolutely not.

Reed   5:34 PM

You're blushing. Sorry. Listen, I know this is weird, but would you like to go outside and—

Transcript of Interview with REED STEWART by Christina Martinez, Bloomville Herald

CHRISTINA:

Hi, sorry to interrupt, you two, but I'm Christina Martinez with the *Bloomville Herald*, and we've been dying for an interview with pro golfer Reed Stewart, Bloomville's own pride and joy.

Reed, this interview is being recorded using the new WriteOn device that automatically transcribes voices into text to make transcription on the go even easier. Is that all right with you?

REED:

Uh, not really. I actually don't have time for an interview right now, I'm just here to enjoy—

CHRISTINA:

Great!

So what is it that brought you to Bloomville a week before what some are calling the most important tournament of your life, after not having won a game in over two years, and your frankly embarrassing losses at Augusta and Doral? Shouldn't you be hitting the gym—or the greens—in Orlando in preparation for next week's Golden Palm?

REED:

I'm sorry, it's really loud in here. I can't hear you.

CHRISTINA:

Sorry, I'll speak up.

Is it love for your parents, Reed? A lot of people are saying it's because you love your parents that you are here in Bloomville at this crucial time in your career.

REED:

I guess you could say that.

Look, even though we're really grateful and appreciative to all the people here in Bloomville who came out this evening to show their support for my parents, they actually do not need financial help, so—

CHRISTINA:

Right, because the charges against them were dropped by Shenanigans International, Inc., which must have been a relief
to you, right, Reed? How much of a distraction has all of
this business with your parents been, Reed, going into the
Golden Palm, which some are saying is the most important
tournament of your golf career?

REED:

Um, it hasn't been a distraction as much as it's been a misunderstanding.

I'm just real glad it's cleared up now, and my parents are
doing great, and I'm going to get onto the course next week
and hit the ball like I always do. I've been working real
hard on my swing and my wedge play—

CHRISTINA:

And just what kind of advantage, if any, has growing up in
a town like Bloomville given you over other professional
athletes in your field?

REED:

Uh, well, I guess . . . the people. The people of Bloomville
are unlike any others in the world. They're so warm and giving and kind and beautiful and . . .

CHRISTINA:

I see that you're directing your remarks at one particular
citizen of Bloomville. May I have your name, miss?

BECKY:

Oh, no, he was kidding.

REED:

Rebecca Flowers. And I'm not kidding. I owe everything to
her. We went to high school together. This high school. We
both graduated from here ten years ago.

BECKY:

He's joking. I mean we did go here, but he's joking about
owing everything to me. He practiced very hard to get to
where he is today.

REED:

Well, she drove the golf cart.

BECKY:

Reed.

He's still kidding. I didn't. Well, I did occasionally, but his success has nothing to do with—

CHRISTINA:

You're Becky Flowers, aren't you? President of Moving Up! Senior Move Management Consultants? We did a piece on you last summer.

BECKY:

Yes, but please don't mention me in—

REED:

You should. You *should* mention her. Not the thing about the golf cart though. That was a joke.

CHRISTINA:

You two dated in high school. Several people here tonight have already pointed that out to me.

BECKY:

Oh, crap. I mean, sorry. Please don't—can you erase that?

CHRISTINA:

No. I don't think so. This device is new, we just got them, I actually don't know how it works. So, are you two getting back together?

BECKY:

I beg your pardon?

CHRISTINA:

You know, rekindling the flame of your high school romance?

BECKY:

What? No!

REED:

Yes. Ow. Did you see that, Christina? She hit me. Can your voice thingy transcribe that?

CHRISTINA:

Okay, I'll disregard the personal stuff. But off the record, seriously, how would that even work? Becky, are you considering moving from Bloomville? Because small towns like this can't afford to lose any more businesses, especially ones offering vitally needed services like yours. Although I would understand it. Running a business in this economic climate isn't easy, and frankly, this town—

(INAUDIBLE)

Oops. I shouldn't have said that. How do you rewind this stupid thing?

BECKY:

Um, no, Christina, Moving Up! isn't going anywhere at the moment, and neither am I. I'm dedicated to growing my client base, and I have family here. I've lived here since I was a kid, and it's the place I love best in all the world.

CHRISTINA:

Really?

REED:

Yeah, really? How do you know? You haven't been anywhere else, really.

BECKY:

Uh, I know I want to spend the rest of my life where my family is.

REED:

But you'd be open to traveling to other places, right?

BECKY:

I guess. On a short-term basis.

REED:

How short? Because in order to qualify for exemption from personal income tax in the state of Florida, you have to live there six months and a day.

BECKY:

What are you talking about?

CHRISTINA:

Is that true? Because I've been offered a job in Florida, and I'm probably going to take it to get away from—

Oh, hold that thought, Reed. It looks like Judge Stewart is climbing to the stage and appears to be preparing to make a speech to his supporters. Rob, could you get a photo? Rob? Rob, seriously, I know it's impossible for you to concentrate even for one second on your job, but could you actually—

(INAUDIBLE)

REED:

Really? So you're never going to leave Bloomville?

BECKY:

I didn't say that. I said I had no plans to leave *for the moment*. What's all this business about Florida?

REED:

My financial advisor said it would be more tax advantageous to live there than California or, for instance, Indiana.

And, like you told my parents, just because you live in one state doesn't mean you can't visit your family back home.

BECKY:

Oh, what a revelation. So could you, but this is the first time in a decade you ever have.

REED:

Not everyone is like me.

BECKY:

Thank God.

REED:

What was that?

BECKY:

Nothing.

CHRISTINA:

You do realize that this device is picking up everything you two are saying, don't you?

                            BECKY:
Oh, sorry.

                          CHRISTINA:
It's fine by me. I just thought you should know. Oh, look,
the Judge is speaking.
    (Applause)

                        JUDGE STEWART:
Thank you, thank you. Mrs. Stewart and I just wanted to take
a moment to say how much we appreciate everything you people
have done for us this past week. Why, if it wasn't for all
of you, it's likely we two would be sitting in the pokey like
a couple of jailbirds.
    (Laughter)

                        JUDGE STEWART:
I especially want to thank Mrs. Beverly Flowers for all
her work on our behalf getting that restaurant to drop the
charges.
    (Applause)

                        JUDGE STEWART:
Guess Connie and I should stay home and order pizza delivery
for a while to keep ourselves out of trouble.
    (Laughter)

                        JUDGE STEWART:
Now I want to address why we're all here tonight. It was
nice—real nice—of Rhonda Jenkins to organize all this for
us. She's a kind woman, and an even better friend. I don't
think we could ask for a better one.
    (Applause, indistinct chatter)

                        JUDGE STEWART:
But the fact is, Mrs. Stewart and I are doing just fine
financially. It's true we've had a couple of little misun-
derstandings with the government about our taxes, but who
hasn't in this day and age?
    (Laughter)

JUDGE STEWART:

And it's true the old house may not look as good as it once did. But Mrs. Stewart and I don't either.

    (Laughter)

JUDGE STEWART:

Why, I remember one of the best days in my life was right here in this gymnasium—forty-eight years ago, it was, and this place was brand-new. It was the first time I ever set eyes on a girl named Connie Duncan, and she was wearing something that was considered a pretty risqué style back then—a miniskirt.

    (Laughter)

JUDGE STEWART:

I knew then that I was sunk—even though, some of you will recall, I'd just been elected Chug-a-Lug Champ of the Hi-jinks Club.

REED:

What is he talking about?

BECKY:

You don't know?

REED:

No. Do you?

BECKY:

No. But I'm loving it.

CHRISTINA:

Shhh, you two!

JUDGE STEWART:

I'll leave it up to your imagination as to what one had to do in order to be elected to a position of such high authority, but suffice it to say, I was already a little unsteady on my feet. I had attained my champion crown earlier that day at a picnic lunch over at Lake Bloomville.

And suddenly in walked this vision with the longest legs—and the shortest skirt—I had ever seen.

Well, it wasn't only my heart I lost that day. I lost my

head, too. In fact, I keeled right over onto that shiny new floor . . . BAM!

(Clapping noise. Laughter)

And when I woke up, who should be tenderly cradling my head, but the very same angel who'd knocked me unconscious with her beauty in the first place, Miss Connie Duncan.

And I knew right then that I'd be resigning my position in the Hijinks Club, and walking the straight and narrow from that day forward, with Connie Duncan at my side . . . if she'd have me, which luckily for me, she agreed to—after I pulled myself up, literally, from the floor.

(Laughter)

REED:

I can't believe this.

BECKY:

You never heard this story before?

REED:

No. Have you?

BECKY:

Oh, hundreds of times. He showed me his Chug-a-Lug Champion medal.

REED:

He did?

BECKY:

No! Of course not.

CHRISTINA:

Would you two mind? Some of us are trying to listen.

JUDGE STEWART:

So at the request of Miss Connie Duncan, who—besides getting suspended from school that day for wearing such a daringly short skirt—took a chance on a boy who also got suspended from school that day, for showing up to a pep rally a little bit drunk . . . on love, of course—

(Laughter)

Kids! You see? Even your most esteemed elders have made mistakes.

But Miss Duncan took a chance on a boy who didn't deserve one, and stuck by him through some very bad times, then provided him with some very, very good ones, including three children of whom I could not be more proud, some of whom have now given me five grandchildren, of whom I'm prouder still.

(Applause)

So I would like to ask, at her request, that all the proceeds from tonight be donated not to us, but a far more deserving organization: the Bloomville Society for Prevention of Cruelty to Animals.

(Gasps, applause, cheers)

                    BECKY:
Oh, my God, Reed. That was so sweet! Your parents are the most—

                    REED:
Yes. Yes, they are, aren't they?

                    BECKY:
And you didn't know any of this?

                    REED:
I had no idea. He's never told that story before.

                    BECKY:
Your dad's the Chug-a-Lug Champ of the Hijinks Club. And your mom got suspended for dressing too sexy!

                    REED:
Kind of makes you think, don't it?

                    BECKY:
Well, I guess . . . I don't know. About what?

                    REED:
Roads.

                    BECKY:
Roads? What road?

                    REED:
The ones that don't have to lead to the same place.

BECKY:

I have no idea what you're talking about. Do you mean the road less traveled, from the Frost poem?

REED:

I mean the opposite.

CHRISTINA:

Reed, do you have any comment on your father's speech just now? As you can probably tell from the reaction of the crowd, they loved it. He really is an extraordinary man. Did you know he was the Chug-a-Lug Champ of the Hijinks Club?

REED:

No.

CHRISTINA:

How did hearing that make you feel?

REED:

I've never been more proud of him.

CHRISTINA:

Really? Are you more proud of him today than when he allowed the Dumbbell Killer to go free?

REED:

Yes. Dad's always been a real class act, but I never thought of him as . . . well, tonight he seemed actually *human*.

CHRISTINA:

I'm not sure I get your meaning.

REED:

Oh, look, there's Rhonda waving to me. I'm going to go over there and say hi. Look, I'll be right back. Don't go anywhere, okay?

CHRISTINA:

Sure. I have plenty more questions—

REED:

Sorry, I didn't mean you, I meant Becky. Can you wait for me here? I have something I want to talk to you about. I think you and I—I think we've been misreading each other.

BECKY:

I don't think so. But okay, fine. I'll wait.

REED:

Good. I'll just be a minute. Christina, end of interview, okay? Maybe another time.

CHRISTINA:

I'm gonna hold you to that.

BECKY:

Sorry. He hasn't seen Mrs. Jenkins in a really long time.

CHRISTINA:

I get it. Let me just finish up here. Well, that was Reed Stewart and Becky Flowers, who are definitely not back together.

So, Becky, let me ask *you* a question. If I was going to move the contents of a small apartment—say a one-bedroom—from here to Miami, how much would you charge me?

BECKY:

I'm sorry, we're not that kind of moving company. I can refer you—

CHRISTINA:

See, I got this job offer in Miami, and I'm not sure if I should take it.

BECKY:

Right. But the thing is, we specialize in managing moves for senior citizens, and you're not a senior, so—

CHRISTINA:

I'm not even sure if I should take the job. It's only free-lance, so there wouldn't be any benefits. You have no idea how hard it is to find decently paying jobs in journalism these days.

On the other hand, it's Miami, you know? So I'd get away from *this* dump. You hear what I'm saying?

BECKY:

Um, I guess. But like I said, we don't—

CHRISTINA:

Then again, what if I got sick? Paying for your own health insurance blows. It's so expensive. And so is rent in Miami.

BECKY:

I hear you. But—

CHRISTINA:

But there are a lot of important stories out there that I could be writing about instead of the crap they make me write about here. I mean, look at me, I'm here covering this stupid thing, when I could be in Miami covering, I don't know, a story on how the glaciers are melting and in ten years the whole place is going to be underwater. You know?

BECKY:

Well, I agree, stories on the environment are important.

CHRISTINA:

Sorry. I mean, stories about pro golfers are interesting, I guess, to some people. But the damn *Herald* only wants me to do local stories, stuff that makes Bloomville look like a positive place to live and raise your children. Like this thing tonight. Tomorrow I'm supposed to cover some book signing at Bloomville Books. A local author, of course. If I don't blow my own head off first.

BECKY:

Well, I mean, local stuff is important, too. To the people who live here.

CHRISTINA:

Yeah, I guess. Rob. Did you get a photo of the judge? Rob? Did you? Or did you spend the whole night taking shots of Tiffany Gosling? What do we need more shots of Tiffany for, Rob? The Shenanigans story is over. How many damned shots of Tiffany do we need?

ROB:

Oh my God, will you get off my back, Christina? It was *one* time!

REED:

Wow. What was that all about?

BECKY:

I have no idea. But it seemed very dramatic.

REED:

Well, anyway. Sorry I was gone so long. You're never going to believe this. I asked Rhonda where she heard that my parents were broke, and she said she's known forever and thought we—me and Marshall—knew, too.

When I said I had no idea until this week, she was shocked. She was, too. You could tell.

BECKY:

Maybe we should step outside, Reed. You don't look so good—

REED:

It all seemed so absurdly obvious once she said it, I felt like a fool for not having put it all together.

Trimble. It's Trimble.

BECKY:

What about Trimble?

REED:

It's her. It's Trimble.

Rhonda says when she was working for my parents, Trimble was always coming around, asking them for money. Rhonda figured we all knew, because it was such a casual thing.

And I mean, I guess in a way we all did kind of know— I know my dad gave Trimble the practice.

BECKY:

What do you mean, he gave her the practice?

REED:

When he retired and started the private practice, he bought the building in Trimble's name.

But that was to be expected because she's the only one of us who did what he wanted and followed in his footsteps and went into law.

Mom and Dad were always helping Trimble out financially because she married such a bonehead—Tony—we call him Too Bad Tony because he makes such bad decisions, and couldn't get a job and was always investing in these dumb business schemes.

BECKY:

Reed, what are you—

REED:

I know they gave her the down payment for her house and probably helped her out financially in other ways, too. That's
why Carly and Marshall came to me for help with their down
payment. They couldn't bear to hit up Mom and Dad for a loan
after they knew how much they'd shelled out to Trimble.

But none of us had any idea—

BECKY:

Are you saying—?

REED:

Exactly. Rhonda says every other week Trimble would come
by to wheedle them for other stuff, too. Tuition for her
kids' private school. Money for their braces. Rhonda says
Trimble even hit up the Judge for the monthly lease on Too
Bad Tony's Audi.

BECKY:

Reed. Wait.

REED:

But get this. My parents are the ones who paid for the restaurant. They bought the restaurant for Tony, not his parents, like we were always told.

And they just bought him a new restaurant, the one up in
Dearborn.

For all we know, my parents paid for the ski trip my sister and her family took to Aspen this winter, too!

BECKY:

Reed, you're shaking.

REED:

Wouldn't you be? *This* is where my parents' retirement savings went—I mean, in addition to the stamps and ceramic cats
and judges' gavels. It all went to my *sister*.

BECKY:

Reed. Oh, Reed. I'm so sorry. Come on. Let's go. People are—

REED:

Yeah, damned right we're going to go. Go get the police and have Trimble arrested for that thing you were talking about— elder abuse.

BECKY:

No, Reed. We can't.

REED:

Why not? I mean, yes, I know they still shouldn't have spent all that other money so stupidly—they still should have paid their taxes and the mortgage on their own house and all their other bills, but . . . what she did, that's elder abuse, isn't it? Isn't that fraud?

BECKY:

Well, no, Reed, not technically. It would be very hard to prove.

REED:

What? Why?

BECKY:

Because it sounds like your parents gave your sister that money freely. There's a witness—Rhonda—who can testify that Trimble wasn't threatening them or holding them prisoner. She certainly didn't steal their credit cards or checkbooks.

And like I told you, your parents are eccentric, but they're not suffering from dementia. It's their right to do whatever they like with their money—such as buy hundreds of cat figurines and gavels, and, unfortunately, give the rest to your sister.

REED:

Are you kidding me? How is that not illegal?

BECKY:

Because it was their money to give, Reed. Your dad earned it. Trimble asked him for it, and he gave it to her.

I agree with you that it wasn't a wise decision, and they shouldn't have done it, because both your sister and her husband are able-bodied adults, and from what I can see, there's no reason that they couldn't have gone out and earned that money for themselves.

But that's what some parents do for their children. They sacrifice everything—everything they have—for their kids. Sometimes they do it for one child over all the others, and in my opinion, it's often because that child is a master manipulator, like your sister.

It's not fair, but I've seen it happen time and time again, and unfortunately, it's not illegal.

What your parents did, Reed, they did out of love.

                    REED:

Love? What you call love, I call a crime. They have nothing left!

                    BECKY:

That's why it's good that you and Marshall and Carly called me. You're already taking the steps you need to in order to remove your parents from what's obviously become a toxic situation.

We'll get your parents away from your sister, somewhere out of her reach, and in the morning you and your brother can make an appointment with an attorney to see if you can have their accounts frozen, and then do what we talked about—try to seek power of attorney to keep your parents from giving any more of their money to your sister.

                    REED:

Yes. Yes, okay, good. Yeah, that sounds like a good plan.

                    BECKY:

But remember what we talked about . . . power of attorney can only be granted by your parents. You're not going to be allowed to control your parents' financial affairs against their will. If you try—at least while they're still fully mentally competent—it's only going to drive an even bigger wedge between you and your father. What he and your mother did, giving your sister all that money, they did out of a strong sense of affection . . . and maybe a little guilt, too.

                    REED:

Guilt? Guilt for *what*? My parents gave us all the best childhood any kids could ask for!

BECKY:

Reed, I'm not a psychologist. I have no idea. But I wouldn't drag lawyers into it until I got the full story.

In cases like this, there's usually something—who knows what—that the child is using as leverage. In my experience, it's usually something that happened to the child that she keeps reminding the parents of, and making them feel badly about, so they continue to give her what she wants.

REED:

Jesus Christ! I always knew my family was messed up, but I never thought they were *this* messed up.

So, what would *you* do about it, then?

BECKY:

Reed . . . are you asking me professionally, or as a friend?

REED:

I'm asking you as someone who allegedly cared about me at one time.

BECKY:

I still care about you, Reed.

REED:

Do you?

BECKY:

Of course. As a friend.

REED:

What if I want to be more than friends?

BECKY:

Well, you might want to start by not dropping out of your friends' lives without a word and then showing up again ten years later expecting to pick up where you left off as if nothing happened.

REED:

Okay. Good point. I might have a little work to do on my friendship skills—

(Loud music.)

REED:

Oh, Christ, not Harrison and the Fords again. Would you look at them? What are they going to do about those earlobes in twenty years when they're coaching their kids' Little League team? Those things are going to be drooping all over the place.

BECKY:

(Laughing.) Reed—

REED:

What? It's not funny. None of this is funny.

BECKY:

I know. Except that you sound exactly like your dad.

REED:

Great. Just what every guy wants to hear. But seriously, if you were me, what would you do?

BECKY:

I would do exactly what you are doing. Get your parents away from your sister. Then let it go.

REED:

Let it go? How the hell am I going to let it go?

BECKY:

Because there's nothing else you can do about it now. And if you don't let it go, it's going to eat away at you. That's what things do, you know, if you don't let them go.

REED:

Well, I don't agree. I don't agree with letting things go. Not things I care about. Not anymore. There's *plenty* I can do about it.

BECKY:

Reed, there's not. Unless . . . what—Reed, ow, you're squeezing my hand.

REED:

Sorry. We're going to Trimble's house.

BECKY:

What? Why?

REED:

Because that's where we're going to find proof of all this.
Remember, Trimble came by the house last night and rooted
around through my dad's stuff. That's why he was so sore all
day, and saying things were missing.

BECKY:

Things *were* missing. I had all his newspapers thrown out.

REED:

No, other things were missing, too. Trimble took stuff out
of the boxes I sorted, but she took papers from Dad's office, too. I bet some of them were important—like the deed
to her husband's new restaurant, maybe, which probably has
Dad's signature on it.

BECKY:

Reed. This is the opposite of letting things go.

REED:

Even if we can't sue her for committing elder abuse, at the
very least I'd like to be able to prove she's been lying all
this time, saying Tony's parents paid for stuff that *our*
parents paid for.

BECKY:

But Reed—

REED:

Come on. If we go now, we can get my niece and nephew to let
us in. Trimble and Too Bad Tony are at some awards ceremony
for the Kiwanis, because he's such a model citizen.

BECKY:

Well, he might be. Maybe he doesn't know that your parents
are broke.

REED:

Becky Flowers, do you ever think ill of *anyone?*

BECKY:

Besides you?

REED:

Funny. Come on. Let's get out of here before Marshall sees us. Carly has some crazy idea that we all have to eat together, to give everyone the impression that we're one big happy family.

BECKY:

I'm not part of your family, Reed.

REED:

Not yet.

BECKY:

Now who's being funny?

REED:

Fine. I know, I'm your client, not your friend. Well, I forgot to tell you. You're fired.

BECKY:

What? You can't fire me. Do you have any idea how much those Dumpsters cost? You owe me fif—

REED:

Oh, my God, really? You'll get your money. Now let's go.
   (Music.)

CHRISTINA:

Oh, crap. Why is this—Rob! Did you see that I'd left this here? And that it was still on? Thanks for the help, Rob. No, really, you're amazing. Did you get enough photos of Tiffany? Did you get any photos at all of—?
   (End.)
   (DELETE ALL)

| BECKY FLOWERS | 9:45PM | 92% |
| TODAY | ALL | MISSED |

Becky F — 8:26 PM
Is Henry on duty tonight?

Nicole F — 8:26 PM
No. I told you, he worked all day so he could have the evening off. He's with me. We're at Authentic. It's 10% off for members of law enforcement!

If you hadn't broken up with the lumbersexual, you could be drinking for free, probably.

Where did you go, anyway? Mom sold all of her Blessie Sticks. She made like $300 for the ASPCA. She's super excited. We brought her here with us to Authentic to celebrate.

Becky F — 8:26 PM
Is Henry sober?

Nicole F — 8:28 PM
Becky, of course Henry isn't sober. It is St. Patrick's Day. 10% off. What part did you not understand?

Becky F — 8:28 PM
There is a problem at Reed's sister's house. I think we might need a cop.

Nicole F — 8:29 PM
What kind of problem?

Becky F — 8:30 PM
Reed's nephew is having a party while his parents are away. He's serving punch with cough syrup in it. Only it is cough syrup for horses.

I think we might need a hand.

Nicole F   8:32 PM
☺☺☺☺☺

Becky F   8:32 PM
It's not funny, Nicole. And it isn't the kids I'm worried about. It's Reed. I've never seen him like this. He's so angry . . . He found out some stuff earlier about . . .

Look, can Henry come or not?

Nicole F   8:32 PM
☺☺☺☺☺☺

Henry says HOLD TIGHT. We will be there RIGHT AWAY.

Becky F   8:33 PM
Please don't come if you're drunk. We have enough intoxicated people here. Besides the horse cough syrup, the kids also got into Reed's sister's liquor cabinet.

Nicole F   8:33 PM
Oh, don't worry, we're not that buzzed. And we're not driving. Leeanne is.

Becky F   8:33 PM
Wait, Leeanne is back?

Nicole F   8:33 PM
Yeah, she just got home and came straight to Authentic to party with you and the lumbersexual, but of course you broke up with the lumbersexual, and Leeanne can't drink. So don't worry, she's driving.

Becky F   8:34 PM
Oh, this is all totally reassuring.

Sweetie Ty

Reviewer ranking: #1,162,355
13% helpful
votes received on reviews

Reviewed

30 in. x 80 in. Molded Brilliant White 6-Panel Smooth Solid Core
Composite Single Prehung Interior Door

As pictured
March 17

So this is my door.

Or at least it's the door I used to have, before my mom took it away,
which if you ask me isn't fair, since none of this is my fault.

She took Tony Jr.'s door away too.

She also took his cell phone, computer, TV, and car keys.

I would say "Poor Tony Jr.," except that I don't feel sorry for him at
all. He deserves it. He's lucky he wasn't arrested by that cop who was
here . . . except that it turns out that horse cough syrup doesn't have
anything in it that can get you high.

Who would want to get a horse high, anyway?

But Tony Jr. DID let all his friends drink everything out of Mom and Dad's liquor cabinet.

He really can't say I didn't warn him, because I told him it was a bad idea.

He blames me for the whole thing—getting busted, I mean.

But how was I supposed to know when the doorbell rang that it was Uncle Reed and his new girlfriend? I just thought it was another one of Tony Jr.'s idiot friends.

So naturally I opened the door as I had been doing all night, and prepared myself to tell them my rules:

- Shoes off (so no dirt/mud/germs get on Mom's carpets)

- Phones off (so no incriminating photos/videos)

- No puking

- No going into my room

Only it wasn't one of Tony Jr.'s idiot friends. It was Uncle Reed.

And now, because I let in Uncle Reed, our lives are going to be 100% completely different.

I was super happy to see him. Really, after having been grounded all week, I was happy to see *anyone* who wasn't one of Tony Jr.'s Tussed-up friends or one of *my* boring acquaintances, who I've really gotten sick of lately. All they ever talk about is whatcollegeareyouapplyingto or makeup.

I'm going to be happy to make all new friends. I NEED to get out of this boring, stupid town.

And Uncle Reed was soooo nice. He said, "Oh, hey, there, Ty. I barely recognized you! You've gotten so grown up," which it wouldn't kill Uncle Marshall or Aunt Carly to say once in a while.

Even his girlfriend, Becky Flowers, said, "Oh, wow, I love those shoes," which shows she has a good eye, because of course I was wearing my nude Louboutins, as one should while entertaining guests.

Anyway, I told them Mom wasn't home.

"I know," Uncle Reed said. "Your mom borrowed some important paperwork from your grandpa's office last night. I was just wondering if we could pop into her study or office or wherever she might keep that kind of thing and have a look at it? Grandpa needs it back. It's kind of an emergency."

I told them sure because I knew exactly what they were talking about. I saw Mom carrying in a bunch of big boxes last night from Grandma and Grandpa's. I asked her what they were and she said her "birthright."

I asked what that was and she said I should try educating myself instead of spending all day texting my friends. So I bought a real nice silver Tory Burch bracelet online with her credit card that I guess she's going to be even more upset about someday.

But right now she's got plenty to keep her occupied. LOLOLOLOLOL.

So then Uncle Reed and Becky went into Mom's study and after a while they came out again with a couple of boxes.

That's when they heard the music from the den downstairs.

Uncle Reed went, "You kids wouldn't happen to be having a St. Patrick's Day party, would you?"

I don't know what gave it away. Maybe it was all the green Jolly Ranchers scattered across the kitchen counter. Really, if you think about it, everything that happened tonight, besides being Tony Jr.'s fault, is also Mom's fault for insisting on having a kitchen that looks out onto a great room that also connects to her office door, so she could "keep an eye" on us while she's "working" (which really means looking up her old friends on Facebook and laughing at their photos).

"Uh, yeah," I said, because you shouldn't lie to your celebrity uncle. "Tony Junior is having a few friends over."

"I'm going to go down and say hi to him. I haven't seen him in a long time. It will only take a second."

Uncle Reed put down his box and went into the basement to say hi to Tony Jr., leaving me alone with his friend Becky. She smiled at me and said, "You certainly have a lovely home."

I smiled back at her because this was the only civilized thing anyone had said to me all night! All of Tony Jr.'s friends had just looked at me and said, "Nice tits," or the equivalent.

This is another reason I'm happy to be leaving this disgusting town.

I said, "Thank you. It was built in the year 2002, which was towards the tail end of the neo-eclectic architectural style of suburban home design, and according to my mom combines Cape Cod, French Provincial, Chateau-esque and Georgian Revival styles. We're quite fond of it."

Becky's eyes got very big and she said, "Wow."

I know people think I'm a dumb blonde but according to my guidance counselor I have nearly 98% aural recall which is why she thinks I should go into telecommunications for college.

I understand the University of Florida has quite a strong department.

That was when I heard shouting, and suddenly Uncle Reed came bursting back up the stairs, holding Tony Jr. by his Polo shirt collar.

"That's it," Uncle Reed said. "We're calling your mom."

Tony Jr. looked more scared than I'd ever seen him.

"No, dude," he said. "It's not what you think."

"It's exactly what I think," Uncle Reed said. "You think I wasn't young once? You think I didn't do lame, idiotic things like this? Your own grandfather was the Chug-a-lug Champ of the Hijinks Club! This sort of thing runs in our blood. But that doesn't mean you shouldn't get busted for it. Everyone gets busted, everyone has to pay the price, and everyone has to choose which road they're going to take in the future . . . the road to success, or the road to the basement."

"But you already busted me," Tony Jr. wailed. "Whadduya gotta call Mom for?"

But it was too late. Uncle Reed was calling Mom. I guess she was kind of crabby when she answered, because Uncle Reed was crabby back to her.

"Oh, yeah?" he said to her. "Well, I don't care how many awards they're giving your husband. There are seventeen intoxicated kids in your basement and if you don't come home right now and deal with it, I'm calling each and every one of their parents to come and pick them up—which I can do because I've confiscated all of their cell phones—and telling them that *you* gave them alcohol, because in essence, you did. How do you think that is going to play in the school's e-newsletter this month?"

Then he hung up on her.

This is much more exciting to write about now that I know I'm moving. At the time, it wasn't that fun, because I was pretty worried about what Sundae's mom was going to say about my mom in the e-newsletter. Sundae's brother was downstairs, even though he's only a freshman.

Uncle Reed found out about that, too. He found out about everything, even that Tony Jr. was charging $4 per red cup of lean.

The only thing he didn't find out is that I still have Mom's credit card.

"But I'm an entrepreneur," Tony Jr. tried to say in his own defense, before Mom got home and sent him to his room (he still had a door, back then). "Like you, Uncle Reed."

"Your uncle isn't an entrepreneur," Becky said, speaking up for the first time. I feel like she hadn't wanted to get involved until then, but it was a good thing she chose that moment to do so, because Uncle Reed looked so mad when Tony Jr. said the thing about wanting to be an entrepreneur like him, I was afraid he might slam him against a wall. "He's an athlete. Do you have any idea how hard your uncle worked at his sport when he was your age? How many hours a day he practiced? He'd get up at five—before the sun rose, most days—and play until school started, then play after school until the sun set, and sometimes even in the dark, with glow-in-the-dark balls. He did it in winter, when it was freezing outside, and he did it in summer, when it was so hot that sweat was dripping off his face. He didn't get paid to do it. He didn't do it for trophies, or to be popular. He did it because he loved the game. He did it to challenge himself, to be the best he could be. He certainly never did it to be an entrepreneur, whatever that means. And he certainly never consciously set out to hurt anyone, which is what you could have done tonight, serving alcohol and medicine intended for animals to minors."

This speech shut Tony Jr. up. It also kind of shut up Uncle Reed, at least for a while. He kept looking over at Becky like she was something very amazing, such as a new Prada bag or maybe even a Jeep 4X4, which I can appreciate because it does take something on that level to shut up Tony Jr.

But anyway that's when Mom and Dad got home and the sh*t really hit the AC unit, if you know what I mean.

Because Mom was SUPER mad—only not at Tony Jr. She only sent him to his room to get him out of the way because he kept whining about how it wasn't his fault.

No, Mom was mad at Uncle Reed. And not even for busting the party. She got mad when she saw the boxes.

"What are you doing with those?" she yelled. "How dare you? How dare you come into my house uninvited and go through my personal things?"

"First of all," Uncle Reed said, "we were invited, by your daughter." He pointed over at me.

This, by the way, is how the whole thing is my fault, and how I got my door taken away.

Mom looked at me like I was a child of the devil, and not hers. I was like, "Holla. What up."

I totally did not get what was going on . . . then.

Then Uncle Reed went, "And we only came here to retrieve Dad's paperwork, which you took from his house without permission. Like this deed to your husband's new restaurant with Dad's signature on it, indicating that he, not your husband's parents, paid for it."

For some reason my mom's face turned bright red. She was wearing her new dress—a navy blue sequined Vera Wang—so with her red face, blue dress, and new highlighted blond hair, she looked a little bit like the American flag: red, white and blue. It was way patriotic.

"Phew," my dad said from where he was standing behind my mom, in his Calvin Klein tux. "I'm glad you guys finally know. It was tough keeping that one a secret. I mean, I get it, your dad is a modest guy and doesn't want people to know he's loaded, so he insisted we say my parents bought the restaurants for us. But I gotta tell ya, I felt kind of guilty about it, especially since my parents cut me off years ago. So who wants a drink?" He went over to his liquor cabinet. "Oh, crap. They drank *all* of it?"

That was when Uncle Reed and my mom started having the worst screaming fight I have ever heard two adults have in my entire life. I know I have 98% aural recall, so if I wanted to I could write down exactly what they said.

But I don't want to, because I don't want to remember the things Uncle Reed accused my mom of doing, and the things she said back to him. They were too terrible. A child shouldn't be subjected to those kinds of things.

And I *am* a child. Becky even said so when she walked over to me and took me by the arm and gently led me into the den and turned on the TV at very high volume and said, "I'm so sorry this is happening right now. I'm going to call for some help."

Except of course when help came, it was a cop and Becky's sister and some Asian lady, and all they did was keep my mom and Uncle Reed from killing each other (and take turns calling Tony Jr.'s friends' parents, and make them come over to pick them up).

For a while I was pretty sure my life was over. I mean, it turns out my mom has been taking money from my grandma and grandpa even though she has a career as a high-powered attorney.

And my dad is crap at running restaurants.

But then something amazing happened:

After all the yelling was over, and all of Tony Jr.'s friends got picked up, and Uncle Reed and Becky and their friends left, and Mom took our doors away and she and Dad got finished with their fight (which Tony Jr. and I could totally hear, since we didn't have doors or our phones so we couldn't put in earbuds to listen to music to drown it out), Dad came upstairs and said that he and Mom were going to be spending some time apart.

Which ordinarily would be super upsetting, except that Dad said he's had this business opportunity to open a real restaurant—not a pizza place—with a friend in Tampa, and he's going to take it, and if we want to, we can come stay with him instead of living with Mom.

He says he won't have much money so we'll have to give up a lot of our creature comforts, such as the hot tub and cheerleading and skiing in Aspen, but he thinks it would be a positive experience for us because the lifestyle we have here has become super toxic and unhealthy, and we need a fresh start.

Um, live in Tampa, Florida, where the sun shines over 300 days a year and no one suffers from Seasonal Affective Disorder or Vitamin D deficiency?

Yes, please.

Do you know who goes to Florida all the time?

Harry Styles.

Do you know who never comes to Bloomville, Indiana?

Harry Styles.

Besides, Tampa is super close to Orlando, where Grandma and Grandpa are going to be. So I'll still be able to see them all the time.

Grandma and I have a lot in common, since we both like to shop.

Also, now that I know about Grandpa's Hijinks Club thing, I feel closer to him than ever. It's obvious that he's the original gangster.

Tony Jr., of course, is staying here with Mom, probably to continue his entrepreneurship. Whatever.

I'm going to use this opportunity to do what Uncle Reed said: Choose a road that leads to success, not the basement.

I swear I'm not going to use Mom's credit card anymore. Because tonight I've seen what life down that road gets you, and I don't want any part of that anymore!

I'm going to be good.

When I get to Tampa, I might even take up golf.

REED STEWART	12:45AM	15%
TODAY	ALL	MISSED

Marshall   6:05 PM

Hey, buddy, where are you? Carly wants us to sit down and eat now.

Marshall   6:10 PM

Whoa, can you believe this speech of dad's? The old man sure does love that microphone.

Marshall   6:20 PM

Reed, I can see you over there talking to your lady love. But you need to tear yourself away so we can eat. The girls are getting antsy. You know what Taylor is like when she's hungry. Have some mercy, buddy.

Marshall   6:30 PM

Yo, dude, what happened? I just saw you run out of here with Becky.

I know you're trying to get into her pants, but Carly was really hoping we could all sit down and eat together as a family. I think Dad was hoping so, as well.

So, not cool, especially on the one good day he's had in a while.

Marshall   6:55 PM

Seriously, Reed, Rhonda just came up to me and said she thinks she told you something that maybe she shouldn't have, and now she's worried because you looked so upset.

But she won't tell me what it was because she doesn't want to upset me, too.

So now I'm worried. It's starting to freak me out that you're not texting me back. Where are you?

Marshall   7:45 PM

Just me, checking in. You better be getting laid, otherwise I can't think of any other excuse for you being such a dick.

Marshall   8:56 PM

OK, so Trimble just called me and told me not to believe anything you say and that you're a lying horse's ass and always have been.

Apparently she thinks that you and I converse a lot more regularly than we actually do.

I did not let on that I hadn't the slightest idea what she was talking about, and pretended I knew everything, and that I believed everything you had not, in fact, told me.

This enraged our fair sister so much that she hung up before I could find out what it is, exactly, that you discovered she's done.

Anything that pisses off Trimble is fine by me. So carry on, my good man. I will use Trimble's wroth with you to placate my seething wife, who hates your guts for not dining with us, but hates our sister more.

Marshall   11:25 PM

So my wife—not me—took it upon herself to go for a little moonlight drive just now, not to spy on you, I'm sure, because my fair wife would never do such a thing. She says it was to "check the ditches to make sure you weren't lying dead in one."

In any case, she has just returned to inform me that your rental car is parked in front of the house of one Beverly Flowers, and that she is convinced you are in the basement apartment of that house with one Rebecca Flowers.

She wishes to know if you intend to spend the night there, and if so, will you return in time for breakfast in the morning, as, it being Saturday, she is going to make blueberry pancakes.

She would also like you to know that she would be happy to make enough for your companion, Rebecca Flowers.

Now I'm going to shoot myself for having been forced to text all that.

Reed   12:01 AM

Tell Carly yes, I'm at Becky's.

Yes, I'm spending the night.

Yes to pancakes. I will force Becky to come too even though she says she'll be too embarrassed.

We're going to have a lot to talk about tomorrow.

Marshall   12:04 AM

You've just made my wife squeal with happiness. It's been months—maybe years—since I've heard my wife squeal with happiness.

Thanks for coming back, bud.

Reed   12:05 AM

I told you I would.

The Bloomville Herald

The Tri-County Area's Only
Daily Newspaper
• Saturday, March 18 • Vol. 145 •
Still Only 50 Cents!

CRIME REPORT

Information in the Crime Report is obtained from calls logged by the Bloomville Police Department.

11th and Main, Bloomville—Resident **Summer Hayes** reported a barking dog. Officer Corrine Jeffries dispatched to investigate. A warning was given to the dog's owner.

Kroger Save-On, Bloomville—Altercation over bacon reported between two men in the meat department. Officer Henry De Santos responded. Both men arrested and charged with disorderly conduct, public intoxication, and misdemeanor assault.

Country Club Road, Bloomville—Off-duty officer responded to a residence at which minors were reportedly drinking alcohol. Parents of minors involved notified, warnings issued.

online

Leeanne Matsumori created chat "Reed Stewart"

Leeanne Matsumori   09:07
Becky, are you up?

Becky Flowers   09:07
I'm up.

Leeanne Matsumori   09:07
WHAT HAPPENED LAST NIGHT AFTER WE LEFT?

Becky Flowers   09:07
I can't really talk right now.

Leeanne Matsumori   09:07
Why, are you at work? It's Saturday. You work too hard.

Becky Flowers   09:08
I'm not at work. I'm at home. I'm just not alone.

Leeanne Matsumori   09:08
Why? Who's there?

Becky Flowers   09:08
Guess.

Leeanne Matsumori   09:08
OMG HE STAYED OVER?

Becky Flowers 09:08
He stayed over.

Leeanne Matsumori 09:09
HOW WAS IT????

Becky Flowers 09:09
How do you think?

Leeanne Matsumori 09:09
Amazing?

Becky Flowers 09:09
More than amazing. Even better than before.

Leeanne, I'm so happy. I've never been happier in my life.

He saved all my letters. And my emails. And my texts.

Leeanne Matsumori 09:09
He saved them?

Becky Flowers 09:09
Yes.

In a binder.

Leeanne Matsumori 09:10
A binder?

Only you would find that romantic.

Why didn't he answer them?

Becky Flowers   09:10
He couldn't. He didn't know what to say.

He knew we couldn't be together, since he couldn't live in Indiana. But he didn't want to ask me to move out to California, since he knew how excited I was about going to school.

And he didn't feel as if it was fair to ask me to wait for him (which he was right about—it wouldn't have been).

So he just freaked out and did nothing.

And then the longer he did nothing, the less he knew what to say.

And then he figured I'd probably just forgotten about him.

Leeanne Matsumori   09:10
How male of him.

Becky Flowers   09:10
Right? I know.

But he's been stalking me on Facebook.

Leeanne Matsumori   09:10
Oh, wow, you guys are perfect for each other. You do the same thing to him and his entire family.

Becky Flowers   09:10
I know. Except I didn't tell him. So could you please not mention it if you see him?

But like I said, I can't really text right now. We're going over to his brother's house to eat pancakes.

Leeanne Matsumori   09:10
You're going over to his brother's house to eat pancakes?

Becky Flowers   09:10
I know. I sound like a freak. Do I sound like a freak?

Leeanne Matsumori   09:10
A little bit. Please don't tell me I came all the way back from Japan only to have you move to LA.

Becky Flowers   09:11
What? NO!!! I am NOT moving to LA.

Leeanne Matsumori   09:11
Then how is this going to work? Is he giving up his golf career?

Becky Flowers   09:11
No. I'll tell you later. Let's have lunch.

Leeanne Matsumori   09:11
Lunch? You're just about to go eat pancakes.

Becky Flowers   09:11
I know. Why don't we meet at Matsumori's?

Leeanne Matsumori   09:12
Sure, why not? I'm still on Japan time. It's tomorrow there right now. What does it matter?

Becky Flowers   09:12
Thank you. And thank you so much for everything you did last night.

Leeanne Matsumori   09:12
Of course. For you? Anything. Although I just have to say after what I saw over there . . . are you sure you want these people as in-laws?

Becky Flowers 09:12
100% positive.

Leeanne Matsumori 09:12
OK. He must be pretty amazing in bed.

Becky Flowers 09:12
☺ 🔥

MARSHALL STEWART	10:45AM	95%
TODAY	ALL	MISSED

Reed — 9:42 AM
Marshall, how many acres come with the old Bloomville Elementary School?

Marshall — 9:42 AM
Where the hell are you? I thought you said you guys were coming over. The girls want to put on some kind of performance for you after we have breakfast, and then I have to take them to soccer.

Not all of us have Saturday off, you know. Some of us have responsibilities.

Reed — 9:42 AM
We're coming. We stopped at Kroger. We're picking up champagne.

Marshall — 9:43 AM
What the hello do we need champagne for?

Reed — 9:43 AM
To make mimosas. You can't have pancakes without mimosas. What are you, a heathen?

Marshall — 9:43 AM
Sometimes I forget that you are the most annoying person in the history of time.

Reed — 9:43 AM
How many acres come with that school you're selling?

Marshall   9:43 AM

Twelve, including parking and the building. Why? And what the hello happened over at Trimble's last night? You know Dad is really pissed. He's called me like four times.

He says Too Bad Tony is moving out and taking Ty with him, to Tampa of all places. That can't be true, though? Like Too Bad Tony would ever hop off the Trimble Money Train.

Reed   9:44 AM

No, it's true about Tony. He's actually a good guy.

Isn't the back of the old Bloomville Elementary on the sixteenth hole of the country club's golf course?

Marshall   9:44 AM

Yes, Reed. A lot of things have changed since you were last here, but they haven't moved the golf course.

Reed   9:44 AM

So if I buy the school and turn it into a junior golf academy, do you think the club will allow me use of their greens? I mean for my pupils?

Marshall   9:44 AM

I'm sorry. It's a little early for jokes, even for you.

Reed   9:44 AM

No joke. I want to buy the old elementary school.

I'm going to expect the city to knock down the price a little because of the asbestos. Removing it from a building that size ain't gonna be cheap.

Plus, I'll be bringing in a lot of business. I plan to make my classes free, because more people should play golf. It's accessible to everyone, since it's a sport that anyone of any size, shape, age, and sex can play.

Marshall   9:45 AM
Reed, have you and Becky already been hitting the champagne?

Reed   9:45 AM
No. I'm totally serious about this. This is all stuff you can use in your pitch when we give them our bid.

My school will keep the youth of Bloomville off the streets and provide them with a safe, healthy environment in which they can learn a game that teaches discipline, respect, honesty, and teamwork, while also helping to hone conversational skills and physical fitness with minimal risk of bodily injury compared to other sports.

Marshall   9:45 AM
Are you on drugs?

Reed   9:45 AM
I'm high on love, man.

Marshall   9:45 AM
You're high on something.

Does this mean you're moving back to Bloomville?

Reed   9:45 AM
Well, not for the whole year. That would be ridiculous. There's snow on the ground here for a good three months. How would I practice?

But for the rest of the year, yeah. My girlfriend has a business and family here. She's not going to abandon them.

And I have family here, too. I may as well start a business, too.

Marshall   9:46 AM

Okay. Yeah. I get it. When you get here we can find out about whether or not the club would give you greens rights.

I can't imagine they wouldn't because you're Reed Stewart. I'm sure they'd be honored.

And then we can draw up an offer on the school.

But where are you going to live? In Becky's apartment in her mom's basement? (Just kidding.)

No, but seriously though. Where?

Reed   9:46 AM

I think Becky likes Mom and Dad's house.

Marshall   9:46 AM

You want to buy Mom and Dad's house.

For your girlfriend.

Reed   9:46 AM

For both of us. What's wrong with that?

Marshall   9:46 AM

Nothing! I'll draw up the paperwork for that, too.

Reed   9:46 AM

Make sure it includes the chandelier. Becky really likes the chandelier.

And I especially don't want Trimble to get it.

Marshall   9:46 AM

I hear you, brother. Anything else?

Reed   9:47 AM

No, I think that's it.

Oh, okay, Becky's back. We'll be right over.

| Marshall | 9:47 AM |

Great. See you in a bit.

| Marshall | 9:47 AM |

CARLY YOU ARE NOT GOING TO BELIEVE WHAT REED JUST TOLD ME.

| Carly | 9:47 AM |

Marshall, I have asked you repeatedly not to text me from the bathroom. It's disgusting and unhygienic.

| Marshall | 9:47 AM |

HE IS BUYING THE SCHOOL.

| Carly | 9:47 AM |

First you tell me your sister and Too Bad Tony are splitting up, then you tell me your brother is buying the old elementary school. Do you really think I'm going to believe all of these lies? I'm happy I'm here to entertain you with my naiveté.

| Marshall | 9:48 AM |

I'M NOT KIDDING. HE'S BUYING MOM AND DAD'S HOUSE, TOO.

| Carly | 9:48 AM |

You aren't as amusing as you think you are, Marshall. Come out of there and help me find the champagne flutes. If they're really bringing stuff for mimosas, we need to serve it in the right glasses.

I don't want Becky Flowers thinking we don't know how to behave like civilized human beings, even though of course we don't because I think this performance the girls are putting on for them involves a war dance by none other than our favorite historical figure, Chief Massasoit.

Marshall   9:48 AM

Reed's moving here. For part of the year, anyway. They're going to live at Mom and Dad's, and Becky's going to run her moving company, and he's going to run a free golf school.

I bet they're married by New Year's. He isn't going to want to mess around this time. He's going to want to lock her down.

Carly   9:48 AM

GET OUT OF THE BATHROOM AND HELP ME.

Marshall   9:48 AM

He did it. He came back like he said he would, and did it. My little brother.

Carly   9:48 AM

And be sure to wash your hands!!!!!!

WITH SOAP.

BECKY FLOWERS	11:45AM	92%
TODAY	ALL	MISSED

Nicole F   9:02 AM

Don't even try to pretend like Reed didn't spend the night last night. Mom and I both saw his car.

I expect a full report later.

Nicole F   9:05 AM

That was fun at his sister's house, but what a byotch! Someone should fully report her to Adult Protective Services. Or maybe Child Protective Services.

Nicole F   9:10 AM

And if later you hear from her (Trimble) that her life-size Dalmatian statue is missing from her yard, it totally wasn't me who took it.

Nicole F   9:14 AM

OK, I might have decided to liberate it. Someone like her doesn't deserve a thing of such beauty.

PLEASE don't tell your new boyfriend that I stole his sister's Dalmatian statue.

Nicole F   9:17 AM

Ha, I guess he's not your new boyfriend, right? He's your new old boyfriend!

Anyway, way to go. He's sooooo much better than the lumbersexual cheesemonger.

Aren't you glad I told you to cliiiiiiiiiiick that story in the Herald????

Mom 9:35 AM

Honey, I'm just so happy about you and Reed. You know I've always liked him so much.

Now, I know you two probably want to spend some time alone, but just in case you're free for dinner, what's his favorite food? Because I'll make it. Is it chicken? Because I managed to get Rhonda Jenkins's recipe for baked chicken and I was thinking of trying it out tonight.

Let me know. Bye now.

Reed 10:20 AM

What if I don't want to go to lunch with your friend Leeanne? What if I just want to stay in your bed and ravage you instead?

Becky 10:20 AM

I think we've done enough ravaging of one another in my bed for one morning.

Reed 10:20 AM

There can never be enough ravaging where you're concerned.

Becky 10:20 AM

I haven't seen her in months.

Reed 10:21 AM

I haven't seen you in ten years.

Becky 10:21 AM

You saw me naked all night long.

Reed 10:21 AM

A thousand nights will never be enough.

Becky   10:21 AM

Stop sexting me in front of your niece while she does her Indian war dance.

Reed   10:21 AM

I'll sext you in front of anyone I want. You're mine now, and I'm never letting you get away again.

Becky   10:22 AM

It would be unwise of you to do so, since I know all of your family's darkest secrets.

Reed   10:22 AM

You don't know my darkest secret.

Becky   10:22 AM

Um, I believe I've known it for quite some time. It involves a certain part of your anatomy.

Reed   10:22 AM

Not that one. The other one.

Becky   10:22 AM

Which one is that?

Reed   10:22 AM

That I love you. I've always loved you. I'll never stop loving you.

Becky   10:22 AM

Oh, THAT one.

No, I think you need to say it a few more times.

REED STEWART	4:52PM	13%
TODAY	ALL	MISSED

Enrique Alvarez   3:16 PM EST

Hey, boudro. Got your message. Yeah, that's no problem. Happy to help out. I'm glad for you, man!

So you finally took my advice, huh? See. I told you. All you gotta do is think back to what you liked about the game when you were a kid. No stress, no playing to win, just doing it for the love of the game.

That's what it's all about, boudro. That's what it should always be about.

Safe travels, my brother.

From: Dolly Vargas D.Vargas@VTM.com
Date: March 18 2:42:40 PM EST
To: Reed Stewart@reedstewart.com
Subject: Lyrexica Offer

Reed, I could kiss you. Thank you, thank you, thank you for the roses.

But thank you even more for agreeing—finally—to the Lyrexica deal. You aren't going to regret this, I promise. The residuals alone are going to keep us in roses for years. Every time they play your little commercial, you're going to get a check. Ka-ching.

And they're going to play it a LOT, because you know how men are about their hair. Well, you probably don't, because you have all yours. But other men.

I can finally buy that little house in Tuscany I've been dying for! After I pay off my louse of an ex-husband, I mean.

We are going to be rich, my darling, so rich!

I love you, I worship you, you are my everything, goodbye and good luck at the Golden Palms, you're going to win, I feel it in my bones.

XOXOX

Dolly
Dolly Vargas
Vargas Talent Management
Los Angeles, CA

From: Trimble Stewart-Antonelli@Stewart&Stewart.com
Date: March 18 4:10:25 PM EST
To: Reed Stewart@reedstewart.com
Subject: You

This letter is to inform you that if you do not cease and desist meddling in the affairs of me and my family, I will take legal action against you.

These actions may include but may not be limited to:

• contacting law enforcement to obtain criminal sanctions against you

• suing you civilly for damages I have incurred as a result of your actions

• anything else that I decide.

Again, you must IMMEDIATELY STOP. You risk incurring some very severe legal consequences if you fail to comply with this demand.

None of this would be happening, Reed, if you'd just stayed out of it. My financial affairs with Mom and Dad are my own business. They were HEARTBROKEN when you left town, and giving money to me and my family made them feel better. Your interference now is only hurting them, not me.

This letter acts as your final warning to discontinue this unwanted conduct before I pursue legal actions against you.

This is your FINAL CHANCE, Reed, before I exercise my rights.

Sincerely,

Trimble Stewart-Antonelli
Attorney at Law
Stewart & Stewart, LLC
1911 South Moore Pike
Bloomville, IN 47401
(812) 555-9721
www.stewart&stewart.com

From: Reed Stewart@reedstewart.com
Date: March 18 4:38:25 PM EST
To: Trimble Stewart-Antonelli@Stewart&Stewart.com
Subject: You

Thanks for the letter, Trimble. I'm going to make sure Marshall, Carly, and Mom and Dad's new bankruptcy lawyer get copies of it, since in it, you basically acknowledge in writing that you've been fleecing our parents for years.

Not that we needed any more evidence of that. I've got plenty of it already.

But it does solve one mystery that's been bothering me:

What was it that Mom and Dad felt so guilty about that they'd hand so much of their money over to you?

Now I know: My leaving.

I bet you played that one to the hilt, didn't you? You were always good at the dramatics. You probably told them if they didn't help you and Tony out financially, you'd leave, too, just like baby brother Reed did. After Tony Junior and Ty were born, that threat worked even better. I bet it got them good and panicked. You really piled on the guilt, didn't you?

Well, it won't work on them anymore. Because I'm back.

And unfortunately for you, I'm staying.

Don't worry about our parents, though. Marshall and I have their backs. Did you know the IRS takes payment plans? It's true! It turns out they aren't any more anxious than Shenanigans to put senior citizens in jail.

Please take all the legal action you want against me. I'll enjoy it. I'll litigate right back.

Your not so loving brother,

Reed

From: Lyle Stewart@FountainHill.org
Date: March 18 5:48:22 PM EST
To: Reed Stewart@reedstewart.com>
Subject: Congratulations

Dearest Reed,

I understand from my brother, with whom I spoke today for the first time in a long time, that congratulations are in order? You and Ms. Flowers are now—how does one put it in today's parlance?—an item?

I'm very pleased for you both.

Your father also tells me that you'll be residing in Bloomville for half of the year, and in Florida for the rest. I think this is a sensible plan. I never thought the California lifestyle suited you, and I agree with your accountant that for those with an income at a certain level, taxes here can be quite painful.

And how nice that you'll be near your parents in Florida, and that Ms. Flowers's business takes her there so often, as well.

I will miss you, of course, but perhaps I, too, will consider relocating to Florida. The weather there is wonderful year round for growing orchids.

(My *Phalaenopsis amabilis* took first place, by the way, in both its category and overall.)

I was sorry to hear, however, that your sister's marriage is not doing well. But to be frank, I'm surprised that relationship lasted this long.

I have no such concerns for you and Ms. Flowers. You have always been a person who loved long, and loved steadfastly—when you chose to love at all.

You will, I hope, have a large wedding, and not one of those foolish small affairs . . . or worse, an elopement. There really are only two occasions for which families gather together anymore, and only one of them is happy, if you know what I mean.

Thank you for providing us with a happy one, and preventing us—in the form of rescuing my brother and his wife—from the other.

Yours very sincerely,

Uncle Lyle

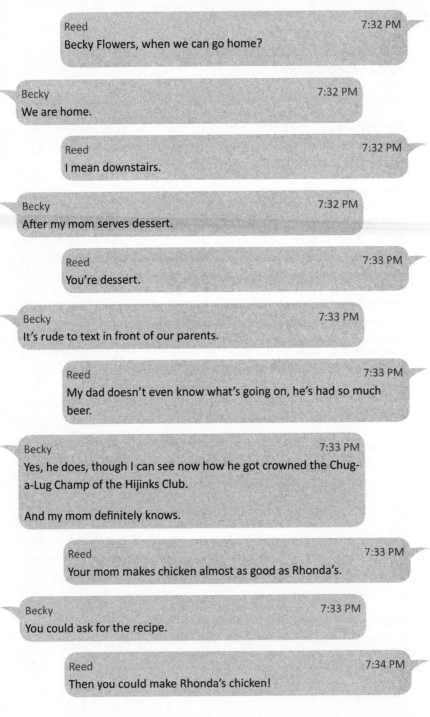

Reed   7:32 PM
Becky Flowers, when we can go home?

Becky   7:32 PM
We are home.

Reed   7:32 PM
I mean downstairs.

Becky   7:32 PM
After my mom serves dessert.

Reed   7:33 PM
You're dessert.

Becky   7:33 PM
It's rude to text in front of our parents.

Reed   7:33 PM
My dad doesn't even know what's going on, he's had so much beer.

Becky   7:33 PM
Yes, he does, though I can see now how he got crowned the Chug-a-Lug Champ of the Hijinks Club.

And my mom definitely knows.

Reed   7:33 PM
Your mom makes chicken almost as good as Rhonda's.

Becky   7:33 PM
You could ask for the recipe.

Reed   7:34 PM
Then you could make Rhonda's chicken!

Becky   7:34 PM
I meant you could ask so YOU could make Rhonda's chicken.

Reed   7:34 PM
Oh, so THAT's how it's going to be.

Becky   7:34 PM
I'm a busy working woman. I don't have time to cook.

Reed   7:35 PM
But you did have time today to sneak back to my parents' house, find my yearbook, and write in it. Don't try to deny it: I found it on the coffee table when I was over there earlier.

Becky   7:35 PM
Maybe I did, maybe I didn't.

Oooh, I just had an idea: Let's hire Rhonda to cook for us!

Reed   7:35 PM
Fine, we can do that.

As soon as you confess that you wrote "You pierce my soul. I offer myself to you again with a heart even more your own than when you almost broke it, ten years ago" beneath my senior photo.

Becky   7:35 PM
Of course I did. I can't believe you didn't recognize the quote. Or my handwriting.

Reed   7:35 PM
Oh, I recognized it, all right. It's just that you stole it from me.

Becky   7:35 PM
How did I steal it? Jane Austen wrote "Persuasion," not you.

Reed   7:35 PM

I know, but now I can't use that quote on you. So instead I have to say: "I have loved none but you. You alone have brought me to Bloomville."

Becky   7:35 PM

Stop texting me and take that beer away from your dad before he spills it.

Nicole F   7:36 PM

Are you and Reed sexting? OMG, that's so cute. Or gross. I can't decide.

Becky   7:36 PM

No! We're just making plans for later tonight.

Nicole F   7:36 PM

Oh, right. You mean like later when he 🔥 ☺ you?

Becky   7:36 PM

No! Stop it!

Becky   7:36 PM

Reed, you really need to stop, Nicole knows what we're doing.

Reed   7:36 PM

Quoting Austen?

Becky   7:36 PM

Well, she thinks we're sexting.

Reed   7:36 PM

She's right. "*I am half agony, half hope.*"

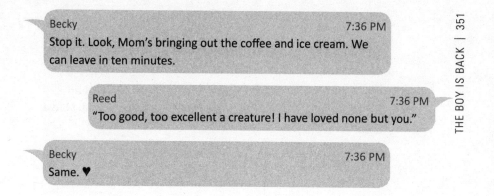

Becky   7:36 PM
Stop it. Look, Mom's bringing out the coffee and ice cream. We can leave in ten minutes.

Reed   7:36 PM
"Too good, too excellent a creature! I have loved none but you."

Becky   7:36 PM
Same. ♥

Welcome to my new online shop,

the Not-So-Crazy Cat Lady

All of the items you see here are available for purchase and shipping in 3–5 business days. Refunds and exchanges are happily accepted. I have over 94% helpful reviews.

Today's featured item is:

Pretty Kitty Nap Time
$29.00 + Shipping

This darling little kitty really does look as if it's stretching out for a midday nap . . . the way my kitties used to, back when I had kitties.

Oh, don't worry, nothing bad has happened to my kitties! I'm just not allowed to feed other people's kitties anymore. I guess that *was* a bit of a naughty thing for me to do ;-)

But who can resist those big eyes, warm, furry little bodies, and soft purr?

My new daughter-in-law-to-be, Becky, however, says I can have a little kitty of my own when I get to my new condo in The Town, which is the name of the retirement village in Florida where my husband and I will be relocating next week!

I can hardly believe we'll be getting there so soon. Things are very different for me now. Everything has been such a whirlwind—but a good one, mostly.

My youngest son is there already—not The Town, but in Florida, getting ready to play in his first major tournament since he lost so badly at his last one . . . well, his last three or four.

Jackie Monroe on Channel 4 says it's really very important to his career that he win, but he says, "No, it's not, Mom. What's important is all of you . . . and that I enjoy the game. And that's what I'm going to do."

He's taken Becky with him. He says it's for luck, but she says it's because the course where he'll be playing is very near The Town, and she wants everything to be just so for my husband and me when we arrive.

Becky is the kind of girl who likes everything to be just so, which is good for my youngest son, because he doesn't care about those kinds of things at all ;-)

That's probably why my daughter and her husband are splitting. Neither of them was very good at making things just so.

It's very sad, but like my oldest granddaughter says: "Don't worry, Grandma, soon we'll be in Florida. Everything will be better there."

I'm not sure that's true, but it's true she's moving there, too, and has promised to come visit me and her grandpa "all the time."

She's very sweet. Much sweeter than my grandson who, like his mother, hasn't stopped by to visit me once this week, even though she knows I've been going through a very difficult time, what with the move and parting with my pretty kitties.

Oh, well!

At least I have all of you . . . receiving your sweet messages of support has meant the world to me, as has knowing my kitties are going to good homes. Thank you, all of you.

And not only will I post photos of the new condo, I'll post photos of my new kitty (when I get her), *and* photos from my youngest son's wedding (when he has it. Who knows when that will be. He's very slow about getting things done. But I have to say, he does get to them, eventually).

Until then . . . stay a little crazy!

The Not-So-Crazy Cat Lady

Blessings Journal

of

BECKY FLOWERS

Today I feel blessed because:

_____

_____

_____

Am I a terrible person? I haven't written in this journal in a week, and it's because I'm so happy.

Is this what happens? When you're truly blessed, you stop counting your blessings?

No. I know who that person is, and I never want to become her, because look how she's ended up: completely alone (well, except for that son, which might actually be worse than being alone).

So I'm going to take the time and express my gratitude.

- I have an amazing mom and sister who, even if they occasionally try my patience, are always there for me.
- I get to do what I love for a living. How many people can say that?
- I have the most awesome best friend in the entire world.
- And I have a boyfriend who takes my breath away—maybe not every single second of the day, but for enough of them to make up for the times during which I want to kill him.

And I'll never stop being thankful to his crazy parents for giving birth to him, and for bringing him back to me.

From: Reed Stewart@reedstewart.com
Date: March 25 4:52:43 PM EST
To: Lyle Stewart@FountainHill.org
Subject: Congratulations

Dear Uncle Lyle,

There's definitely going to be a wedding. I'll make sure it's large. And of course you'll be invited. I can't wait for you to meet her.

Thank you for encouraging me to take the same road as my father. I know now that mine won't lead to a dark and gloomy basement, but a garden as light-filled and sunny as yours, and bursting with Becky Flowers.

Love,

Your Favorite Nephew,
Reed

The Bloomville Herald

The Tri-County Area's Only
Daily Newspaper
• Monday, March 27 • Vol. 154 •
Still Only 50 Cents!

STEWART WINS

BY CHRISTINA MARTINEZ Herald Staff

Orlando, FL—Reed Stewart earned his first PGA Tour victory in over two years on Sunday, posting a final-round 68 to finish the week at minus-15.

The win gives Stewart a two-year exemption on the PGA Tour, a spot in the Masters, and a $1,230,000 prize.

Stewart was one of the youngest players in history to win the US Open, but this week's win at the Golden Palm is his first after a series of what his long-time friend and caddy, Enrique Alvarez, calls really, truly humiliating defeats.

Stewart, 28, is the youngest son of Judge Richard P. and Constance D. Stewart. Now retired, Judge Stewart and his wife will soon be relocating to Florida, where they told the *Herald* they hope to "make many new friends, but that also many of our old friends and relatives will come to visit us in the wintertime."

The Stewarts' eldest son, Marshall Stewart, 32, co-owns Stewart Realty Company, along with his wife, Carly.

Last week Stewart Realty announced the sale of the old Bloomville Elementary to Reed Stewart, who—with the help of Becky Flowers, 28, president of MovingUp! Senior Move Management Consultants—will be renovating it and turning it into a junior golf academy.

Flowers, in Orlando to assist the elder Stewarts with their move, said she believes Stewart hopes his golf academy will inspire others to find the same love for the game that he has.

"Did Reed want to give up?" Flowers asked. "I'm sure he did. But he didn't. That's a valuable lesson for all of us who might feel like quitting from time to time."

Next week, Stewart will be playing for what is traditionally referred to as "the green jacket," the PGA's "Masters tournament" at Augusta National, a $1.8 million prize.

When reached by phone for comment—in the same hotel room as Flowers—Stewart blamed his previous losses on "failing to follow my heart."

"Sorry for the tears," Stewart said, apologizing for what appeared to be a sudden post-victory burst of emotion. "I didn't know it was possible to be this happy."

ACKNOWLEDGMENTS

This book would not exist without the help of so many talented, hardworking people that I couldn't possibly list them all here (without going over the data limits on my phone). But here are just a few to whom I am endlessly grateful:

- The tireless crew at William Morrow, including Lynn Grady, Brian Grogan, Nicole Fischer, Doug Jones, Jennifer Hart, Rachel Levenberg, Carla Parker, Liate Stehlik, Molly Waxman, the unflappable Pamela Spengler Jaffee, and my extraordinary editor, Carrie Feron.
- Friends and media consultants Janey Lee, Ann Larson, and Nancy Bender.
- Authors Michele Jaffe and Rachel Vail.
- Beth Ader and Jennifer Brown.
- My mom, Barb Cabot, who is nothing like the mothers in this book (except in good ways).
- My ever-patient agent, Laura Langlie.
- And finally, my husband, Benjamin Egnatz.

ABOUT THE AUTHOR

Meg Cabot was born in Bloomington, Indiana. Her books for both adults and tweens/teens have included multiple #1 *New York Times* bestsellers, selling over 25 million copies worldwide. Her Princess Diaries series has been published in more than 38 countries and was made into two hit films by Disney. Meg's numerous other award-winning books include the Mediator series and the Heather Wells mystery series. Meg Cabot (her last name rhymes with habit, as in "her books can be habit-forming") currently lives in Key West with her husband.

BOOKS BY MEG CABOT

"She is the master of her genre."
—*Publishers Weekly*

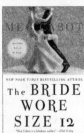

ROYAL WEDDING:
A Princess Diaries Novel

HEATHER WELLS MYSTERIES

SIZE 12 IS NOT FAT

SIZE 14 IS NOT FAT EITHER

BIG BONED

SIZE 12 AND READY TO ROCK

THE BRIDE WORE SIZE 12

QUEEN OF BABBLE SERIES

QUEEN OF BABBLE

QUEEN OF BABBLE IN THE BIG CITY

QUEEN OF BABBLE GETS HITCHED

THE BOY SERIES

THE BOY NEXT DOOR

BOY MEETS GIRL

EVERY BOY'S GOT ONE

THE BOY IS BACK

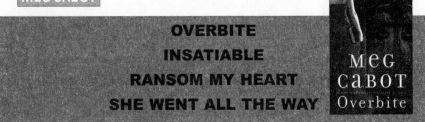

OVERBITE

INSATIABLE

RANSOM MY HEART

SHE WENT ALL THE WAY

For a complete list of Meg Cabot's books, available
in paperback and eBook, visit www.MegCabot.com